Peter Muirhead is the third son of the late William and Julia Muirhead and was born in Aigbirth, Garston Liverpool in 1928. At the age of 11 he was sent to St Joseph's College, a seminary at Upholland near Wigan.

Not a particularly willing student, he left there when he was 17 and following his father's footsteps he joined the Royal Navy where he trained as a wireless operator. He then joined the Western Approach's Fleet aboard HMS Loch Fada and after the cessation of hostilities he was demobbed.

After a 5 year service in the West Sussex Constabulary he left to become a self-employed salesman. A small legacy enabled him to purchase a property in Wokingham and he started his own business as a caterer.

He 'retired' and moved to Hereford where he continued his selling with Allied Dunbar.

He started writing small stories for a Kent Newspaper called the Focus, when he ceased operating he began writing novels.

THE KING'S BASTARD CHILD

Dedications

This book is dedicated to my wife Dorothy and my son
Graeme, whose support has been invaluable

Peter Muirhead

THE KING'S BASTARD CHILD

AUSTIN MACAULEY
PUBLISHERS LTD.

A CIP catalogue record for this title is available from the British Library.

ISBN 978 184963 416 8

www.austinmacauley.com

First Published (2013)
Austin Macauley Publishers Ltd.
25 Canada Square
Canary Wharf
London
E14 5LB

Printed and Bound in Great Britain

Acknowledgments

Christopher Hibberts's 'The English, A Social History 1066-1945'

Alison Polwden for her 'The Tudor Period'

David Whitehead for his treatise on Hereford Castle and Green

Reader and Critic

Doctors T and J Roderick, both of Lampeter University

Preface

Fate is an unpredictable spirit, interfering in all of our daily activities without any invitation, as it did to these two young people who are central to our tale, which events hereto recorded changed their lives forever.

This time they lived in was probably the most sexually depraved Tudor period, when most men made themselves out to be the superior sex in all aspects and particularly towards women, and generally took full advantage of them whenever and however they chose. They were led from the front by their own ruler, King Henry VIII.

These two people, who are central to our tale, were both socially and in distance, poles apart, Yet Fate enabled them to meet.

After another row with her father, Elizabeth decamps from Hatfield house down to Hereford, where she meets someone there and falls in real love for the first time.

On her return, her frustrated and assumed lover Robert Dudley, suspecting that she has had a dalliance with someone whilst she was away, and that maybe she has returned to Hatfield Palace unknowingly carrying his child, as one of his many spies had told him.

Dudley's so called love for her was actually an attempt to marry her and become her co-ruler, then he would no doubt kill her and if these rumours are true, then this means that both this man and their child must be killed, to finally quash the rumour of her mysterious child.

Finally, in their middle age, when all was forgotten, the rumoured father (Gad) was betrayed by a neighbour and so, after this long and tortuous chase of twenty odd years, which proved to be useless, the whole issue was resurrected.

All this was watched over by the Queen herself, who was frustrated by being unable to help directly. Her memory of the whole affair though, was never far from her mind.

Chapter One

The little ten year old girl was terrified. She had been taken from her friends in Greenwich Castle and was put into a barge and was being taken down stream towards Richmond.

It stopped at a small landing stage which led up to the huge mansion of Hampton Court, which was completely surrounded by wonderfully laid out gardens, including a recently purchased cherry orchard and a mysterious brick structure known as the Mount.

The lady from the court, who was dressed in a long black dress and cloak, gripped the frightened girl's hand and the girl was almost dragged like a 'prisoner' along the thin paths that meandered through the flower beds and up to the front door, via a hard surfaced driveway. Inside, the young girl was led into to a small anteroom next to the Main Hall. Here, she was told to take all her clothes off and "Wait".

This awful demand caused her bladder to react and she peed on the carpet, then she curled up in the foetal position in another part of the room and covered her genital area instinctively. Immediately her fear and anxiety was very quickly changed into anger and temper that she should be insulted and humiliated like this she resolved to talk to Kat Ashley, her friend and Court Guardian, about it when she got back.

There was another door in this room leading into the Main Hall and suddenly it opened with a loud bang followed by the loud noise from the other people there who all seemed to be talking at once.

Then, a short line of men entered the small room, all dressed in their finery. As they walked in, each was trying to out do the other with the size of their ruffs. When the door was closed, they all circled her like predatory wolves watching their prey.

"Stand!" she was ordered and she obeyed, slowly into a half crouching position.

As they passed the girl, as she stood up, each man in turn felt her back and her buttocks, and she cringed in both fear and anger. Then one of them gripped her shoulders, twisted her around and tweaked both of her tiny nipples.

That was it! Enough was enough, she thought. Gripping her fists like she had seen the brawlers do on the street fights on the foreshore in Greenwich, she punched him hard in the face. Initially he just yelled and then, a tiny trickle of blood ran down his mouth and chin, and stained his ruff. There was an instant shocked silence from the other watching men, and then they all erupted into howls of derisive laughter, pointing at the little man's stained ruff and his bloody discomfort.

The Guardian also seemed to be struck immobile, but she soon recovered. Then, gripping the offensive little man, she rushed him out and into the Main Hall.

When the people saw his messed ruff and asked him what had happened, then they too howled with derisive laughter at the young Spaniard's pain and discomfort. He ran out, raising his fists and uttering foreign and obviously incomprehensible and blasphemous oaths as he went. A churchman standing there made several signs of the cross.

Back in the anteroom, Elizabeth was hurriedly dressing. When the other men came over to help and offer her their commiserations, she gave them a withering look which sent them quickly back.

On her return to her friends at Greenwich Palace, she recounted the events to them, much to their great amusement. Kat secretly worried that there may be repercussions, as the man she had hit was the young son of one of one of Spain's senior Admirals.

Henry too was initially highly amused, until he realised that this would make his marrying her off a more difficult thing to do, so he shelved the idea.

When Elizabeth became Queen and was facing Spain's huge floating Armada, she smiled as she remembered the incident. She told her friend, Captain Drake, to go to Cadiz and give them a bloody nose, adding quietly to herself, "another one for my nipple twister", having a huge grin at the memory.

Like all gossip, the whole of the initial incident was flashed around the Court, so when she returned and started to grow, the number of 'accidental touches' of her breasts by the more aggressive nobles at Court irritated her.

Lord Seymour was the exception. She had initially liked his tactile attentions when she was very young, but later she had to admit, only to herself, that it did awaken her lustful thoughts. These were soon quashed, however, when she saw what happened to a friend of hers, who's bloated, pregnant body was found floating in the River Thames.

Despite this, or maybe because of this, she did remain almost pure for many years, growing up to be a highly intelligent and unattractive woman.

The incident that changed her life forever happened when, at the age of fourteen, she asked her father to do something for her. Unfortunately she had picked the wrong moment, as he had just returned from his lands in France and was about to put his feet up and enjoy a well-earned goblet of wine.

"Go away, child!" he said rather brusquely, and turned away.

But she was not to be denied and stood in front of him.

With her legs apart, her hands on her hips and a much more determined look in her eyes, she shouted, "Listen to me, Father!"

Oh dear! Henry's response was unfortunate, to say the least. Gulping down his wine, he said somewhat tartly, "Will someone not rid me of this bastard child?"

The deadly silence lasted a couple of seconds, until Elizabeth, swivelling on her heels and with a flick of her head and a dismissive wave of her arm, strode off, followed by her silent, nervous retinue.

As they tried to settle back in Hatfield to where she was sent, she turned to her Guardian Kat Ashley.

"So he wants rid of me, does he? So where can we go?"

After a few silent mutterings, Blanche Parry, a recent lady in waiting spoke up.

"I comes from Herefordshire, My Lady and not only is it a very nice quiet place, it is also on the very edge of our Kingdom, next to Wales Land."

They waited as she thought about it, and she said, "What a good idea, Blanche. Ye and Mistress Parry can make the travel arrangements."

She walked off, humming to herself.

So they did, and two days later three coaches and a party of troopers left the old Palace and headed west. The first stop was Gloucester Cathedral, where the elderly Bishop bored them near to death, but soon they were on their way again with fresh horses. They dozed as the coaches carried them up Crow Hill and past the mysterious wood of 'a hundred trees', which never increased in number.

The coaches slowed as they reached the top, and the bright sun made them cover their eyes as it shone quite harshly through the coach's windows.

As they the small village of Ross-on-Wye, with its quiet waters, which sparkled like a floating bed of diamonds in the morning sunshine. Soon they turned at the top of another hill and prepared to go down the steep lane into Hereford. Elizabeth called a halt at the small hamlet of the Callow, as they all wanted to stretch their legs and relieve their bladders.

When the troops returned to their barracks some few weeks later, they told their mates that they had never seen so many bare arses before, as the ladies got out of their coach and lifted their skirts and squatted in a group.

Then, as they crossed the lane, they were open mouthed in amazement as they saw the dark and menacing Black Mountains appear out of the mist ahead of them, almost ghostlike. The mist rolled slowly down the darkened hillside onto the bright and colourful fields below. The dazzling mixtures of yellow and green with splashes of red told them that spring had arrived here.

Elizabeth too was open mouthed as she ran across the lane and peered through the tangled growth.

"Look, Kat," she cried. "The trees are bowing to me."

All the new young saplings bent towards her, caught in the morning breeze.

She smiled as she said, "I will call this place my 'Golden Valley'."

A quiet cough behind her made her turn, and she saw a young trooper blushing nervously, standing there chewing a small hawthorn twig. He was holding one out to her.

"We calls this our bread and cheese tree, Milady."

They all watched quietly as she took it, and everyone was wondering what she would do. She chewed it for a moment and then a smile crossed her face.

She said, "How interesting. Kat, try some."

Soon they were all laughing and chewing the twigs of the small hawthorn tree's twigs, which were also thought to protect people against thunder and lightning and witches and all sorts of evil creatures. But as none of them were there and time was getting on, they had to re-embark on their journey to Hereford again.

At the same time as this young girl was being introduced into the real world, a young lad of a similar age was growing up too. They were both at opposite ends of social scale.

He was already living in Hereford and, like Elizabeth; he too was having difficulty entering the real world as well, as he was more interested in hunting and killing wildlife such as coneys/hares for food as he was now in charge of his family, as his father had been executed. He faced a very unusual start to his life called 'work', something he had never even considered in his poverty stricken life.

This introduction into the real world started when his Pa said he was to go real hunting with him.

He stood in front of him in their poor, dilapidated hovel as his Pa said, "Get yer boots on, lad. It's about time ye saw some real hunting, not yer little coney chasing."

Nervously he got ready and, although it was still dark and dawn was an hour or more away, they left and struck out, a bit too fast for Gad's little old legs, so his Da had to slow down, begrudgingly.

Earlier, Gad had watched his Pa lovingly polishing his short, powerful bow. He occasionally smeared it with what smelled like pig's fat on the wood, and then began polishing it very vigorously.

Now it was sitting on his shoulder and he carried a cloth bag for his arrows and hopefully some food, as he hadn't eaten for nearly two days.

They crossed the lane and over the dilapidated city wall. After a stumbling run up and across the Widemarshe Common, they sat on a low wall. As they rested, they could hear the rustling of one or two of the early rising creatures, who looked out at them, no doubt annoyed at this unexpected early morning disturbance and the unwarranted and unusual interruption to the start to their moving on. They entered a marshy wasteland and keeping to the edge, they both crept quietly up the field. Gad saw that the dawn also waking up, just as thin streaks of red began to appear in the distance ahead. The wet, musty smell of the damp field changed to a fresher smell when they crossed a small bridge over the River Lugg, into a clean smelling field.

At the top of the hill ahead of them, they could see the dark bush-packed wood. He was nearly at the end of his strength and he thought that his legs were about to drop off, so his Pa stopped once again and Gad thankfully dropped to the ground.

"Tired, lad?" his Pa asked with a smile. "We be nearly there."

Ahead of them was a stout hedge, planted no doubt by the farmer to keep the cattle in, but Tom for that was his Pa's name knew the area well. He moved along the hedge until he found a weed covered stile. They both climbed over and dropped onto a thin and dusty lane.

The remarkable silence didn't come as a shock to Gad after the noise and rustle in the fields they had crossed, as he was used to this change during his coney hunting. His Pa put his finger to his lips, which told Gad to keep quiet.

As they crept up the lane, they came to a hillock and they stopped and Tom sniffed the air.

Gad tugged his Pa's coat and said quietly, "What be ye smelling, Pa?"

Tom leaned down and said equally quietly, "These deer, they shits and farts see and that's what smells see."

They were just about to move on when Tom held Gad back and unshipped his bow. Ahead of them was a darker clump of bushes. They could just make out a movement there.

It was the up and down movement that told him something was eating grass, and quick as a flash he unshipped his bow, fitted a bolt and fired all in one smooth movement.

What happened next would be engraved on Gad's mind for the rest of his life. As the arrow hit the shape in the bushes, they all exploded four men dashed from the nearby undergrowth and grappled with Tom.

As he fell, he shouted, "Run, lad!" and Gad ran quicker and harder than he had ever run. He tossed his coat as he ran to make his running easier. This probably saved his life as, looking over his shoulder as he ran, he saw two large dogs chasing him that had been sent after him by the forest Wardens. The jowls of these hounds dripped saliva, and their large teeth would tear Gad into little pieces. As they reached his coat, the hounds changed their attention to it and started ripping it apart, which enabled Gad to get away.

He stopped on the bridge over the River Lugg and looked back and listened, but there was no sign of any dogs. How was he going to tell his Ma? He dissolved into tears.

The whole family was shattered by the news, and Gad tried to comfort his young siblings. As time moved on and they waited for the bad news they expected, Gad realised that there must have been a traitor among his neighbours, who no doubt heard Tom bragging to his friends in the local hostelry about how good he was, and that he was going out soon to get a deer to "'ave a feast".

As they all left, they patted him on his back, save one of them who didn't, but they had turned Judas and told the Forest Warden for the reward. The next few days were tense as they waited for the knock on the door. Eventually it arrived. Tom was going to be hanged the next week.

When the day of execution arrived, Gad took his weeping mother to the courthouse, which was opposite the jail on the other side of the town in a long tree lined road called Bye Street.

The crowds were already there, all wanting to see the hanging, and Gad stood with his mother at the back, crouching with his arms round her. He had covered them both with a shawl in case that Judas saw him and reported him.

Then a small band of ill-assorted men, in different clothes and with similar musical ability, announced the slow arrival of the Mayor, who was followed by other officials and the hangman.

Gad watched as his Pa with the other criminals. He was paraded in front of the crowd. Eventually, they put all the men on the hastily erected scaffolds and the charges were read out.

Gad saw with pride that his Pa stood tall and erect and seemingly fearless, whereas both the others cried and begged for their lives and forgiveness, hoping for a reprieve. But it was not to be and Gad's Ma began to shake in repressed terror.

A nod from the Mayor, a trumpet sounded and the trapdoors were opened.

The silence was broken by the snap of Tom's neck and he was instantly dead, followed by loud "aahs" from the ghoulish crowd. The others were not so lucky and, as they dropped, they began to swing. They screamed and choked. Men were brought out to hang onto their legs until they stopped moving. As they choked to death with blood and fluid dribbling out of their mouths and down their fronts, Gad and his mother crept away.

She had stopped weeping now, but hung onto Gad fiercely, realising now that she needed to care for her family without her man's support. Young Gad would have to provide an income, or at least food. Then, almost like help from heaven, they had a visitor. Fate had seen the events and no doubt wanted to level things up.

Ralph de la Haye ran a small leather goods and repair business near the castle, in a large barn-type building. Directly opposite this was the dilapidated entrance to the castle where, no doubt one day, the promise of a better entrance would be built to the cathedral next to it. He knocked on their hovel's door. He explained to them that several months ago, Tom had saved his life as he was attacked by two men in the High Town. Tom had grabbed them both and beat them to give them a lesson. When he offered Tom a reward, he said, "Nay Master, but I 'as a son and I would take it kindly if ye would give him a job."

He turned to Gad and said, "I offer ye two pence a day, and maybe a small gift from my profits once a week, which can be as much as five pence. Ye will have a bed, regular meals and ye will learn a trade.

Gad was overjoyed and thanked him. His new life had begun.

Chapter Two

It was now 1589 in London, some years later. Gad, like his Pa, without any court formality, was tortured by Dudley, who had been chasing him for many years to discover whether he and Elizabeth had lain together and produced a child. Unfortunately, other things had interrupted the chase – things to do with the Scottish Mare.

So this sudden capture of Gad was welcomed with great pleasure, and he wanted to make sure he got the whole truth out of him. Until now, he had been badly served by his so-called helpers, so his surprise and delight were euphoric. When even torture did not produce a result, perhaps a period on a scaffold might do it. He was put on one of the many scaffolds around the city of London's dock area.

This one was up the hill above the huge Tower and wooden bridge over the large river called the Thames. One such gibbet had several men standing there, already awaiting their fate, and an extra one called Gad wouldn't be noticed.

Like his father before him, he had been arrested by the Earl of Leicester, so it had seemed that time and history had caught up with him.

"It had to be raining," the man thought.

His brow furrowed in annoyance as Gad stood on a scaffold with his hands tied behind his back. He could feel the spots of rain on his face becoming heavier as the storm began to build.

"It's goin' t'be a bad 'un today", he prophesied to himself as though in his present situation, the rain really mattered.

The dark, heavy clouds were full of mischief, even hate, as they hung over the river like a doomsday warning, coming in off the Channel and backing up the Thames to fulfil their threat.

They were sweeping over the docks with increasing fury, rushing towards the grim fortress and up to him in case they missed the show, while the ships below danced to their tune.

"It should keep the lookers away too, "he added, as if they too were of any importance.

The well-built, thickset man with iron grey hair stood on the old trapdoor of the scaffold, and both swayed together slightly, as they anticipated the storm. He was just fifty nine years of age.

There had been many who had trudged up to this infamous place to mount the scaffold; some in a trance, not knowing, and others fighting and screaming in terror, much to the delight of the ghoulish crowd of onlookers. The people liked a good show, and those closest to the structure could watch the turmoil in a man's mind, as well as when he was about to be taken to meet his maker.

Some of the more adventurous among the onlookers shouted, "When ye meets our maker, mention we was kind to 'ee."

Others suggested that Beelzebub be spat upon, or cursed. Experienced watchers would make bets with those new to the show by shouting, "Half a penny to a shilling that he pisses his pants afore he goes up the last climb", and as the poor creature either struggled or was dragged up the well-worn steps, a cheer would go up as his pants stained widely, or worse still, the smell of a more extreme emptying of their bowels brought cries of disgust and a small movement away.

The oft-used structure began to respond to the storm, groaning in sympathy with the old man's thoughts. He shivered in his thin shirt as the quick bursts of the storm's preemptive rain cooled his torn and fevered body.

Many days of brutality and torture had reduced his once proud and strong body to a torn and ravaged wreck. He sucked his badly mutilated gums, which still bled, his badly broken teeth having been either smashed or removed with pullers. His hair though, was still as thick as it ever was, and rested on his shoulders, grey and with a curl or two, as was the fashion.

Gad remembered with renewed hatred the man called Waad, the senior torturer and of 'Dud' Dudley's remark, as he was tied to one of the blood-stained supports deep in the Tower's dungeons.

Thought ye could get off by your hiding all these years, d'int ye? But we ad 'ee, sir, we 'ad 'ee. Fornicate with our Queen did ye? Well let's see what ye have that pleasured her so."

He then had ordered Gad's pantaloons to be ripped off and also his thin undergarment. All was then displayed for the gawking attendants, who giggled like little girls. His penis lay flaccid and uninterested against his inner thigh, and Dudley lifted it with his sheathed sword and then let it drop.

"Not much for a royal gigot, eh?"

This was greeted by a half-hearted cheer and, like all bullies who were brave in a crowd, the thinness of their laughter showed. As they cast fearful eyes around the walls of this evil place, it was obvious He would have liked to be able to have killed this man one day, but now that he was to be hanged and it was impossible. However, it didn't stop his mind conjuring up many potential scenes of what he would do to him as he stood there awaiting his death.

The rope alongside his head began to sway with a slow metronomic beat keeping in time with the wind, although too soon, the hemp would be around his neck.

As the storm got closer, it began a macabre dance next to him. As the tempest's noisy forerunners hit the flags on the fortress below, stretching them out and looking like as though they were made of wood, the scaffold creaked and moaned in its song of death.

"God's tears, I suppose," Gad thought, with a wry smile, as he blew the drip off his nose, his hands having been tied behind him.

He saw the savage birds of prey being buffeted high above him, as they tried to stay in touch with their promised grisly meal.

Gad was a simple man with little self-importance, despite his significance in Elizabethan England, but more of that will be mentioned at a later date. Nevertheless, he would be less than natural if he didn't hold out the thought still that maybe his 'love' would save him at the last moment. No, it was too late now, as he reconciled himself to his imminent death.

Then he thought of Meg, dear Meg, his wife, a simple woman who was devoted to him. She never once queried what he did and why he had to go off for so long all those years ago, nor had reproached him when he returned after such a long absence of nearly a year.

She was his real love. She had always looked after him, suffering the many hurtful indignities of Dudley's spies as they looked for him after he had gone; although worse than that was the lack of information she had about him. Had he been killed? Was he in prison? Nothing. Several times she had found herself being followed as she visited friends, and on one occasion a friend of hers was accosted by a man who claimed to be Gad's friend and asked where he was, so that he could send him some money he owed him. Her friend had smiled as she recounted it to Meg, and they had both laughed when she said how she had asked the man his name, so she could tell Gad next time she saw him.

"He ran quicker than a drain rat," she had said, and they both laughed, a little thinly.

As he looked around, down towards the river, as with the perversity of the damned, he reckoned he could count the twenty arches over London's river Thames. In reality, he only saw a few. However, he did see the billowing sheets of the women linen workers as they stretched their cloths, until his eyes watered. When he looked again, the sheets had disappeared as they drew them in away from the impending storm. The only thing that upset him was that his dear Meg would be hurt badly by his execution, and his son and grandson would be shamed too. Had his own mother been there, she would have had a feeling of déjà vu.

No doubt the rest of mankind would soon forget him, so they did not deserve his thoughts.

What he had done was to sire a child, unknowingly and in an act of pure lust, but with someone of great renown. When everyone was against him and his lad, he had saved him and kept them both free for over thirty years. Now at least he had hoped his son would be safe. Not as a royal bastard because he was unaware of his real mother, but as his son, a man of England and someone worthy of his trade, a boot maker.

It had been the treachery of one of his so-called friends which had finally betrayed him, probably for money. That meant the anti-Protestants had won, and that saddened him too. He hoped that his death would not embarrass his own dear Beth; she had more than enough of her own problems with the aftermath of the Armada's costly battle, and the dire financial state of the county in general, without having him reappear like a bad coin.

The hunchbacked hangman came up the scaffold and into the wind, moaning and complaining as he adjusted the knot again, and catching the rope as it swung back and forth.

"Don't wan' 'e swinging like a bell, do we nar? Make as much clamour too I shu'nt wunner."

He cackled at his own black humour. The watchers were getting restless as well, and several were calling out to this deformed hangman to hurry things along.

"I 'as my drinkin' to get in yet."

The crowd laughed at the humour of it, but he was used to this and just ignored them.

Meanwhile, John Shakespeare, William's brother had not been idle. He had reported to his master, Lord Francis Walsingham, who looked after Elizabeth's security. John was one of his men. He quickly called on Elizabeth, who was resting in Windsor Castle.

"What is it, Francis?" she said a little testily.

"It is Dudley, Your Majesty."

Elizabeth frowned. "What's the man doing now?"

"Well, it appears he is using the country's scaffolds to execute his enemies without recourse to the courts, putting himself above the country's laws. Oh, and a man's name has been given to me for your attention. A common workman called Gad O'Hereford."

Elizabeth could not avoid her sudden start which, despite her quick recovery, was noticed by Walsingham.

"Damn the man," she said. "Get him here immediately, Francis, and stop all those executions."

As he left, she prayed she was in time to save her shoemaker. Hanging was an operation with very mixed results in those troubled times, particularly as regards to the length of time it took for a man's soul to leave his body and take its journey to face God's final punishment. Many figures had faltered on the way up or, like Gad, had marched firmly up the many well-worn steps. Over the years, bad people and good people, the guilty and the innocent, aristocrat and commoner alike had swung unhappily from this and other gibbets, although aristocrats usually chose the axe. Gad was both good and innocent. During Gad's stay in the cells for the condemned below the Courts and among the other candidates for the rope, the more feared would try to bolster their confidence by telling tales of bravado.

Men and women who had nothing to lose, except their lives in most cases, were fully deserving of the punishment.

Some of them with a twisted sense of humour would tell of evil hangmen they knew, who deliberately let a man dangle for hours, twisting and jerking in their final agonies. Those with friends had hired men to hang onto their legs to hasten their end.

Often the faces of the condemned would turn blue and violet under the rope, with eyes bulging, and mouths were dribbling a mixture of blood and spittle. Then the crowds would jeer and parody the noises just out of fun. As they listened to the gurgling and watched the bleeding when a chafing rope broke the skin, they took bets on how long he would take to die. It depended on where the knot was placed so he was told -supposedly it was behind the left ear, but in the rain the rope would swell and refuse to slip, so it wasn't a good day for hanging today. He smiled. Was there ever a good day?

One chap, he was told by a fellow gaolbird with a sadistic turn of mind, was still alive when they cut him down after three hours. But as he was so near to death they buried him just the same.

Buried alive! That really scared him, and he shivered at the thought. He was becoming a victim to his own morbid thoughts now, which was a dangerous thing to do. He shuddered again, his mind playing the 'teaser' on him, and in spite of his efforts, the black thoughts kept filling his mind.

He was cold, bitterly cold after the heat of the fires in the dungeon from where he had been dragged, to stand in the cells, which were open to the cold north westerly wind.

So many things had happened since that fateful day in Hereford – some he regretted, others not. Occasionally people were drawn and quartered, their insides pulled from their bodies before they were dead. 'Twas just like dressing a bird; except the fowl had their necks wrung first, and despite the cold and the rain, his forehead was wet with the sweat of fear.

"Stop it!" He commanded his brain to stop tormenting him.

He hadn't got much time for praying, being Independent, but he felt that perhaps now was the right time to do so if there was ever going to be one.

"I hope there's a God. But if so, was what I done so bad tha' 'e can't forgive I? Still," he added, "as I ain't sorry, I 'spose he won't forgive I."

However the hangman seemed to know his job, was very attentive, almost fussy and, despite his deformities, he did not appear to be a bitter man as most of his kind were. Although his present victim had no money to bribe him with, Gad would try and persuade him to put the knot in the right place when the time came, or to find him two men to hang onto his legs as some do, to hasten his end.

The lenticular hangman appeared again. He was irritated and tutted with a frown of disappointment.

"Seems like we'll 'ave to wait a mite longer till 'is Worship comes, sir. Sorry about tha'. But 'tis dinner time, I 'spect."

Gad was wondering whether the hangman was more upset at maybe losing his 'money for his rope fee' he could sell for a shilling a length, after the.

A few hours later, there was a noise outside Elizabeth's door as men tussled. She was alarmed as two men burst into her holy of holies.

"What on earth…?"

She started as she saw Dudley and her Sergeant-at-Arms fighting, as Dudley tried to push his way in without first asking permission, which was almost a hanging offence.

Recovering her harsh composure, she said, "Silence, My Lord. Sergeant, put his Lordship against that wall."

Delighted to get her permission, he grabbed Dudley and pushed him hard against the wall, making him squeal. The picture above him fell slightly at an angle, but still remained there, slightly crooked.

"Now, sir," she said to Dudley. "I need to talk to you."

He also was recovered, and said in a plaintive voice, "What is amiss, Bet… Er, Your Majesty?"

Frowning at his lapse of respect, she said in an ominously quiet voice, "I am advised that you are putting yourself above the law, sir, by hanging people you do not like without the use of our courts."

A deadly silence followed, as Dudley had no answer.

Eventually Elizabeth said, "Because of our previous friendship, I will not have you executed this time. However, if these hangings are not stopped, or you repeat these actions, you will feel the executioner's axe yourself."

Turning to the Sergeant, she said, "Rid me of this man. Now go!"

Gad, meanwhile, stood with his legs spread resolutely apart – more in defence against the wind, he would say until they would be tied together, than any bravado. He looked down at the crowd again around and below him, at the noisy expectant people. They were ghouls, all of them, as they gathered closer to the gibbet. They, like Gad, had been made to wait a longer time than usual, and they were both cold and they crushed up against the Gibbet, partly to get out of the coming storm and also to get a better view. He sighed.

"Is this what I have come to?" Then he cocked his head to one side. "Was that a prayer, I wonder? and he grinned again.

The misshapen face of his executioner below, squinted his one good eye up at his customer and wondered what such a man had done that he could still smile – that was twice now, he noticed. He was a brave man and nodded approvingly. He would make sure that he would die quickly. Always a hard working man of the journeyman class, Gad had been 'arrested, tried and sentenced to hang' by one of England's most powerful men just for loving the wrong woman. But that was nigh on forty years ago, and the son they had produced was a man himself with his own son now. Could hate last that long?

All he ever wanted to be was a bootmaker and mender, and he had no pretensions to be anything else. How he cursed himself for relaxing his guard, as well as keeping everything to himself, even from his Meg and his son; but surely they had forgotten after all these years?

He had named his son after his own dearest friend from childhood, and had allowed his grandson to be named Gad after himself. However, had he known the sleepless nights he had given those concerned with the throne's successors; he might have taken some satisfaction out of his misfortune.

That was another regret, too that he could not be with his two men and teach them to be strong and honest; to face life squarely on and become fair and true tradesmen, treating their fellows all the same, giving good worth for their money. He smiled as he remembered his young grandson wanting to be educated, and how he had taken to Latin and Greek among other subjects so easily. At first he had wondered where he got his brains from, and then he remembered the boy's grandmother and what a sponge for knowledge she had been.

They say when you drown, all your past life flashes before you. Funny, the odd things you begin to remember. The times when you were young and carefree, when your only problem was getting something to eat for you and your poor family they seemed such good times now, even if then they were awful. Perhaps hanging was the same.

Eventually there was a disturbance among the gathered men who supported Dudley. He had returned, much to the relief of the people gathered there, including the security people, who were worried that this disturbance might be exacerbated and a full-scale riot might start.

Suddenly there was a movement among the crowd as a Sergeant-at-Arms was seen, clutching a fluttering piece of parchment as he approached the gibbet. Gad's stomach tightened. Was this it?

"Bring 'im down, Jethro, they've let 'im orf."

The crowd was most displeased and shouted their anger and frustration, as some had stood there for hours.

Consequently, a bewildered and relieved Gad had to suffer many knocks and swipes as the angry crowd jostled and pushed to get at him not that he felt any of them.

He was shaking, and it took him a little while to readjust his mind to realise he was not going to hang after all. Perhaps his Beth had got wind of the arrest, the subsequent torture and death threat.

His hands and arm and legs were like jelly, and he had to take Jethro's and the Constable's arms as he was led back to the courthouse along the rutted, muddy and smelly road. When finally he reached the steps of the courthouse, where he had been dragged from much earlier, he sagged and slowly he slipped to his knees, with his head still reeling and his body racked with pain.

As he drooped and fell, with the two men trying to lift him up at the foot of the steps of the old courthouse, he saw his arch enemy, 'Dud' Dudley, the man who had caused him all his suffering and near hanging, standing there in all his elderly glory.

He was posing on the worn top step, trying to act like one of his young acolytes who surrounded him. He was dressed in a large hat with a white feather in it. His multi-coloured doublet and hose was topped by a brilliant cloak of many colours half across his shoulders. His face, though, showed the signs of the Sergeant's rough handling of him, and it was blotchy with dried blood.

One varicose leg in white hose was on the top step, and the other had been carefully placed on the next one down. Both steps were covered in filth and mess that had accumulated there from its use as a pitch for flower sellers and the like.

A clean space had been made by his flunkeys so as not to dirty his lovely attire and his shiny buckled shoes, which contrasted with the dirty rain-soaked approach road. One hand held a lace kerchief, and the other was on his sword pommel. His disdainful sneer was evident. He kept the smell of the crowd at bay by flicking his perfumed kerchief in their direction. This sight gave Gad a new energy and made him stand upright defiantly, somehow getting the strength to show his adversary that he was unbroken and determined not show fear. 'Dud' Dudley, son of the late Lord Dudley, now the Earl of Leicester, stood amused as he watched the wretched man's struggles, making quiet comments to his friends over his shoulder, who laughed obsequiously.

He was affecting a nonchalant pose, feeling secure as he no doubt was, surrounded by his toadies and lackeys, watching this broken man approach.

Now that his own father was dead, Dudley felt he could act without restraint and yet, he of all people should have had some sympathy for Gad. He was not legitimate either and even 'God cleanse my mouth' Thomas could have been his son had he married Elizabeth. Maybe that was the reason, except the only thing that he had which might have interested her was his mind, because until fairly recently he had been studying in Balliol College at Oxford.

He had suspected for years that someone had had some mysterious hold over Elizabeth and when he had found Gad, he had wanted to use him against his sovereign, attacking what he thought was her weak link. He should have known better; she had no weak links, as his own chopped neck later on would testify.

This woman was 'sometimes more than a man and in truth sometimes less than a woman', as her Chief Minister Cecil would say quietly to friends.

This time however, Elizabeth had got wind of the execution and stopped it. Although Dudley thought she could hardly arrest him, he had a sneaking, odd feeling that there was more to this man Gad than he knew, which the great Queen Elizabeth, his one-time Bess, would rather keep quiet about. How little he really knew her.

"It seems you still have friends, shoemaker – or perhaps one friend," he said in his squeaky voice, making reference to Elizabeth, "Anyway, ye have been pardoned."

Then, with a swish of his hand, he held back his pox-ridden acolytes, who wanted to jump on Gad and no doubt stomp him to death. The crowd surrounding them, sensing this, moved forward instinctively and started to murmur.

One or two shouted, "E as more friends' than ye," and another, "Even now, 'e'd make more of a man than ye."

People were getting closer to the aristocrats and Dud's friends closed ranks with their hands poised, hovering above their sword pommels. The constables had stopped smiling. Their numbers had been increased, with the military put on alert. At that moment, a clod of filthy mud sailed over the heads of those watching, and took the arrogant Dudley full in the face. He staggered back, dropping his kerchief and was held up by his friends, who also suffered from the mud.

The crowd erupted in howling laughter and delight as the mud splattered over all his friends and his fancy hat went down into the muddy lane. For a moment, the two factions stood toe to toe. Dudley with his friends, their drawn swords on one side, and an angry crowd bent on attacking the others. The constables closed in.

Gad shook himself free from one of his attendants and held up an arm using what little strength he could dredge up.

"Friends! No! Look at him. He ain't worth your sweat. Go home. It takes more than a puffed up dandy like him to put me down, or hang me up."

He was cheered loud and long -not that any of them knew why, but it was a chance to get at the 'aristos'. One or two came over to Gad and patted the now slumped man on the shoulder, and the crowd slowly dispersed.

Dudley, now brave added in his high-pitched courtesan type voice, "Rabble!" Unable to hide his anger, he pointed at Gad and hissed, "Keep away from me and shall we say, our mutual friend."

With a flick of a new kerchief in front of his nose, he ignored his ruined hat and swept off, followed by his own rabble and accompanied by the howls of laughter and the curses of the men as a hail of mud and stones hit them all, covering them with mud and cuts from the stones.

Another man who had watched all this was pale, in thinly dressed in breeches and shirt. He came over to the crumpled reprieved man. His hair was thick and long too, just like his father's. But its red colouring was covered up by a cowl-type hat with its ends tied beneath his chin, so that it could not be seen. The long back was tied in a ponytail and tucked up and under the cowl. They could hear someone in the crowd mimicking the effeminate voice of Dudley, which made the people scream the more with laughter. The irritation that they had felt at having missed an execution was soon forgotten, and they made full use of the opportunity to hound Dudley and his friends. Mud, stones and other filth was rained on them as they ran for cover. The watch with its constables was called over, but when they saw who the butt of the fun was, they smiled too and were loath to interfere until the crowd had had their fun.

Thomas, son of Gad, pushed through towards the fallen man, still conscious of his lifetime's admonition never to call him father in public.

"Gad! Oh Gad!" he said. "Did ye not know that he only put you up there as a sort of charade? You were never going to be hung. The Queen had forbid it."

His voice held the awe in which he mentioned the Queen in connection with his father. He had yet to learn of this relationship.

He flung his arms around the shaking man who was quickly led away between his friends to a small carriage, which rushed off at speed. It slipped and slid along the cobbled road, which was slippery with all sorts of filth, and the rain just added to it.

The small covered wagon, for it had no springs, made the ride a painful and a tortuous one. Thomas sat with his father cradled in his arms and helped to alleviate the bouncing, jerking ride. He wept as he watched Gad's mutilated face, which seemed to have been taken with the fever as he sweated the whole time he was being carried back to their lodgings.

Gad never remembered this last journey, as his injuries and mental torments were enough to finish a weaker man. The expert torturers had tried everything except the rack to make him tell them where his bastard son was.

Dudley was beside himself with frustration as, having finally got his quarry, after years of trying, he was unable to kill him. They needed the information to discredit Elizabeth, but unknown to him, he was to be arrested himself soon for his involvement with the treacherous dealings with the Scottish cause and also the Catholics.

He was beheaded not long after this episode. However, this did not let this man off the hook, as other traitorous groups took over the hunt in the hopes of bringing Elizabeth down.

Meg, his wife, was ecstatic at his return, as she had never really expected to see her man again. Her mental torture when they had taken him away two weeks ago had begun to wear her down and her friends feared for her sanity. Will Shakespeare, her grandson's friend and tutor, comforted her all he was able and by seeing as many people he could in an endeavour to get help. He had been mystified by Gad's remark as he was taken which was, "Tell the Queen." Why her? What could she do for a commoner? But he had asked those he knew in any sort of power, and somehow it had worked. Will was astounded and determined to ask Gad later – why would the great Queen interfere on his behalf?

Meg alternated between crying and laughing as they all settled themselves down in their cramped rooms, with her arms around him, daring anyone to touch or take him away. Slowly Thomas prised her off him, saying she would suffocate him else.

"Let us just have a quiet evening Ma."

Gad had been carefully lifted into a hastily made up cot by the fire, and Meg still fussed about him 'like an old hen', as Gad used to say. After many days of their beatings, his finger and toenails had been half pulled out; the torturer must have been drunk, so his efforts were worse than just crude. His teeth had been smashed and the rest had been removed with pullers. He had had no food, and just sufficient water to enable the rest of his body to survive, which made it all the more remarkable for him to be still alive.

Once he had been a powerful and taut muscled man, and now he was reduced to a quivering, shaking shadow of his former self. He had accepted the offered broth greedily as he had not eaten properly for over two weeks, and was immediately transformed by the heat and succulence of it. But it did not last long and he soon sagged again and then, heaving painfully, he brought it all up.

His ravaged stomach was not used to such richness, but eventually he managed to eat a crust of bread later, after it had been dipped in the broth, which he could suck as his empty gums were still bleeding.

Standing and watching this was young Gad, the old man's grandson. His eyes were alight with righteous anger and his long red hair, which was tied in a knot behind his head like his father's, bobbed as he reacted to his grandfather's torment. He was all of sixteen years of age and, despite his humble beginnings, he was already learned in Latin and Greek like his Grandma.

Slowly the injured man's body relaxed and its quaking movements stopped. He felt completely tired out, as Meg, holding him against her bosom, soothed him like a baby, stroking his rough cheeks and carefully cooling his brow with a cold wet cloth. Then, just as he was dropping off in his wife's tender arms, there was another knock at the door. Meg couldn't help her violent start, as her fears of more trouble from Dudley's friends was always a possibility.

Her start awoke Gad, who tried in vain to struggle up in into a sitting position, but Meg held him down and he didn't resist.

All the occupants became alert and poised with swords drawn, and Meg's arms were wrapped tightly around her man. This time it will be over my dead body, she avowed to herself.

"'Tis but just a friend in need,' Will said, as he entered with a flourish.

Everyone relaxed with a smile, as the house was always being invaded by some thespian or other and aspiring actors reading or learning their lines.

Even Gad seemed to come to a little, and he smiled as Will knelt by him and held his hands.

"Thanks my young friend," Gad said quietly.

He knew that it was Will who had got through to Elizabeth after Gad had been taken, and was instrumental in the execution being called off.

Will and his young grandson were almost of an age, Will being the older by a year, and they had become good friends. But Will, ever the showman, was still crouching next to Gad and turned his head to the assembled group smiling at the welcome companionship. Then, unable to resist an audience, he stood and said with great feeling, one arm across his chest and the other held outstretched in true thespian style,

"And these few precepts in thy memory
See thou a character.
Give thy thoughts no tongue,
Nor any unproportion'd thought his act.
Be thou familiar, but by no means vulgar."

He paused and looked around at his captivated audience to get the most out of them.

"Those friends thou hast, and their adoption tried, grapple them to thy soul with hoops of steel."

The silence was broken by the croaking voice of Gad, almost smothered by Meg, but strong enough for all to hear.

"Aye, and neither a borrower nor a lender be;
For loan oft loses both itself and friend."

The roar of laughter that greeted the quotation showed that Gad was on the mend. Will had borrowed money off Gad to help in the making of the costumes for his next drama and some for acquiring second hand gowns off lady's maids, wanting to earn a shilling or two. Tales were told that often, when the ladies of the court were visiting the play and a particular dress was recognised by the poor lady's friends, it brought howls of laughter. Then she had to say, in her great embarrassment, that it was given to the writer.

Will stood and roared the loudest, and then he dropped to his knees again and hugged Gad with tears rolling down his cheeks.

Despite his youth, the young actor loved this man like a father. William, like so many others, had admired Gad's love and determination that had originally rescued Thomas from death as a child years ago, and brought him back against all the odds. Young Dudley had at the time set up a chain of spies throughout England to find and report back that both him and the 'bastard' had been killed, which was fruitless. Time had passed, but not Dud's anger and jealousy.

This attempted hanging by Lord Dudley's son was the result of a traitor who had disclosed Gad's whereabouts.

"My debt to thee, dear Gad," said William, "transcends all fickle gelt."

His long thin delicate hand and fingers, almost feminine, stroked the rough hollowed face of his sick friend. He was a man in a boy's body.

Then, turning to Meg, he said quietly, "Dearest Meg, should I meet one as fine as ye, let her be mine and please make sure this gentle man regains his health and strength. England's might depend on it."

She smiled at the intense young man.

"England's might indeed," she sniffed.

Then Will quietly left, as did the others, realising that most of all he needed rest and care. Then Gad lapsed into a coma and his body shook with the ague. Sometimes he sat up and called out names, strange names Meg had no knowledge of. It seemed as though he was beginning to live out his old memories of the finding and the bringing home of his son. The days that followed were slow and anxious, fearful at times as well as painful, as the fever swept over Gad and eventually relented. His strong constitution overcame what would have killed a lot of other people, but he said later that it was just his old stubbornness and Meg nodded with a relieved smile. Many friends came and went, and occasionally they felt an enemy had joined the throng as well, but at all times there were strong men at hand to keep a watch over this bravest of men.

Tenure of him to the care of Will, saying, "Aye, ye are a good man, Will, and mark my words, lad – when ye sort yerself out, ye'll make yer mark as an actor and maybe even a writer."

Will read it with tears falling down his cheeks, as it was a cancellation of his and his debts father's debts to him.

Then tragedy struck yet again. Gad relapsed into a shallow coma, and as he drifted in and out of consciousness, so did his memory of times past. He saw his friend Thomas, Beth and his villainous encounters with different people, and he began to relive all his previous adventures.

A fearful Meg smoothed his sweating brow again, not knowing what else to do. An apothecary living close came in, looked at his head and made a tactless rejoinder.

"The fever is in him and rarely let's goes. He may recover, but that is doubtful. Perhaps it would be better that he dies, as what would be left might not be worth having."

That changed Meg. It was just what she needed to shake her out of her torpor.

"Not worth having, indeed!" she stormed back at the man, her hackles raised she roused herself to the defence of the man she loved, which was fine to see. "He's more a man now than ye are in ye normal health," she stormed.

The pan in her hand was close to becoming a dangerous weapon. Then taking a grip on the ear of the 'herb mixer', she steered him to the door.

"Out, thou man of bad news."

She busied herself with stoking up the fire and when that was done, she put the big black kettle over it and prepared herself to give her man a bath.

Watching him tossing and turning in his fever, she said to herself, "I wonder what he is dreaming about. I have known thee for many years, my love, and really I know so little about ye. Even our son. Who is he?"

When he had brought him to her, the lad was thin, small and underfed, and he had been misused badly by those who took him from his stepmother. The Lady Dorothy, his guardian, had been killed.

When Meg washed him, he had asked in a frightened voice which trembled in fear, "I don' wanna go in they chimneys again."

Meg hugged him and talked to him as well, explaining he had a Mum and a Dad now, who loved him and the bad days were gone. That same little lad was a man himself now, with a child of his own, "so, with love and care, we can do most things, eh my sweet?' But he never heard her in his mumblings and mutterings.

"Not worth having!" she repeated, reliving the confrontation with the apothecary. "All the saints, I'd rather have a little of him than a lot of many others."

She looked up as her man mumbled, "Not me sir... Poacher."

She shook her head as she busied herself again, filling the big tub with water. The house they were living in was one used by many of the actors in London at the time, a big rambling place off Cheapside. Meg was constantly being spoken to in the most peculiar languages as various actors came by to try their lines out on her. Will was often there with his head stuck in a book most times. He and her grandson would get together, as Will taught him grammar and the use of words and phrases.

Every now and then, young Gad would rush up to Meg and hold out a piece of much used slate to show her what he had written. He was a more than apt pupil, as Will said often enough, but where did 'ee get such brains from?"

Had she known then who the lad's grandmother was, she might have begun to understand, as Elizabeth had been an exceedingly bright child as well and who became a wise and very erudite woman and Queen. But as Meg couldn't read or write, it meant nothing to her.

Now that Thomas, the young lad's father, was grown up and with a wife, Meg spent a lot of time with her; she was quite a nice girl but a terrible cook, and there were many arguments and tears as the poor girl tried to learn her culinary arts.

Bread was her difficulty, as she did not appear to have the strength to knead the dough sufficiently. Meg tried to teach her the art of pastry making and she began to find her metier. She would beam with pride when Gad asked Meg which pastry shop she had bought these from.

Her pride was good to see, and Meg smiled as the girl said shyly, "t'were all my work sir," giving Gad a little curtsey. Meg nodded with pleasure. The girl had some talents then, so perhaps she might make her lad a wife yet.

Gad still lay in his cot and, on the advice of another local friendly apothecary, who was just passing through and who told her she ought to move her husband and turn him over a lot, else bedsores would start and they would be awfully painful and difficult to heal; so that was another chore she had to do, and she was to do it every day, sometimes twice.

The better he got, the more he liked it, and there was much giggling and slapping of bare flesh as he improved in health. His son Thomas had taken over Gad's trade as a boot maker, and with the money it brought in, they were able to pay rent and live fairly well. He too was showing a great aptitude for leather, and was soon experimenting on gloves.

Slowly, Gad's colour began to change, from a puce to a grey to a dirty pink. His eyes looked less rheumy and his voice stronger. But every now and then, and this more often these days, he would go back into some sort of coma, and they feared for his sanity, and even his life. He was still unable to sit up without help, but the mumbling in his sleep continued.

At night he was worst, and he would sometimes shout out names, or lapse into a quiet, shallow sleep. His lips would move quietly and the occasional smile would flit across his face. He seemed to be living his life all over again. Meg realised then how little she really knew about him, and one day he would recount it to her, but until that day she was quite prepared to leave sleeping dogs to lie.

She loved him and he her. That she understood. It was the kind of love that trusts and never asks. If he needed her she was there, just as he was always at hand should she ever need him?

Her world was small and simply encompassed by her family's needs, but with a trusting understanding that she let her man step outside of it if needs be, knowing that only in extreme cases like now, would he ever bring his troubles home. When that happened, they drew strength from each other and survived.

Meg watched Gad as he struggled with the covers of his bed. He seemed to be trying to hide, and then he would reach out twisting them with his still bony fingers in his dreams, as though he was being chased or attacked by someone or something. Meg would go to him immediately, dropping whatever she was doing and put her arms about him, which seemed to calm him, as though he knew he was safe there.

Will had discovered a chirurgeon, who had visited him backstage one evening. He was a small bespectacled man with a sharp pointed beard and piercing eyes, and by his language he was a foreigner. Will had explained to him of Gad's drifting in and out of sleep in a coma-like state, mumbling and shouting and then peaceful. He even woke sufficiently to sup a broth his wife kept hot for him, but his lucid moments were short-lived and they were all worried about his sanity.

The doctor, who was called Wulfren Saxe-Goben, came from Vienna and seemed quite knowledgeable about Gad's condition. No doubt pleased to put Will Shakespeare in his debt, he came around to where Gad was living one wet and windy afternoon to their hovel in east Cheapside. He listened to Gad and examined him thoroughly. His pince-nez bobbed disconcertingly on his nose as he hummed and hawed, tapping his nose and making various noises, much to the amusement of Meg who had the greatest difficulty restraining her giggling. He wore a mixture of two pairs of breeches and two coats that flapped when he moved, and his shirt was tied at his neck with a kerchief.

She constantly had to leave the room to get over an attack of hysterics, but when the good doctor finally diagnosed that there was fluid in the cranium, which was affecting his brain and suggested removing this fluid, she was not so happy.

It sounded very perilous to her.

"Is that dangerous?" she asked him, her voice quiet and fearful.

After all he had gone through; the last thing she wanted was for him to be killed by a 'quack' cure.

The doctor seemed impervious to any of their hints as to his professional abilities, and he did not take offence from Meg's less than charitable remarks, saying that he had successfully operated on a member of the Austrian Emperor's family, a young girl, and it was entirely successful.

"She had had a fall from an 'orse and then was kicked by it, but when I removed ze fluid from her head, she vos soon distracting her farzer as young girls do zumtimes in their gaiety."

Meg turned to her son Thomas and asked him and Will what she should do, and Thomas asked the doctor what would happen if they did nothing. The doctor removed his glasses and violently polished them several times, before answering with his nose twitching like a rabbit constantly.

"My eenglish is not good, yes? But your answer will be that he will die. Zis fluid it vill grow and ze brain will soon cease to work. It 'as no uzzer cure."

The short, curt answer alarmed everyone, and so Meg reluctantly agreed. However the good doctor held up his hand by way of a caveat.

"But verst, you will feed him well. He must be stronger before I do zis operation. Ja?"

They all looked at the subject of their discussion as he tossed and turned and mumbled about poaching, and then his voice tailed off as he remembered.

The cold, penetrating wind bent the small scrub trees and defiant shrubs and probed its icy fingers into the very bones of the watching boy as he crouched, shivering, tense and frightened in the reeds and rushes on the bank of the large river.

The year was now 1545, and the river was the one called the Wye, which was a natural border between England and Wales. The time was early on a dark November evening and the place was outside the walls of the city of Hereford.

The boy shrunk himself lower from the searching men. Some were on horseback and others walking in front of them, circling outwards from the mounted men and coming closer to him. They were not more than forty yards away from their quarry.

"Damn the boy!" one of the walking men said as he slipped up to his calves into the mud.

He was one of twenty men on foot who had been alerted by the watch after a dead stag had been found on the road from Hay Wood. It must have been dropped by other poachers, as they were challenged by a gamekeeper.

All Gad had, was two scrawny rabbits. He had been caught much earlier in the woods by the gamekeepers, while he was trying to reclaim them on land belonging to the Crown Estates. But, well versed in the art of using the apparent frailty of his age and size, he slipped away when they relaxed their grip.

A sympathetic chaser thought that Henry VIII was a bit more interested at this time in saving his syphilitic body from the attentions of the apothecaries, physicians and chirurgeons, than a few scrawny rabbits a hundred and thirty odd miles away.

His young twelve-year-old daughter, the Lady Elizabeth, too was unconcerned. She was more than a little agitated by having to constantly defend her young virginity against the pretended 'fatherly' touching and clasping of Lord Seymour, who had earlier expressed a wish to marry her.

It would get even worse when he had married the Lady Jane Grey as she, by way of pandering to her husband's little depravities, joined him in trying to indulge in 'horse-play' with her, touching parts of the young Elizabeth's body she had always and instinctively regarded as out of bounds to others.

He was nearly forty years of age and she was a blossoming fourteen-year-old girl. Although a pleasant man, she was scared to death of him. Then, when he started getting into to bed with her in the early hours of the morning, she decided that was far enough and put a stop to it once and for all. She began to dress herself much earlier, so that when he appeared dressed only in his nightshirt, to his dismay he would find her fully dressed and working on her embroidery.

This was a ploy not told to her, but it was her natural instinct for self-survival, which was to stand her in good stead in her future battles with men. When things got a little more out of hand, Catherine tried to have Elizabeth sent to a court Physcian, Sir Anthony Dennings' House in Cheshunt, out of the way, as her husband, Lord Seymour, was becoming infatuated with her.

So even at a very early age, she was all too aware of her ability to arouse men, and indeed her own arousal too by Seymour, which sometimes alarmed her.

This, of course, was his downfall, and he was eventually executed for this and other misdemeanours.

Meanwhile, the scrawny youth Gad had no difficulty in slipping his captors when he had been grabbed earlier, and he raced free like the creatures he hunted.

They had been trying to stop unlawful poaching which was classified still as a hanging offence, but with youngsters like Gad, it was a hopeless task.

Poverty in Hereford was no worse than anywhere else, but it was still in abundance there.

The ground south of the river was marshy and treacherous, but it was teeming with small game and was in the care of the Master of the Estates for his Lord, who held it for the Crown. Nothing could be taken by anyone without his authority.

Young Gad, despite his age and size, could run and stalk like a man, but stags or deer were out of his class of course, as he had no means to carry them back, and certainly there was no place where he could butcher them afterwards. Although his mouth watered as he thought of a fat, juicy joint of venison.

It was a difficult time in England. With the recent marriage of Henry VIII to Catherine Parr, and the vicious fighting between the Howard family and the Seymours, most noblemen's families were in constant fear and confusion about which group of courtiers to adhere to.

Money too was in short supply, and castles such as Hereford's were in desperate need of repairs, so all sources of revenue – and that included the selling of game – were consequently of great value.

But to a poacher like Gad, who received 2d per day as a boot maker's apprentice, his catch was life itself. It took two days' pay to buy half a pound of beef, and with these rabbits, he could feed his dependent family for two whole days, or exchange for beef, and so Big Henry's financial worries were not his concern.

"Give me a hand then, Ruskin!" the trapped man shouted a little peevishly to his friend who laughed at him.

"Not so agile, are ye, my city friend?" he said scornfully. "Mind, this is the young lad's territory", he added with a certain admiration, heaving his irritated friend out of the sucking mud.

Although showing his sympathy for the plight of these poor people was something he kept to himself, he was glad the lad had got away.

"Come on, ye men less chattering and more looking."

The strident voice of the following rider sounded irritated and tired. The rider approached them, standing up in his stirrups and holding up his flaring torch high above his head. He tried to see further into the marshy wasteland surrounding south of the river, close to the city and bordered by Hay Wood.

The wind streamed the flaring torch and was almost useless beyond a few feet. The boy knew the paths and byways in this morass of weeds and mud along the riverbank like his own hand so, keeping to leeward of the men and the flaring torch, he was not seen by them.

Then suddenly, with a cheeky grin, he stood up and doffing his imaginary hat.

He bowed and said, "Good day, sirrahs, hast thou lost ought?"

Then, with a laugh, he raced off along the bank, still bent double, zigzagging among the thorn bushes and rabbit holes. He quickly and simply disappeared, his silvery laugh growing fainter by the second, which only added to the men's discomfort.

His sudden popping up like a jackrabbit had caught the searching men off guard, and as night had already fallen, they resisted the offered challenge.

Then, with a resigned, "Hold back, lads, we'll not find him now", they halted.

With drooping shoulders, tired wet legs and aching arms, they scrambled back onto the rutted roads leading into the city.

The thought of strong home brewed ale or mulled cider awaiting them by the roaring fire was of far more interest now, and so was getting somewhere warm and dry for a change.

These roads out of the city were once made of wood, and now, with the holes made when the wood rotted or was smashed by a heavy carriage being filled in with earth, which was soon washed away by the rain, they were in a parlous state of repair. These large, deep holes appeared everywhere, making carriage riding and even riding or walking a dangerous game at night. There had been a practical reason for the use of wood for the roads in earlier years, as after constant assaults from over the border by the marauding Welsh, as this enabled the watch to set fire to the roads as soon as they were warned of a major assault being threatened, thus preventing them being used. Even the stone bridge over the Wye was changed to wood at one end, so that they could quickly dismantle it if they were threatened. Drastic, but effective at the time. It worked for a while, and when the Welsh marauders found the garrison there too much, it stopped any of the surprise attacks from these bandits and prevented their easy access to the city. Circling the Black Friar's Monastery, which was a depressing structure close to the river, the lad doubled back towards the city.

He had crossed the river in one of the many small craft which were hidden along the banks of the Wye among the rushes. He had mastered the fast current the river had this time of the year, when the rain soaked Welsh water from the mountains emptied into the river in a flood, and he knew where the coracle would end up on the other side.

This was a feat not many men could do as easily, but as Gad would say, "When y'ume desperate you can walk on water like." The fourteen year old lad had a competence and strength beyond his age, both of which had been acquired over the years by his poaching, which was now encouraged by necessity.

As he passed the outer wall of the monastery, he could hear the chanting of the monks singing their office. He shivered, not just with the cold, but with the fact that these monks put the fear of God into him, with their hooded garb and continuous mumblings. It was enough to make Gad give them a wide berth.

It was thought in those far off days that if they caught you, they would crucify you, like their master was done many years ago; and as religion was a mystery to Gad, the sight of a crucifix simply terrified him.

Climbing the city wall to avoid the pike men at the Friar's Gate was no real problem either to a young active lad like Gad, and he was greatly relieved to be free of those men and monks. In fact, most of the walls were in such a bad state of repair you could have jumped a horse through the holes. Anyway, the boy knew the patrolling guards would be supping warm ale at the larger inns by now, more than likely, and drying off their wretched wet clothes at places like the Green Dragon, or the Duke of York's Inn.

The sharp wind was not felt nor heard now as he dropped down on the city side of the wall into Plow Lane, by the side of The Duke of York's Inn, whose rear wall was actually the city wall too, with a 'plop'. The sudden quiet was broken only by the squelch of his homemade boots and the occasional gust of wind.

In the morning, he knew this lane would be made almost impassable by the quagmire of stinking mud, added to by the daily disposal of human rubbish from the houses into the street outside. The early coaches and horses would be passing along too and splattering a new layer of filth onto the walls of those houses, and in some cases, throwing back the rubbish dumped earlier.

He wondered what the time when a church bell chimed the hour was. Eight o' the clock! He was late, and his master had strict rules about being out after dark, but he shrugged his shoulders; and, like in all his adventures, he made sure he had his back covered by using a system of stone throwing to arouse his friend Thomas, who would slip down and let him in.

The domestic and other smelly filth on the rain-soaked lane was difficult to avoid, as there appeared to be little control over what people threw on the streets, but his agile feet and good strong boots helped to protect him from the worst of it.

The town's fathers had made a new by-law and soon this practice would be stopped by law, but for the moment he had to avoid the rubbish by careful dodging about.

He knew that around the corner in the King's Ditch it would be stinking mire by now, but his boots were strong and well made. And so they ought to be -that was his trade. Almost the first thing his master did when a boy joined him as an apprentice was to get him to make boots or belts, or whatever they wanted to specialise in, for themselves. Then, if it was a bad job, they suffered from their own ineptitude.

They learned *fast.*

He patted his day's catch swinging from his belt, knowing he could get two pence each for them after they had hung a day or two. Both the rabbits hit his side as he crept along the wall towards the few lanterns being lit, and home.

As an apprentice to the Guild of Saddlers and Leather Makers, this home was also his master's house under the lea of the castle's forbidding walls and moat, and it was still several minutes of fast running away.

Just as he got to Kings Ditch as he left Plow Lane, opposite was one of the many smaller city ale houses. Known as 'The Woolpack', its door was flung open and a man, obviously the worst for wear with drink, was tossed out into the mud with a splash and a cheer from the inmates.

In the beam of the smoky light which covered him, Gad could see that there was some sort of gathering inside and, being nosy, he moved across the road to look.

He had slipped through a hole between the city gate and then over wall, and had intended to make a run towards St. Ethelbert's, where his master's house was, but this was a diversion he rarely saw. He stood transfixed, with his mouth open and his eyes popping at the scene in front of him. He knew he should move on and quickly, but it was really the fascination of what he could see that had frozen his movements. They were obviously group of n'er do wells and without doubt a bit like him, only 'grown men', he thought, and they were up to mischief. Then, without warning, a large hand grabbed his arm and he was swung into the lighted room like a skinny rabbit.

"Well, well! And what have we 'ere then?" the man said to no one in particular in the crowded bar and kicked the door closed. "Name, lad!" the stentorian voice demanded.

"Gad, sir," the boy replied in a frightened high, pitched voice. It was still unbroken and he knew when to sound pathetic.

This news was greeted with a roar of laughter from the assembled men, and by way of an explanation one voice said, "When 'e were born, 'is Da' 'ad asked his wife where 'e'd come from and she were 'eard to say, 'By Gad Sir, I nerra know'."

The laughter erupted again, and the big hairy man let the little shrimp of a boy drop to the floor.

Lying on the dirty smelly rushes, his animal cunning advised stillness. A mixture of ale and urine assailed his nostrils, as men rarely went outside to pass their piss in this weather. The boy known as Gad waited for the opening to run.

Someone threw him a wing of cooked fowl and his captor said, "Now, don't 'ee move lad, mind."

Not that he could have if he had wanted to, as there were men all around him and the door was closed fast. It did not help that the unshaven, misshapen face of the villain brooked no argument either.

The situation he had interrupted was some sort of ceremony, he thought, and as he squatted, gnawing the meat off the wing, which was an unexpected and much needed feast, he watched this group of men. The alehouse was known as The Old Woolpack Inn, one of many throughout the city where beer was often brewed in house.

It was a small yet cosy beer house, much frequented by shepherds, sheep shearers, cattlemen and others, like vagabonds and beggars, who frequented there to spend their ill-gotten gains. This was one where the beer was homebrewed – not very clean, but strong and cheap.

The men here were mostly shepherds – you could tell that by the smell and they were surrounding another couple of thin, scrawny lads of about fourteen years of age. They were both dressed like Gad in torn breeches, old waisted jackets and dirty blouson shirts. Unlike Gad, they were shoeless. Their hunger was etched on their skinny limbs, and sunken cheeks and washing were not in their daily routines.

On the wall in front of them, about three feet up and in a circle of light thrown by the smoky lanterns, were pinned two items taken from clothing, a purse and a pocket. Fixed to each was a little sacring bell and a variety of hawkers bells were near their openings.

Gad became scared because this was a den of villains, a veritable thieves' kitchen, and to be caught here, he guessed, would mean certain death. He was sure. The landlord was a big, muscular, unkempt man, and he was clutching a small pile of coins, which Gad assumed were the proceeds of gambling and thieving. He also realised that this was an 'appointing' of a regular cutpurse or 'foister'.

This habit of groups of men training and setting up young lads as professional foisters had been imported from the big cities like London, where it flourished under Henry, and had even been encouraged. But here and now, it was regarded as a serious offence, and was heavily punished by the City Fathers. When they were caught, it usually meant a hanging.

The big man who had grabbed Gad was talking to the other lads. "Ye have one minute to bring me the contents from one 'o they pockets, but should we 'ear a single tinkle..." He made a slicing action across his throat.

Both boys licked their lips either from anticipation or from fear, Gad could not tell which, but in his case it would have been the latter. Bets had been made and the landlord held the stakes. By now the full attention of all the men was on the boys, and a comparative silence descended on the gathering, with just the occasional belch or fart and the crackling fire which sounded loud in the unnatural quiet.

The larger of the two boys was smirking.

"Easy, master," he said with a little too much arrogance.

It was then that Gad saw a look pass between the big man and another in the crowd, who took out something from his pocket, and held it closed in his hand behind his back. It was very small bell. A sudden belching brought a swift, curt admonishment to the culprit, and once again the silence became heavy. The group of men leaned forward, their beery eyes wide in anticipation. Some had their mouths open, and others took advantage of the drama to pinch their companion's beer.

Swiftly and expertly, the first boy slipped his fingers under the purse's flap and through to the inside and withdrew a couple of coins.

Tinkle, sounded the bell.

A roar of disapproval came from the crowd. The boy protested sharply that he hadn't touched the bells and received a cuff around the head for his trouble. He sullenly made way for the next boy, rubbing his ear ruefully. The man in the crowd had surreptitiously swung his hidden bell, which Gad saw.

Gad stood up, and as he had a natural aversion to cheats which had risen to the surface, he thought he would do something about it without worrying about his own safety. He gently but firmly pressed forward and, taking the greasy skin from his half-eaten morsel of chicken, he quietly moved his hand to the cheat's back and waited.

The second boy was not as quick as his predecessor, which was made worse by his obvious terror of what would happen to him if failed the test. He managed to get his hand inside the pocket under the flap and as he withdrew it, the bell man opened his hand. The young contender swiftly withdrew the coins, but this time there was no sound from the bells. The surrounding men cheered – a win at last.

Gad slunk back onto the floor and tried to look innocent. The big man's accomplice looked down at his hand as he had felt it being touched, and saw Gad slinking back.

He looked inside his bell and saw that a wad of greasy chicken skin was neatly jamming its action. The man roared his angry disapproval and told the big man what had happened behind his hand as the locals chattered about their win.

But their game was up, as not only Gad had seen the trickery, but the landlord's hand was already on the second villain's collar. Meanwhile, the crowd were patting the winning young lad on the back and pressing ale on him and making enough noise to alert the watch, whilst one or two blocked off the exit to the two villains and picked up their shepherd's crooks.

Gad felt a tap on his shoulder and, turning around, he saw the landlord's wife, who said quietly, "'ow much?"

Pointing to the rabbits, Gad, not one to miss an opportunity, said, "I gets five pence each".

Without a murmur, she passed over ten pence and Gad handed over his night's catch, tucked his money in his belt pouch and smiled to himself.

"I must come here again," he thought. But his luck was about to change.

Swiftly, the big man grabbed Gad and thrust him forward into the pool of yellow light.

"This lad wants to try his hand it seems," he said harshly to the crowd of assembled drunken men.

He looked around expectantly, trying to stop his imminent thrashing.

"What say ye? Double or nought?"

"I'm no foister, master. I'm a poacher, sir," Gad said, in his highpitched, squeaky voice.

The men laughed but nodded good-naturedly.

"By Gad, he has a warbler's voice," one man said, to add to the merriment.

But the big man was not pleased. "Nay young lad, ye try, and if we hears a tinkle mind, 'tis yer hide they'll put up the chimney".

Gad gave a frightened look towards the red-hot fire, then looked at the purse and knew he could not win by trying to do what the other boys had done. The beery eyes of the men surrounding him, encouraged by their win, shouted for him to try his hand.

The young Gad trembled.

Looking about him at the eager flushed faces of the excited men, and knowing only cunning could save him, he took out a dirty kerchief he kept for wrapping any cuts he got. He then pretended to wipe his forehead and, offering up a quick prayer to his saint, he swiftly pressed the cloth over the bells above the pouch opening. Then, with a deft swish of his free hand, he sliced the bottom off the purse with his razor-sharp hunting knife and caught the coins as they fell. He left his kerchief over the bells until he was acclaimed as a winner and then he removed it during the cheering.

The two villains were going to be soundly beaten and were not too pleased, and one, knowing what might happen to Gad, hustled him out by the back door and told him to run, "like the devil was after ye mind."

Gad fled through the archway and into Kings Ditch, dodging the puddles of putrefying rubbish as the rain began to sluice down in earnest. With the wind behind him, he made a good pace.

He knew that he had been lucky to have escaped two captures and made a fervent prayer to his patron saint that it might hold. He had to get back into his lodgings yet, undetected, which at this ungodly hour was, to say the least, very difficult.

The old church bell sounded nine times and Gad almost flew, as the thought of a beating from the housekeeper was not a pleasant prospect. The old dragon would be there, unless she was drunk or making funny noises with her friend the gardener and her horny hand was a weapon to be feared.

The other punishment he would get if he was caught was worse than any his previous captors would give him, as it included the ice cold douche without his clothes on, outside at the communal pump.

His master was very experienced in the art of cooling the ardour of young men, and the indignity would be as bad as the cold wash itself. The anxious lad crossed the shallow dip at the end of the ditch by jumping onto and over an abandoned cart, and then he stopped in front of the forbidding, dark, half-timbered structure of St Ethelbert's Cathedral.

Chapter Three

Ahead of him and attached to the cathedral were the dark and fearful graves which fronted the main road, and already he could see movement among the freshly dug graves. He stopped and licked the rain off his lips. Fear of the spirit world was a real thing with people then, as what they couldn't understand frightened them, and ghosts and all things spiritual were the same thing. What Gad could see was a dog nagging at a corpse, which had only been lain in the ground a dozen inches below the surface, probably done secretly and without permission.

This was often done to save the expense of a proper burial, but the body below in its casket would be left open to the sky when the dogs had devoured what was on top. Gad took a large stone, and a well-aimed throw was rewarded with a series of yelps.

It was time to go, and dodging the mud and dips of old burials, he scampered across the darkened area, his slipping and sliding feet carried him swiftly over the uneven ground. As he ran, he saw a rush torch held by a paid nightwalker, for a home going group appeared. Grateful for the company, he followed them until he had to leave their trail. He took a left and a right turn towards his master's house and home.

In the darkened dormitory, Thomas de Witt paced the rush-covered floor and listened to the rain beating on the skylight. His friend Gad was still out in it, or maybe worse, and his heart gave a start as he imagined all sorts of terrible things that could have happened to him.

Footpads still roamed the streets of Hereford, using the darkness and now rain, as a cover for their activities. If they were desperate enough, they could have grabbed Gad, which Thomas had already imagined.

Then they could have sold him into slavery in some Moorish country and he could, at this very moment, be being thrown into a pit full of snakes and scorpions and, and, his imagination began to overrule his common sense not an unusual thing with Thomas.

Then he stopped when he heard a noise, but it was only a servant clearing up in the kitchens.

Where was his friend? He heard the clock in Master Rolfe's room downstairs strike the hour. One, two, three, right up to nine. Christ's bones! He was late.

For years, Thomas and Gad had been friends, even before they came together at his master's house, and he was like a brother to him.

He had seen the activity at the castle yesterday as he had been watching when he should have been working, and had had his ears boxed for his nosiness. He had seen a large group of troopers and fine ladies of the court, and a pair of magnificent carriages rolls up the lane outside their house on their way to the drawbridge and the entrance to the castle. That could auger more work for his master. .

He started pacing the floor again until a well-aimed boot hit him in the back, as one of the other boys in the dormitory complained at his noisy walking about the room.

"Gerra' bed, you noisy bletcher." Thomas grinned nervously and was tempted to overturn the mattress of the complaining lad, but refrained from too much disturbance or the old bat downstairs would come up and find that Gad was absent. As he sat on his palliasse covered truckle bed, he put his head in his hands and wearily had to admit that Gad had already been caught by the watch.

'Thomas…"Gad's voice trailed off as he tossed and rolled in his delirium.

Meg was there by his side instantly, with a cold cloth for his head. He did this often during his illness, speaking names she hardly knew, although she knew that one, as they had given their 'son' that very name.

"Dear Virgin," Meg cried quietly, "make him well again."

Will visited him again the next day, concerned as to his welfare, to give Meg a break, and to reassure her again about the operation. She reluctantly went out to get some vegetables and meat, and left Gad in Will's care.

He sat at the side of the cot and when Gad awoke in a sweat, he saw Will, smiled through his cracked lips and ran his tongue over them, indicating his need for a drink.

Will readily obliged, carefully holding his friend's head and, lifting it gently, put the goblet to his lips. Gad looked at Will with a great tenderness and nodded by way of thanks, and slowly closed his eyes again.

Will took his hand and said quietly, "Dear Gad, when this life's tales are told and time permits and history's stories writ, a mention will be given to thy town of Hereford to keep you always in my mind. My heart is yours."

During the painfully slow recovery, Gad returned constantly to how and where it all began. Although time had marched on and things had changed, his heart still pined for his hometown and the friends that he had known there.

He could still see that little frightened boy, not dissimilar to his own grandson a few years ago, who was now on his own too, and he remembered. He wondered too how God's hand had fashioned what he did, if there was such a person and asked the eternal question. What would he have done differently had he the option to do it again?

His health and strength was helped by the fact that it had been nurtured by his past, hard life and his trade was one which enabled him to have a decent life. So maybe not any, perhaps he wouldn't change a great deal, if anything at all. He rarely philosophised, but there had been many times during his escape and rescue of his son Thomas that had seemed beyond him at the time, but somehow he had always managed to get by.

His association with the present Queen was something he was not sure about. As a commoner, he thought the lives these aristocrats led were shallow and uninteresting, as most never knew the joy of the early morning dew shining through spider webs. Nor had they ever heard the cry of an owl at night, hunting or calling its mate or watching the fox slipping quietly through the undergrowth, stalking its prey and returning with it between its jaws.

He remembered all those things and smiled to himself. No, he thought, perhaps I wouldn't change even the bad times, as those had their place in my life too, if only to prove to myself I could beat them.

With the two lads helping, Meg managed to get Gad into and out of the tub and finally onto warm blankets and thick linen bed sheets. He had hardly moved since they had bathed him, and at one time they both thought the worst had happened, but he still breathed.

He opened his eyes and smiled at Meg.

"Thank 'ee lass."

His voice was tired and croaky, but she was thankful he was back among the living. Slowly she fed him some more broth, then he lay back, smiling. He sought out her hand and held it firm, like he was frightened to go to sleep and needed the comfort of her.

But eventually he slept, drifting back in time again, still clutching Meg's hand.

When he was sleeping deeply again, she released her hand, covered him over more completely and stoked up the fire again. This was going to be a long wait for her, but she didn't mind, as she kept telling herself, 'He must get well, he must...'

The sick man still tossed and turned; both his body and mind were in violent torment.

The bats had joined the wind and had started to swoop in their nightly ballet, flying in and out of the spires of Hereford Cathedral. Their chattering and squawking was drowned by the noisy trees fighting to be heard over the wind, in a sort of macabre fight for supremacy. They seemed to be calling Gads' name as they busily whistled through the half-timbered top of the building.

'Gad,' they called. 'Gads'.

The city of Hereford, a small community much reliant on cattle and sheep, glove making and leatherwork, had gone to sleep long ago, except for such nighthawks as miscreants, the hobgoblins, witches and all manner of creatures of the dark. And Gad.

The black, stark structures of the surrounding buildings made the young boy feel squashed by the darkness, and with no moon yet, it was as dark as Hades. Gad shivered again, because although he was only comfortable in the countryside at night or indeed any time, he was mortally afraid in the city and at night particularly.

He knew that the human animal was the more dangerous species, and there were plenty of the more evil ones around now that the wars had ended. Bands of cutthroats roamed at will it seemed, and few ordinary people moved abroad after dark.

These trampers were made up of soldiers disbanded after the war, sailors beached when their service time had ended and, like a lot of their ships, they too were just battered hulks, often missing a limb or two, or an eye.

Since the ravaging and sacking of the churches and the beheading of the Papist priests and religious people in Big Henry's reign, 1553 was not a good time to be out at night in such a place. Despite the fact that Hereford's Cathedral Church was exempt, because it was not owned by the Church, it was still in Gad's eyes a place of mystery and danger with a great deal of 'mumbo jumbo'.

Soon they would have Tudor Mary on the throne in London if the young Edward didn't make it, and the cycle of killings would turn the other way round. It would be a time for revenge. The Catholics no doubt would want to exact a far fiercer retribution than the Protestants. But that was a few years off yet. All this was above the understanding of this lad, as he was a simple God fearing, fourteen-year-old boy.

He knew only that grown-ups were sometimes not nice to know, which is why he preferred the company of the animals and the companionship of the trees in the great forests surrounding Hereford.

Small of stature but strong and as sharp as a knife, to him church people were just dark mysterious figures, which spent most of their time muttering to them. They were on a par with witches and hobgoblins and Gad swore he had seen those aplenty.

There was one notable exception – Brother John, who was tutor and doctor and everything else to the twenty odd boys of the small cathedral school.

When Gad was eight years of age, he had been taken on as an apprentice to the good Master Rolfe de la Haye, a leather merchant and boot maker to the nobility. He had a house just off Castle Street, under the lee of the lower walls of the castle, near the moat.

It was a rare privilege indeed to be taken on, as there were many applicants for positions with him. In fact, he was only taken on as a favour to Gad's dead father, who had at one time saved his master's life when the King's soldiers visited the Cathedral Church, chasing Papists.

Gad and eleven other boys like him were at various stages of learning the leather trade – some on tack, others on wearing apparel. In Gad's case, it was the art of boot making, and he was paid a penny a day.

His poor mother lived in a hovel the other side of the city, near the Widemarshe Common. It was a crumbling, damp wattle and daub place framed with rotten timbers, hidden among other such places behind the Jewish cemetery, although the Jewish community had long since been disbanded and dispersed by the people of the city, to their shame, just outside the city wall. It was comprised of one room with a fireplace and a soil floor, and was really just a lean-to adjoining a smelly slaughterhouse.

Her neighbours also were not of the too savoury kind either, as poverty breeds its own kind of criminal. Some were evil through necessity, but also there were those who were just basically bad. There were too many children and dogs, they were always hungry, and the slaughterhouse encouraged both.

The smell and the damp were all too pervasive, and it was not surprising that everybody in the area suffered from either rickets or other diseases brought in by nature's parasites, already living on the not so young, nor too clean carcasses of meat in the unsavoury abattoir.

Dogs too, scavenging for food, were known to carry off unwatched babies. Accidents as well carried off their fair share of the unwary young and old, causing accidents themselves by bystanders, such as the military man who, seeing a dog grab an unwatched baby and in his rash attempt to skewer the dog, unfortunately pierced the small baby.

Consequently, Gad tried at every opportunity to help with the feeding and clothing of his six brothers and two sisters. He was the seventh child of a seventh child, so his mother had told him he would one day be someone important. He was a man to be feared, as he had the 'powers', whatever they were. She told him he had the power to foretell the future and would one day meet Merlin the Wizard, and this amused Gad, as Merlin had been dead for years and years, if he had ever existed. Gad was not so gullible as these grown-ups, and he was of the firm belief that once you're dead, that's it – and not even Merlin could come back from the dead. At least, he hoped not.

There was no doubt though, that he was a lot different from the rest of his family, as he was quick, skilful and sharp in his reactions. One day he might be famous, if only for making boots, but even he had his doubts about that. Maybe he would become a cutthroat! He had laughed at the thought.

The rest of his brothers and sisters were just scavengers or crippled, and could only beg or steal. But as to what he might become, that was for the future to decide. All he knew now was that his catch tonight of two rabbits, he had already sold for the money to buy some presents for his mother.

Gad loved his mother dearly, and at every opportunity he would try and bring her something special. Once he found a shawl, no doubt dropped by a wealthy lady, or lifted and then dropped by a foister in panic, and another time he bartered two pheasants for a small keg of local made cider.

Christ's birthday was near, and it was a special time for giving. He had been cleaning and tanning an animal skin, which he had removed from an animal he had found dead in the woods. It was a dark and light mixture brown fur, and he hoped it would make a warm cover for her aching legs.

His master had let him use the garden to hang it out to dry.

His mother was old before her time and crippled with stiffening of the joints which we now know as rheumatoid arthritis, and despite her forty years of age, she was unable to walk or move without pain.

He always tried to find a special a gift for her during the celebrations at Christmas; last year his present had been a scarf made from scraps of material from a gown which he got from a lady who made them by smiling at her. However, his father had been caught stealing a sheep with some friends a few years back and had been hanged on the common, so he was the main breadwinner.

It was not so bad now that he had become apprenticed, and when that period was over he could earn a lot of money, he told her and then they would move into a proper house. Sadly, she died long before that prophecy was realised. It had been a bad time for this young orphan, so Thomas and he became closer and they grew up like brothers.

His sisters and one brother were put into an orphanage, where they too died. Soon, he passed the huge mound and lower outer walls of the castle and felt dwarfed by their very height, despite their poor condition. The castle itself was still imposing even in its crumbly condition, but tonight that was the least of his worries.

Right now all he wanted was to be let into the house by his friend Thomas by the usual arrangements, when he was away 'foraging' as he called it, and perhaps he could get a few hours sleep.

The wind whistled and droned as he sped the last few yards to his master's house and hoped his delays had not made his friend give him up as being caught and awaiting a flogging in the town gaol.

"Not yet, dear saint," he muttered to himself and looked over his shoulder, expecting a visitation no doubt from his guardian angel, as he saw the bats whirl with the wind around the roof in their nightly entrechat.

He reached the wall below the window and, picking up a few small pebbles, he hurled them at the window. No response. Again, he tossed a few larger ones, praying they wouldn't break this valuable glass so recently installed.

As before, there was no answering face at the window and he sighed. No doubt by this time his friend had finally fallen asleep fully dressed on his truckle, "I suspect not able to keep 'cave' any longer."

Unfortunately for Gad, the room they all slept in was just off the centre of the house with a single boxed 'dormer' type window high up above him, and quite a distance from the boys' beds.

Unlike most houses of the period, it was a stone building up to the first floor and then a wooden first level and sometimes a second floor above that. He shivered – this time it was from the cold and he brushed the rain from his nose and eyebrows whilst a trickle of water ran down his neck, making him squirm.

Ah well! His luck had to change. So, with a resigned shrug of his damp shoulders, he made his tired way over the garden wall and dropped quietly into the small yard.

Standing still for a moment as he had been trained to do to see if he had disturbed anyone, he listened with his sharp ears, but he was safe so far. He ran towards a building which, although attached to the main house, was kept separate.

His master wrapped this building in mystery and said it was not a place to stay too long in. It was hidden at the rear, shrouded in trees and bushes, and usually was very dark inside, even in the daylight. If he could get in out of the rain and cold wind, he might sleep until morning and slip back in during the morning ablutions, providing the old bat's sharp eyes and hearing didn't spot the fact he was not inside the building.

The church bell had sounded ten times by the watch-keeper some time ago and that meant he had less than six and a half hours to sleep left. The building he was approaching had been a sort of burial vault at some time, and he had always been told not to tarry there, as demons visited the occupants occasionally on their perilous way back to Hell.

His laugh of disbelief always sounded a bit hollow and was not very reassuring. It was an eerie enough place in the daytime, but at night it gave him a dry mouth and he shook with cold and fear. Fortunately this was a place rarely visited by new boys without the dire warnings, and was avoided by all the staff.

"There was no need to tempt the fates by ignoring the signs," the cook had said one winter's evening.

For all that, it was just a store shed for the keeping leathers and dyes and suchlike, and thankfully was kept dry and weather proof and airy to avoid mildew, but it still made him apprehensive.

Picking the large lock was no problem to his nimble fingers despite the rain and cold, and soon the creak of the door told him he was in. He knew the layout of the store blindfold, being the oldest apprentice and the one trusted to store and retrieve the leather when it was required. His courage was beginning to ebb ever so slightly, as he stood shivering with the cold and fear – a light would help.

Chapter Four

He swept his hands over a barrel of grease used for softening the leather, and picked up a doused glim, one which he knew was always kept there. It was not that he was frightened, you understand, he reassured himself, but it was a comfort to have some light -he could manage without of course, but well...

These glims were homemade lamps, used a lot in those days to give just a glimmer of light, hence their name. They used grease made from rendered fat, which burned with a nasty smell using a wick made from twined hemp.

It took a moment to light, and soon the darkness gave way to a glow brightly enough to see his way by. Already, the acrid smell of burning goose fat made him feel quite at home.

He skilfully avoided the stone pots, rolls of leather, bags of hemp and bags of coloured dyes, and made for the back of the building. At the very far end of the shed was another pile of leathers, large rush covered jars and an assortment of boxes and leather straps. The shadows danced all around him when he moved quickly away from the closed door.

It was like the shadow theatre games he and his friends sometimes played when sleep was slow to come, using their hands to reflect them onto the wooden walls of their bedroom in the candlelight.

He could hear the scurrying of the rats and mice moving away from his path as he crossed the floor, but these were old friends of his, and they certainly held no fear for him. Animals he could cope with; they only attacked if hungry or protecting their young. Gad brushed a selection of these leathers off the top of the old stone sarcophagus at the back of the building, reputed to be last resting place of Merlin the Wizard, and he took a deep breath.

Not that he believed such old wives tales, despite his mother's forecast that he would meet him one day, he hopped up. His tiredness overcame any concerns he had over mysterious visitors he may have, and he yawned as if to prove it.

All new apprentices, two of whom Master Rolfe took in nearly every other year from local poor families, had to be 'sacrificed' on this old stone slab in a symbolic gesture of acceptance within the fold at every Halloween, as a kind of initiation ceremony that took place.

He shivered at the memory of his own admission into the trade some years ago. Then, he had been tied and blindfolded and laid on top of this stone tomb, and he could hear the moans and groans of his fellow apprentices.

When the scarf had been removed from his eyes, he found himself surrounded by dancing lighted demons, whereupon he had screamed, he minded.

These glowing faces had been carved out of marrows and turnips, with lit candle butts inside them, later to be taken around the town; but the sudden lights and faces glowing and dancing eerily and with all the moaning of his friends, it was a big shock to the system.

He was ashamed to recall that he messed his breeches that night. Now, all he wanted to do was to lay down and go to sleep.

He got onto the top of the slab to avoid the rats' sharp little teeth, and he curled up into a tight ball, wriggling himself against the rear wall as a support and to give himself protection, and tried to doze. However, a good half an hour later he was still moving about and fidgeting, as he could not get comfortable. He could hear the whine of the wind through the roof timbers, and every now and then a little flurry of dust settled on him as a particularly strong gust hit the roof.

He was not happy, so he sat up and felt around for a neck rest like the soldiers have on bivouac duty, which he had seen, as he had watched them prepare for battle on the adjoining fields.

In the deep recesses of the shed, his hand touched a stone cross of about nine inches in height, seemingly fixed to the end of the tomb. It had a circular cross member and was like the ones the monks carried at church processions, easy to grip. He held on to it firmly as he tied to swing across and down over the edge, when suddenly he felt it give a little.

His first thought was that he had broken it, and he feared the consequences if it was discovered. However, surprised at its movement, he pulled it again. This would do, he thought, as it is broken; and once more it moved, so he knelt on the slab, and with two hands pulled it towards him.

To his shock and horror it wasn't broken, just hinged, and the slate slab, which was the top of the tomb's lid he was lying on, started to move sideways. At first it just shuddered, then it tilted and finally it slid off in a flurry of dust and a heavy thud.

Odd bits of leather were sent flying everywhere, and Gad hit the floor unceremoniously on his backside. His glim went out, and in the panic to relight it, was made worse by the smell that assailed his nostrils. His bravery had gone out with the light.

Death and destruction seemed to fill the air about him, and he stumbled back from the tomb, now open. He expected a visit from Merlin or his cat at the very least, and perhaps a spell turning him into a frog. He whispered a prayer to his saint again, 'Help!'. The hairs on the nape of neck seemed to be standing out like cut straw and with his stomach churning and tightening alternatively in terror, he could taste his vomit. He was sweating, and yet he was cold. Then, in abject fear, he felt his own body to see if he was still a boy. He let out a long held breath when he realised he was still himself.

Slowly, as nothing had happened – there was no spell, no apparition, just lots of dust which made him cough – his poaching skills reasserted themselves, and his breathing became normal again. He stood crouched and alert on the balls of his feet. He was still moving his eyes left and right, although he could see nothing in the dark as he searched for the flint.

The light from the glim, now rekindled, showed him that the lid of the tomb was standing on its short end, half on and half off the entrance to the main body of the tomb. As if in a dream, he walked slowly over to his now disturbed sleeping place, and despite his chattering teeth, parched mouth and fearful mind, he held the light above his head and peered over the edge with his mouth open. His eyes were bulging in a mixture of terror and suspense, not knowing what to expect.

Despite all his protestations about not believing in all this mumbo jumbo and Merlin and all that, his teeth were chattering and his mouth was as dry as dust. But despite his aversions, the compulsion to look overpowered his feelings. The same ones he had that he couldn't resist looking in at the Woolpack Inn, which nearly did for him earlier. "Curiosity killed the cat" was what his mother would always say, and so far it had twice nearly done for him.

The bad memories of that place had long gone from his mind as he approached the tomb. However, to his disappointment and relief, all it contained was a set of steps going down into the ground – no cobwebbed skeleton, no collection of bones nor grinning skulls, just a descent of steps. Terror was replaced by excitement.

Holding his kerchief to his nose which was wrinkling at the still evil pungent smell of rotting vegetation emanating from the depths of this long unused hole, he climbed up and over the edge and started to descend.

Years after, he never quite understood why he actually climbed in to find out what was there, as any other person would have run like the devil. He thought the noise his heart was making as it pounded against his chest would wake the dead and he realised he was holding his breath.

The dead! He looked carefully around as he bent down to look ahead and saw he was entering a kind of low tunnel.

Every nerve in his taut little body was at breaking point and all his brain was saying was 'Go back!' But oh no, not him his body seemed not to belong to him as he continued down the steps.

Then he relented as common sense took control again, and he climbed back over the edge of the sarcophagus and onto the storeroom floor.

Now, he had this terrible urge to urinate and, losing his pantaloons, he enjoyed the relief it gave and watched the steam rise from the dusty floor.

Once more however, his curiosity got the better of him and he climbed back over the edge more easily this time and descended the steps slowly, holding his glim in front of him with one hand and grasping the hilt of his dagger with the other.

Well, there was nothing there, so where's the danger? Then disaster struck. Halfway down to the bottom of the steps, he missed his footing on a loose piece of stone and slipped. He had the presence of mind to hold onto his glim, but in his fall he dropped his knife as he grasped hold of one of the many supports in the wall for assistance.

His cry was pathetic. Caused no doubt by his dry mouth, it was just a whisper really and he started to cough as the dry air and a cloud of dust filled his face. Suddenly, with a growing sense of despair, he noticed that what he had grabbed hold of had moved disconcertingly to one side and to his renewed horror he heard and felt the sliding back of the lid above him, until it gave a dull 'crump' back in position.

He had still held onto his extinguished glim, but it seemed to take an age as he tried to get the flint to strike a spark and as it did, his nervous exhalation of breath made the light flicker quite alarmingly. So he covered it with his free hand to protect it. The feeling of abject terror once again began to rise in his throat, as he looked up and saw just a ceiling of slate – solid, heavy slate!

All he wanted to do was to shout for help, but nothing came. He had lost his voice temporarily and all it did was croak. His only escape route had been cut off and he was alone, more afraid than he had ever been before. He felt the roof and pushed it as hard as he could, but it was solid and would not move with his puny efforts.

All sorts of thoughts crossed his over active mind as he thought of himself dying there and his skeleton being found many years on, with his skull showing the open mouth of sheer terror. He shook himself and told his mind to stop over reacting.

Moving slowly along the passageway, bent double, his hand which was holding the light was shaking in fear and trembling as he began the slow climb up the steps at the other end.

The small passageway became narrower too as he walked, with both his shoulders touching the walls on either side. Now the light he was holding began to flicker alarmingly, as in his fall he had lost most of the fat in the dish, and soon he would have no light at all. That brought on another feeling of terror as alone, trapped and in the dark, might be more than he could cope with.

He was in a place not visited by anyone for years, maybe centuries; in fact, it was positively avoided and it was too enclosed to let anyone hear his shouts. This was a boy who was used to the freedom of the woods and fields, and so to be trapped in this claustrophobic tunnel made him sweat with fear. It felt as though there was a huge pressure on his head and he would be squashed flat quite soon.

Not a person to panic easily, he felt his confidence and self-assurance begin to dissipate.

The tunnel was quite long, about thirty feet, and went up steeply, bending around the foundations of the house until he came to another steep rise of steps. At the end there was a blank wall of slate and he was on a platform also of slate. With nowhere else to go and before the glim went out completely, he saw that the facing wall was not stone nor soil, but more like wood. He realised too that wood meant it was made.

The complete darkness, when it came, although he was expecting it made him cry out, and he fell forward against the wall opposite in panic. As he fell, he dropped his light and he instinctively grabbed the wall in front of him. He was panic-stricken for the first time in his life.

Then suddenly he felt the wall give slightly and a wonderful draught of air hit his face. Oh, the blessed relief! It was almost tangible. He collected himself and moved his hands over the small wooden door in front of him. It was swollen and covered in cobwebs, but was moving very slightly if stiffly, showing it had not been used for a very long time. The light too was better.

From a tomblike blackness, it was now a blue colour and getting lighter. Where he was he had no idea, but there was no shout of surprise from the other side so, taking his courage in both his hands, he heaved as hard as he could. The next thing he knew he was looking face to face at his friend Thomas who, not surprisingly, was more terrified than him. What he had done was to discover a priest's hole and escape route, and the various struts and supports, apart from giving the tunnel its strength, also hid the secret levers needed to open and shut all the exits and entrances. It went from their dormitory to the tomb in the shed.

So that was why his master kept everyone out of the shed. Merlin indeed!

His friend Thomas had fallen asleep on his cot and when suddenly he was awakened by a noise in the corner of the room, he got up. Like his friend, he approached the wall of the room opposite him with all the trappings of fear.

Something was moving there he was sure. Oh, God! He saw the wall panel above the washstand begin to move, and he was only just in time to catch the washbasin, jug and table top as it all tipped forward by the action of the tunnel's entrance flap.

Saturated with the water from the communal washing bowl and shocked by this apparition in front of him, it changed from what was a moment of terror, until he realised who it was, to a moment of relief, and they were attacked by a terrible fit of the giggles.

Thomas pulled his friend through the hole and both boys hugged each other, laughing and crying and trying not to make a noise.

Meg felt Gad move and start to sit up. "Thomas! 'Tis ye lad."

Then he lay back with a smile on his face, totally exhausted.

She wiped his face with a cool cloth, and Gad slowly opened his eyes. "Meg" was all he said, and the sound of him mentioning her name was like sweet music to her ears. She bent forward and kissed his rough unshaven cheek.

Soon she would go to sleep herself. The weather outside was cold and windy with the smell of rain in the air, but inside their little room it was warm and comfortable, and they were together.

Whatever he had been dreaming about, she couldn't hope to guess, but sometimes as she watched him it was so terrifying, although at other times he was smiling. One day maybe he would tell her all about himself, but she would never ask.

It was Sunday and as Meg awoke, she heard the church bells and the sun shining through the open doorway guarded by her grandson, a strapping lad of sixteen. He must have returned while she slept, and the lovely boy just kept guard. There was no sense in taking any risks with what had happened to his grandfather, and their neighbours would have no compunction about stealing, even the food simmering by the fire.

Just like his grandfather, his body was short, but promised strong arms and broad shoulders. His red hair was tied back into a knot behind his head and uncovered. He turned and looked at Meg.

"Grandpa's awake and seems to have stopped sweating," he said with a smile. "I 'ad a look at him a while ago."

His smile tore at Meg's heart, as that too was just like his Grandpa's, lopsided. She got up and went over to Gad's cot, but he was still sound asleep.

Too deeply, Meg thought, and made a note to wake him if he wasn't so in an hour's time. Despite the law making attendance at church compulsory, there was no time for that for her. She would say just a quick prayer and she knelt to ask her own mysterious God, which was what Gad called him, to make her man well again – although, like him, she had no time for the preaching and the pontificating these priests did.

"Please find it in ye kindness to spare my Gad, dear Lord. I know 'ee don' hold much with prayin' and the like, but per'aps I can do enough for both on us."

Young Gad smiled. He thought, how strange grownups were.

Chapter Five

The following day, young Gad attended his workshop and during the break, they were surprised to see another fine coach and horses outside in the lane. As they watched, they saw one dainty foot appear, followed by another, and a vision of beauty descended from the coach.

As she turned to see who was watching her, she tripped and fell forward. Gad reacted instinctively and rushed over and grabbed her around the waist, followed by a handful of young firm breast.

It wasn't just her breast that startled him, but the diamond encrusted necklace that nearly came off, almost hitting him in the face.

She stood up and thanked him, with her cheeks colouring with the deep red of embarrassment, and took off like a startled hare and ran into Master Rolfe's house.

Thomas and Gad looked, smiled and then grabbed each other in a frenzy of playfulness.

"She's mine," Gad said.

"No she ain't, I saw her first," said Thomas, and they wrestled each other to the ground in fun.

As they stood up, a rough voice sounded behind them. It came from the distorted mouth of the villain whom Gad had caused to have a beating at The Woolpack Inn.

"Lovely, ain't it?" he said. "Not her titties, mind, they'm two a penny. It's her jewels I wants."

He came up to Gad, his fists balled, ready to have a go at him.

"I wants money off you or your fancy boss fella."

Gad froze. He could lose his apprenticeship if Master Rolfe found out about his staying out late at night.

Quick as a flash, he said, "I ain't got any money but I can get that jewel for 'e if ye wants."

Behind him there was the voice of Master Rolfe, 'Gad, where are ye?'

The villain, realising he could be in trouble if he was caught here, 'Gerrit it then', and moved away. Without thinking Gad said, 'alright, be 'ere about eight o' the clock tonight.'

He froze. What had he done? How can he get that jewel?

Chapter Six

Gad told Thomas what had transpired the previous night at the Woolpack and how he had found his way back via the Priest's hole. However his first priority was to attend high Mass at the Cathedral, which was what Master Rolfe wanted, to make sure his two main boys went. Gad and his friend went somewhat reluctantly, as Gad had this problem to solve.

Normally, their listening to the previous year's new intake of choristers at the cathedral school was a time for great merriment for the other boys. This time however, they sat there quietly watching but not listening as the choristers gave their hard learned repertoire an airing, while the two boys sat unmoved.

Hearing their so far unbroken voices stumbling over the long phrases and pauses in the Plain Chant should have amused and entertained the boys from Holyrood House, which was the name of Master Rolfe's 'sweatshop', where Gad and his friends worked and lived.

But the Mass for St Cecilia, patron saint of music, where there is quite a particularly difficult section in the Gradual, did not amuse Gad and his friend as they sat sour faced and silent.

The rivalry between the various groups of boys was usually vented on the football field, and it was down to Gad this year to make and stitch the small leather ball stuffed with all manner of cloth remnants. Gad faced a more pressing need though, as he gnawed his knuckles and tried to think of a way out of his present dilemma. Last night he had escaped detection by a hairsbreadth, then, unfortunately, on his visit that morning to the leather storage room to obtain material for the day's work, he had been interrupted by an encounter with the very man he had caused to be punished for cheating at a foisting ceremony at The Woolpack Inn in St Nicholas Street. He had come wanting revenge.

The very thought of losing his apprenticeship made him sick with worry, and the two boys had racked their brains to find a way to get the evil man either arrested or somehow stopped from telling Gad's master about the poaching that Gad did, which would have cost him his apprenticeship.

Watching the boys from the cathedral school inattentively, through a haze of his preoccupation, he was not really listening to the high warbling as the choir moved across towards the chancel. They followed the Dean in his flowing robes, and then, dividing into the two halves of the choir, they faced each other.

He vacantly watched their quiet wraith-like movements in the candlelight as they gave a fair impression of ghosts in...

Gad sat bolt upright with the sudden realisation of an idea that had just flashed in front of his eyes. So startled were his movements that a Liber Usualis clattered to the floor, making everyone turn to him. Master Rolfe scowled alarmingly.

Thomas looked at him as well, but instead of alarm he saw a smile cross Gad's face, and immediately realised that an idea had been born. He knew his friend of old and his penchant for ideas – some had been no more than hilarious, but others were positively dangerous. As they left the cathedral, they didn't join in the banter between the two groups of boys, but hurried off.

Hereford was the most important centre in the west for all the judicial, commercial and educational activities in that region of England and Wales. The cathedral school too should have benefitted with a higher status, which unfortunately would have precluded the poor from attending. But it didn't and so they had to take their share of the clever poorer children.

The city had the only bridge over the river Wye for many miles either way, so trade and commerce was beginning flourish and the population had recently risen to two and a half thousand. The cathedral school was situated then in Broad Street, which meant that as they travelled to the Minster Cathedral across the graveyard each day and they regularly met the boys from Master Rolfe's Tanning and leather workshops, among other apprentices of the city.

A healthy rivalry developed and many a black eye on both groups appeared, as did a swollen nose or two and not only the others. Gad had his fair share of cuts and bruises.

Gad and his friend left the boys behind and they walked quickly across the Close towards their home, leaving the cathedral Boys to make their way back clear of any hassle.

As they approached the lower castle wall, they ducked down below the somewhat ruinous east gate of the castle and sat quietly in a disused sentry stand below the badly worn drawbridge.

"For all the blessed saints, Gad!" Thomas whispered gripping Gad's arm, "will ye please tell me what ye 'ave in mind? Ye've been grinning like a drunkard in his cups ever since we left the Minster."

Gad turned to his friend and, with his eyes alight with merriment and mischief, said, "It was seeing the choir boys in the candlelight and thinking how eerie they all looked in the flickering light."

He paused and looked over his shoulder and dropped his voice. "I bet that muttonhead I met at The Woolpack who wants me to steal fer 'im is more frit of they spirits and hobgoblins than most. What say ye?"

He sat back, grinning, and waited for Thomas to reply.

His friend was a big lad, with an unruly mop of black hair and a face full of freckles. He screwed his mouth up and wrinkled his nose as he suspected more trouble and tried to understand Gad's train of thought.

"No, ye have me there. What d'ye mean?" he said slowly, not having Gad's quickness of thought.

"Well," Gad said, but before he could say another word there was a shout and the watch was approaching on the double towards them. They were on forbidden ground.

Because of the ruinous state of the lower walls, nobody was allowed too close, as many a hovel was built from stone taken from the walls and that just made the rebuilding of the castle and its curtilage that much more expensive.

Gad and his friend nimbly hopped out and jumped up onto the path by the moat and swiftly left the scene and not a moment too soon, it seemed.

They arrived breathless at their lodgings just in time to see Master Rolfe helping another customer down from a very expensive looking carriage and four.

Gad whispered to his friend, "I'll tell 'ee later."

The chirurgeon arrived with Will and another man who looked strong and fierce. That worried Meg, and she said so to Will.

"Fear not, dear lady, he is there only to hold him down if the brandy does not dull his pain enough."

Meg was sent away by Will, as what was about to happen would only distress her, and a distraught woman would not help the operation.

Gad was awake now, if only just, but the surgeon started to ply him with the rum until Gad's beatific smile told him it was having an effect. He was an extremely clean man, the chirurgeon, and insisted that all his saws and drills and levers were kept in alcohol. He spent a long time preparing himself. Had he been a Naval surgeon, he would have saved more lives than most of his contemporaries ever did just by his cleanliness.

At last, Gad seemed to be unconscious. The big man stuck a knife in Gad's arm to see if he flinched. The surgeon tut tutted.

"Not there, Matthew! Watch me."

He took the knife and tapped the mutilated tips of Gad's fingers. The hand twitched, but he didn't wake. The assistant cut away the hair from the places designated by the chirurgeon, as he assembled a hand operated drill which he said he had invented; but as the bit had only straight edges and channels, he would have to keep removing it to clear the debris away and slowly the drill bit into the skull.

Gad moved and moaned.

The big man held his shoulders down and the surgeon held his head between his knees. Slowly the drill was removed and a dribble of fluid came out mixed with blood, which he collected in a bowl. For nearly an hour they stood drilling and holding him as four thin holes were made in his head, two on one side and two on the other. The bowl was about two inches deep in a pale red fluid.

Eventually the dripping stopped and the surgeon straightened his back with a groan as the assistant began to wrap Gad's head in white linen bandages, which soon turned red as blood continued to seep through.

Soon both of them stood back and looked at their handiwork as Will came in.

"So! All is done is it? The man lives?" He went over and listened to Gad's breathing. "Is he truly still alive?"

The Austrian looked slightly miffed at the very thought that he should have died. "Of course, my friend, but no, I do not let my patients die," he said a little haughtily.

Still in his drunken stupor, Gad had returned to his youth again as the pain in his head dulled by the drink began to throb.

"Come in young Gad and get ye self-tidy," the master said in his fussy voice. "There is someone I want ye to meet. Hurry now."

He beckoned him to go in front of him and tried to straighten the boy's blouse and twist his hose straight.

Master Rolfe patted the boy's jacket and pressed down his unruly hair, hurrying him along as he did, and Thomas was convulsed with repressed laughter at the fuss and trouble his master was going to, and at Gad's discomfort. His dark, wiry hair was as rebellious as its owner and, despite spittle, some strands stood up defiantly.

They stopped outside the door to his main room and Master Rolfe said quietly, "She is a lady in waiting to the Princess Elizabeth, so behave yerself. She wants a pair of soft leather shoes for Court wear."

They went in respectfully, and Gad's first gaze fell on the two young gentlemen, resplendent in doublet and hose of the finest material, gold insets on brown. Their legs were covered in hose of several violent colours, with each foot posed carefully one behind the other. Each had a hand on his hip, clutching the hilt of his bright, probably unused sword, making a pretty sight.

A pity they smelled so foul, thought Gad. Did they never wash? Was his next thought as he wrinkled his nose at their unwashed odours? He was right, they rarely did. It was reckoned to be unhealthy. And yet he washed every day in cold water from the pump, sometimes using a rough cloth to remove stubborn dirt, as did all the apprentices, although the soap was so hard it had little soapy lather.

These two young courtiers, who were no older than Gad, wore casual demi-cloaks embroidered with the finest gold thread around their thin shoulders, and their long curled hair hung about their necks. They were both laughing in a very nervy high-pitched way, and they constantly handled their dress swords.

Gad thought that if put to the test with those prickers, they would drop them and run.

The girl sat on a high backed chair, the one his master's wife normally occupied, with her feet supported on a small cushion. One of her hands held a fine linen white handkerchief, which she kept swishing past her nose as though there was a smell she didn't like – probably her companions, if not her own. The two bald headed men she kept in her bodice bobbed disconnectedly below her chin and began to become a focal point for Gad's eyes.

Master Rolfe introduced Gad to her with a flick of his hand. "This is Gad, Milady. He is my finest shoemaker."

She smiled at Gad, who was by now reasonably calmed down.

"Such expertise in one so young," she said. "Well, here are my feet, boy," she said and sniffed. "What do ye want me to do?"

He ignored the 'boy', knelt in front of her and gently removed her walking shoe, which was, as the London Fashion dictated, too small for her.

He noticed the beginnings of a lump on her big toe.

"With your permission, Milady," he said, and gently felt the whole foot. He noticed she squirmed slightly as he felt the

84

sole of her foot. It was hot and smelled unwashed, and was no doubt very sore and tender to the touch. Boy am I?, he thought as he squeezed he foot making her yelp.

"Sorry, Milady," he said, with a slight grin on his face. He carefully measured the tiny foot in all the prescribed ways and did the same to her other. Then he produced a piece of cloth and laid it on the floor.

Looking up at her, he said with a smile, "Perhaps Milady would not mind standing on this cloth for me to mark out 'er feet."

Her helpless look was signalled. She tried to get up without much success, as her dress had imprisoned her. The two men rushed over to assist her, and she eventually stood quietly on the cloth as Gad marked around each foot with a piece of charcoal.

The whole episode was related in every glorious detail to his friend, and they both sighed with their hands to their mouths, then they laughed at their own surrender, clutching their bosoms in mock dismay.

Later that evening, with more serious things to do, and having instructed his friend in what he wanted him to do, they both began to prepare their trap.

Thomas was a fairly clumsy lad and his nerves were not as taut and sharp as Gad's. Consequently, getting the whole charade correct took several tries, each one worse than the other. Poor Thomas – he was more nervous than Gad, whose whole life was hanging by a thread.

At about a quarter to eight, they excused themselves and went upstairs to their beds. Quickly they stuffed fresh straw under their blankets to give the false impression they were asleep. Their only worry was for their own friends, and they listened for anyone who may be coming up the stairs. Then they went to the washstand at the end of their dormitory.

Thomas was nervous and shaking like a leaf, and nearly sent the jug flying in his anxiety.

While Gad removed the jug and bowl and placed them on the floor gently, he said to Thomas, "Take some deep breaths,

Thomas it 'elps, I knows and don' 'ee forget what we planned."

Thomas quietly leant the stand over, and despite his shaking hands, lit a glim. Then he descended into the passageway, carrying the assorted trickery he and Gad had arranged earlier. Gad could see him gulping air as he went and shaking his head he replaced the bowl and jug. Then he slipped out of the dormitory and went downstairs again, and because now he had a reason to go there, having asked permission to go and get some more leather for the morning work earlier, he went out into the storeroom.

As he went in, almost immediately he smelled the ale from his adversary's breath.

"Ye got it?" he asked roughly to the seemingly frightened boy.

"Aye, of course, sir," Gad said, hoping his friend was starting the trickery. "But I 'as to warn ye, sir, 'tis a full moon tonight, and…"

"Don' 'e worry about Master Merlin." Cackling, he added, "'e's long gone. Give it 'ere."

He leant over towards Gad with his large, rough hand spread out in anticipation.

Gad 'accidently' kicked over a metal jug he had placed conveniently near where he hoped was a place where they would do their transaction. That was the signal to Thomas. The smell of burning sulphur permeated the air all around them, and a low moaning could be heard coming from the direction of the sarcophagus.

The big man froze. His outstretched hand seemed to curl inwards and his battered face looked ashen in the low light.

"Oh my God!"

Even though Gad knew what to expect, he felt his scalp prickle and his mouth went dry as they both stood stock-still.

"What's tha'?" the big man cried again in a hoarse whisper.

Gad now cringed on the floor and pointed with a shaking finger towards the dusty sarcophagus in the dark corner. The sound of the sliding lid and the increasing sound of moaning, coupled with a dim glow of light showing wraith-like figure in a flowing drape, miraculously appear from inside the tomb. They had spent ages trying to make a wig and a beard for him, and Gad prayed it would look realistic in the poor light.

Gad had to admit that the sight of this tall, long-haired and bearded apparition rising slowly from the dimly lit tomb was a fearsome sight.

Then Thomas touched the lighted taper below the firecracker in his other hand and tossed it out. The crash of the lid and the bang of the firework was just too much. With another hoarse cry, the thief took to his heels and disappeared out into the night, never to be seen again.

Gad shifted in his cot and smiled at Meg, who had just come in from the street, loaded with washing in a basket. His head still hurt, but he was feeling a lot better, that was sure.

"I think I'll get up a bit today," he said, and Meg frowned.

"Perhaps!" she said, using her cross voice.

She knew that Gad was still in a very emaciated and weakened state and could hardly stand up, let alone walk, and the thought of him meeting any of the friends of Dudley who had thought him long gone disturbed her, as in this neighbourhood spies and informers were two a penny.

He had been at death's door for nearly four weeks after the operation, and had been visited twice by the little Austrian surgeon. She knew he needed to strengthen himself a lot more yet, and it worried her.

"Perhaps I could ask around a bit first, eh? Then we'll see."

Gad conceded and sighed his disappointment.

Later, he smiled, sat up and supped the ale she had brought him. The bread fresh from the oven across the street was making his mouth water, and his eyes began to show interest in the things around him. Meg felt he was on the mend at last. Meg saw himself consciously feeling the back of his head, which was still covered by a large, thick bandage, and fervently hoped it did not pain him.

The narrow lanes and dangerously overhanging buildings with their accompanying rubbish, disease and rats made him unhappy, and he felt depressed again.

Then he thought of his Herefordshire home not that he had one as such but the freshness and openness there made him yearn to leave and return there even more.

Chapter Seven

His young grandson came in and they hugged each other gently at first, but the old man's impish sense of humour returned as he squeezed a bit tighter, making the boy squirm.

"I bets ye make the lasses dance a bit, eh?" he smiled, as his grandson blushed.

"Grandfather!" the boy said with a pretend shock.

They both laughed. Then the lad said his name, again only this time as a question.

"Grandfather?"

"Yes, lad?"

Gad recognised the signs and smiled inwardly as he waited for the conversation to start.

After a pause, the young Gad shook his head and said, "Oh, never mind," and tried to walk away.

The older man smiled in recollection and remembered Brother John, who was long gone to his Maker no doubt, and the talks he had with him.

"Come 'ere, lad. Let's ye and I 'ave a man's talk, eh?"

So long ago, thought Gad, looking at his grandson, I was just about the same age too. He remembered that he too had been confused at this age and he could do with Brother John now.

So far in his short life, Gad had met with and overcome all sorts of obstacles, even a brush with death itself more than once, but never had he felt as mixed up as he did now.

He had always known self-preservation as a way of life. In those early difficult days of 1547 in rural England, a boy of sixteen, near seventeen, was regarded as a grown man. He could take arms, get married, be hanged and have many other adult pleasures and pursuits. But since his mother's death, which devastated him more than he cared to admit, and his apprenticeship with Mr Rolfe De La Haye as a leatherworker, he had led a busy and full life. But he knew he wanted something more.

His mother had been afflicted with a painful disease caused by her terrible living conditions north of the city, which crippled her and made the bringing up of the young children, four of whom had died either in childbirth or soon afterwards, making her daily existence almost an impossibility without a man about.

Her condition was not improved through having to live in this daub and wattle lean-to, which leaked like a sieve, and with a soil floor, her damp clothes froze in the winter.

Nearly all the houses in the city of Hereford were of the timber-framed type, and were neither particularly warm nor safe. Those in Caboches Lane Church Street leaned alarmingly towards each other so that the top windows were almost falling, and one day they probably would.

After Gad's father had been convicted for poaching and was hanged on the common, he had had to become the breadwinner at seven years of age, and he had learned the art of survival quickly. It also made him into a strong, able and adroit young lad, which in turn produced a quick-fingered leather worker, particularly in the making of shoes and boots.

He could have become a glove maker, which was another of the trades popular in Hereford, and he had even approached the Guild of Glove Makers, but the conditions there and the looks on the faces of the workers put him off. Those were the unhappy faces of overworked children. Since his mother's death, when he was only been an apprentice for nine years under the kind Master Rolfe, his sisters had been removed to an orphanage.

He had lived in Master Rolfe De La Haye's large, mostly stone built house under the lee of the high forbidding walls of Hereford Castle, which was a rarity, because it was one of only a few houses which were half-timber framed. At least he had regular food, warmth and even a copper or two to spend – another rarity.

Recently, his master had made him a journeyman, which was a most unusual step, as it was customary in those days to keep the apprentices to their indentures until they were twenty four.

Now he boasted four pence a day and his keep, which was a good wage in those difficult times and, like Thomas, he had the good sense to recognise it.

His confusion had started he remembered with an instruction to go the castle in his capacity as boot and shoemaker, and take the measurements of a young lady's feet, with view to making her some indoor shoes.

She was a young lady of quality called the Lady Elizabeth, and if she was anything like the one he had measured a while ago when he had ruined a perfectly good set of hose defending himself against the local stonemason's apprentices who wanted to rip up the shoes he was carrying, then he was not in for a treat. He had given as good as he had got, he remembered with a satisfied smile.

A southeast wind ruffled his hair, freshly washed at the outside pump that morning, and it teased the pink, hairless cheeks of the young lad. He hurried across a rickety wooden bridge and onto the outer bailey, thinking what to get for his sisters for a Christmas gift this year. As he approached the castle proper, he could see the ten tall turrets glistening in the sunlight, and their individual flags flying taut in the breeze. He had always been brought up to believe the turrets were built to represent the Ten Commandments, and he often wondered which ones were which.

The boys suggested that the shape of the turrets showed that they ought to be all about fornication, only they called them by less respectable names than that.

As he reached the main gate, a short, thickset man stood in his path.

"Hold back there," the Guard commanded. "Who are ye, and what is yer business here?"

Gad laughed at the man's pomposity. "'Tis I, Master Barton," he said cheekily. "What be ye doin' 'ere?"

At that moment, three other men whom Gad did not know and who were dressed in short armour covered by tabards he did not recognise, stepped smartly out with hands on their sword hilts.

"Less of ye impudence," one said. "What is yer business here?"

Gad hefted his bag onto his shoulder more comfortably, and said with equal abruptness, "I am here to measure the feet of the Lady Elizabeth for a pair of shoes," which made him feel really important.

The result acted like a magic wand as the men parted and bade him quickly follow them.

Although he had lived in Hereford all his life and most of that not thirty paces from the castle walls themselves, this was the first time he had been inside the castle legally, that is.

Several years ago, Thomas and him had decided to have a go at getting in and having a look around, but it was doomed to failure, as their preparation did not include avoiding the large dogs with teeth like daggers and claws like knives, which roamed the bailey all through the night.

At least that was how they saw the barking hounds as they discovered the two boys' entrance. They reckoned they had run faster than anyone else had ever done in the world before.

Her Ladyship and her party must be powerful rich, he thought, as he scuttled after the fast marching escort.

He entered the main hall and was amazed at the crowd there. There were dozens of people of all kinds milling about, with several horses and lots of dogs. In fact, the noise and smell must have made conversation very difficult indeed.

Gad found the bag he was carrying getting heavier and heavier the higher they went, until they stopped outside an impressively studded door. The loud knock announced their impending entrance, and after being invited to "Enter!", the soldiers opened the door almost with reverence. Keeping Gad between them, they came to attention, bowed then turned around and left.

Gad was out of breath, hot and sweaty and in the sharp light a little disorientated. He could make out three arched windows in front of him looking out down onto the river below. There were three shapes too in front of him and he blinked to regain his focus.

Then, when his eyes became accustomed to the light through the window opening, further away were the forests of Hay Wood, and had he looked beyond them he would have seen the distant hills of Wales, the Black Mountains. This was the place where demons roamed and hobgoblins too, who would either eat you or cast spells upon you. The quick, small, dark men who always looked wild and untamed very occasionally came into the city on their short sturdy horses and traded. But everyone crossed themselves when they appeared, and most pulled their children in out of their way.

Over the centuries, they had invaded and ravaged the city and memories were long, when stories were told around the fires so it was understandable that they feared them.

Three ladies were sitting on the window seat, and although initially they were just dark outlines against the bright sunlight, when his vision realigned itself he could see that two of them were not much older than he was. The one in the centre was younger, and another was matronly figure, tall and imperious, whom he was later to find out was another Herefordian called Blanche Parry.

Two of them were smiling and sniggering, but Gad could see by their dress that they were definitely young ladies of quality. One of them wore the fashionable half hats, which seemed no wider than a band and was ringed around the brim with bright beads, which continued around the neck and disappeared down the front of her gown. Mistress Blanche was frowning, and looked very severe in her long, black, featureless gown and white cap as the other two girls giggled.

The colours of their gowns were beautiful too, and his heart gave a start as he realised the girls were smiling at him now. In his confusion, he felt his cheeks redden. The young lady in the middle had the most gorgeous red hair which he had ever seen and, uncovered by hat or veil, she spoke first.

"What is your name, sir?" she said in a quiet, polite voice without emotion.

She shooed her companions away in the same instant, although another lady, not as old as Blanche, called Kat Ashley, her governess, demurred a little and did not go far as Elizabeth waved them away.

Gad looked at the sole remaining lady and said to the girl with the red hair, "Gad, my Lady." Then he looked back at his feet.

The Lady Elizabeth fiddled with her overlarge sleeves, which were fitted tightly at the wrist by a ruff, as though they were uncomfortable.

Smiling coyly, she said, "Well, come here, sir I will not bite thee."

One of her companions who was still in earshot, giggled loudly but was quickly hushed up, by the older lady no doubt. Gad looked up and moved towards the young girl. As he moved closer, he became more confused and stared rudely at her, and it was then that he saw her properly for the first time.

Initially he had only thought of her as a young girl trying to make a fool of him, and then he realised who she was.

"I have been sent to measure your feet, Your, Highness and show ye some skins," he gabbled and put down his heavy bag gratefully. I

It fell over, spilling its contents everywhere. The girl in the anteroom, who was obviously still watching the scene, giggled loudly again at his discomfort.

Elizabeth turned her head and scolded her and suggested they had other things to do, as she too was embarrassed herself at this young lad's discomfort.

They were shushed away by Kat Ashley, who followed them out of Elizabeth's hearing to give the girl a reprimand for showing such a lack of manners.

He spent an uncomfortable few minutes gathering the bits together in some sort of order, when Lady Elizabeth spoke again. "Well, get on with it, sir," she said, not unkindly and Gad crouched down at her outstretched foot.

He noticed that, unlike the other feet he was used to touching, her foot was not only warm and tiny, but did not smell foul as most of the other ladies' feet did and that pleased him. He took from his bag his charcoal and cloth for measuring, and placed the tiny foot on it.

Then he stood his small stool upright again and also a quantity of skins, still dropping most of them on the floor in his anxiety. He picked out a few of them again and layered them along his arm and, still crouching, looked up at the girl. He raised his arm so she could make a choice. Being so close to her, he saw that her smile was genuine and her face as pretty as one he had ever seen. His heart did a couple of somersaults, while his voice became restricted and at that moment, he became her slave.

That feeling would last for years and would very nearly cost him his life. He remembered that if she had asked him there and then to jump out of the window and dash himself on the courtyard below, he would have done so willingly, and that too confused him.

She selected a lightly tanned goatskin, stroking the soft fur, and then held it against her cheek. How he envied that goat. He stood up and laid the other skins on the ground in front of her, his hands shaking with a mixture of emotion and nervousness. He did not step back, anxious to keep as close to her as possible; the smell of her perfume was like a drug to him.

Then Elizabeth, unthinking perhaps, bent down to rummage among the other skins on the floor. As she bent forward, Gad had a full and unrestricted view of her lovely young breasts, not yet filled out to their full potential; but it was a sight that constricted his throat again and did unmentionable things to his libido.

They twisted Gad's heart a further few turns as he gazed on their soft creamy shape, and he looked at them with mouth slightly agape and felt a tightening in his groin. Then, as she continued to grovel amongst the skins on the floor, possibly unaware of the turmoil above her, her young and burgeoning nipples came into Gad's view, and his body reacted sharply.

This made him even more confused and embarrassed in his tight fitting hose. He had slapped and tickled the local town girls when out with his friends, but somehow this was different. These were like delicate, precious works of art unsullied, and were so desirable. They were like sensuous porcelain globes of artistic beauty, and his mind was racing – they were only to be treated with reverence and not sullied by the hot sweaty hands of some 'sack' soaked lad.

As he stood back, her voice came over much more harshly. "Hast thou seen enough, Master Gad?"

Nevertheless, her hands did not cover up her modesty, nor did she straighten up.

"I am sorry, Mistress," he said.

The colour on his face deepened to a dark red as he stammered his apology, but when she saw the confusion in his strained groin, she was convulsed in a high silvery laugh at Gad's predicament, holding a delicate hand across her mouth.

Then she added cheekily, "Are thou disturbed, Master Gad?"

He looked straight at her, seeing the green eyes crinkled in laughter, and boldly said, "I have never seen anyone so beautiful before, Milady."

Then everything stopped. Had he gone too far? His heart was pounding, and his mouth was as dry as a summer's lane, with his mind full of the emotions he had never experienced before.

The silence between them was broken by a deferential cough and turning around, Gad saw a tall man wearing a fur-trimmed coat who had entered the room unnoticed by the two young people. He wore a cap edged with the same fur, and he was holding a long silver knobbed staff.

"Shall I have him whipped, Your Highness?" he said calmly, as though he were talking about the weather.

Gad instinctively backed off with his hackles rising. In his thoughts, he was saying, 'just you try, sir'. In reality, he said, "I am sorry, Milady."

The girl stood and, smiling at Gad, said, "I hope not, Master Gad." However, the full import of her meaning was lost on this callow youth and she continued, turning to her protector. "No, Master William, our shoemaker was just taken aback that is all. Is that not so, sir?" she said, turning to Gad.

Gad's full understanding of her first comment was for the moment ignored by him, as he felt a lady of such quality could not mean what he now thought she meant, but it would return later. Gad nodded and asked quietly, "May I measure your other foot now, Milady?"

Elizabeth sat down again and lifted her dainty foot. Gad was a good shoemaker and, placing her foot on the skin on the floor, he took the charcoal in his hand and marked it true as he measured her foot on the skin. Despite his disturbed frame of mind, and his trousers now wet with the marks of his disturbance, he made no mistakes.

"I shall return the day after tomorrow, Milady," Gad said, taking his emotions in hand with a great deal of effort and trying to gather his spread about tools and leathers together, "and we shall have another fitting – if that is all right, Milady?"

His voice sounded in the distance to him as his mind was also saying, 'Please! Oh yes, please can I see you again?' He carried on collecting his skins and the tools of his trade together and packed them, ready to leave. His embarrassment was mainly at his coarse thoughts and not what she may or may not have meant, seeing his stain spreading across his pantaloons.

Had he had the eyes of a grown man, he would have seen that as he spoke to her that same look was returned by her, as she appeared to be smitten too.

Even princesses have emotions, and the sight of such a young handsome, unpretentious boy so disturbed had so affected her that even she, with all her worldly knowledge was surprised; although at fourteen she was very court wise too, and changed her expression quickly. She knew the problems concerning her father, the great King Henry, and if he died and her brother could not succeed him, as her sister Mary was older, she would be left out in the wilderness.

Little did she know that that battle she would lose, and even spend a short time in the Tower, although it would be the only one and it would not be for another twelve years before she became Queen Elizabeth I. But for the moment, she had been enjoying herself until William spoilt it.

"We may have to return early, Milady," he continued, "so Master Gadulf may have to send the shoes by horse." He coughed again. "Your father's health causes us great concern."

Elizabeth looked up at her protector sharply. Although fond of her father, this was different. Then she looked at the simple country lad, living in a way off border town at the far end of her father's kingdom, and wondered why she felt as she did.

"We must have at least one more fitting, Master William," she said, her composure temporarily restored. "We cannot spoil Master Gad's excellent work by skimping on time now, can we?'

With that, she dismissed her protector, and Gad's emotions were bouncing around like a ride on the top of a fast coach, at first despondent and then elated.

Quick to seize on the final approval and before William could return and maybe cancel it, he said, "Very good, Milady, until the morrow."

As he left, he covered his confusion, which was still very obvious, with his hastily filled bag in front of his disturbance, and backed out of the room.

Inside, and before her ladies re-joined her, Elizabeth sat on her own with her hands cupped over her exquisitely painful breasts, and wondered what it was that was happening to her, and why her crotch was so hot and swollen too.

Chapter Eight

As for Gad, he floated down the steps in the castle and surprised those he passed by saying in a loud voice and raised fist, "I shall make the finest shoes in all England. Shoes fit for a Queen." He skipped along with the sheer delight of his new emotions, leaving a startled Master Barton, the guard on duty, with an open mouth. His mood continued as he ran back to his workshop and lodgings.

He slapped Thomas with a hearty thwack on his back as he entered, saying, "Make way for a master shoemaker, Thomas, one worthy to make shoes for our next Queen."

Later, the master looked at Gad with a soft expression. Having noticed the stain on his pantaloons, he smiled and said equally gently, "Is there ought ye have to tell me, Gad?"

Gad's embarrassment when he finally came down to earth became acute, as he said in a whisper, "No, Master Rolfe."

His employer was a kindly man, not given to that period's tendency, recorded by others, of always beating his apprentices. Rather, he looked upon them as his children and as his rather sharp wife would remind her friends, "'E's far too soft and easy with them. A hard beating would do them all a power of good."

The remark would be accompanied by much nodding of shawls and bonnets as they sipped their homemade apple wines from goblets and nibbled their cakes.

The finished shoes were handed back to Gad with a "Well done" by Master Rolfe, but as he turned to go Master Rolfe said quietly, "Ye know that one day she will be Queen of England?"

As Gad hesitated, saying quietly, "I know, sir, "his master added, "There is nothing there for ye, my young friend."

Later as the two young lovers were sitting together again with Mistress Kat Ashley, who was doing some needlework in the corner trying to look invisible, except for her sniffs, they looked at each other for all the world like lost puppies.

The shoes had been made exquisitely, with all the love and care he could muster, and he even found himself kissing the inside of the shoes, before he carefully wrapped them in soft lamb's wool. He hugged them to his chest as he carried them back to the castle for their final fitting.

Young Gad's eyes prickled with emotion as he thought over the events of the previous day, when he might have lost the love of his life, as it had taken him an extra day to finish the shoes.

On his way back the previous day, he had been accosted again by another three young lads apprenticed to the masons who were out for revenge, and they gave him a beating. Not that they got off undamaged, as for every bruise and cut he had, they also had plenty to rub with balm later. But what was worse was that they ripped his Lady's shoes.

He chased and caught all three, and the beating he gave them individually was so violent that two had several broken ribs, and the other was unconscious for ages. Love could be a great stimulant for the wrong reasons too.

As he knelt before her with his hand around her tiny foot, trying to fit a shoe on one of those pretty feet, she looked across at her governess and moved her head sideways, indicating that she should leave. Kat looked disapproving, with her mouth pursed, but she went and closed the door quietly.

He gently caressed her tiny foot into the first shoe and held it for a moment as though sorry to lose it into the shoe. At the same time, she looked down at this boy with affection and stroked his face with her hands, cool and soothing. As her hands touched his face he froze instantly, like a mummer in a silent play, with his hands still around her tiny foot. He savoured this moment of tenderness, not wishing it to stop and she placed her other hand on his soft head, gently stroking his hair as she would her pet dog, but with infinitely more love.

"Ye have a great hurt," she said with the concern in her voice, emotion overriding her caution, as she saw the cuts and bruises supplied by the mason's boys. Then she remembered she had dismissed her chaperone, Kat although she was probably still in earshot.

"Just a slight difference of opinion with the ignorant, Milady," he said about the battle with the other apprentices.

But it had taken him a further day and a night that time, and he fretted the whole time that she might have been taken back to London and away from him. He resumed the gentling of her foot.

"Please, Gad," she said, her voice suddenly breaking with emotion, "call me Beth."

He looked up with his eyes glowing with love, and not knowing how to control it.

"Beth," he whispered. "Beth," he repeated, as his world changed and went topsy-turvy. The name was like the sound of music to him.

Knowing the danger she was putting Gad in, she lowered her face ostensibly to inspect the shoe. Her cheek brushed his and Gad's hand took hold of hers and held it. This must be what Heaven is like, he thought.

The cough! It startled Gad so much that he actually sat down before he scrambled to his feet and, expecting a crack with the staff on his head, he turned away cowering slightly.

Elizabeth smiled at the by-play, and whereas she was now fully in control of her emotions, Gad was still in a state of confusion. As the daughter of Anne Boleyn, she had had a hard schooling in controlling her emotions and masking her true feelings, although she did not remember her mother, because she was only three years old the year her mother Anne was beheaded. Consequently, she always felt that she was someone less than acceptable by certain groups within the Court circles.

Her two ladies in waiting also returned and the older one, Blanche Parry, looked decidedly cross at what she had heard had gone on in her absence. She decided to have a word with her lady at the first opportunity she could. For the moment, she had to return to her home in Bacton near Hereford, Newcourt House.

On one occasion, Elizabeth had even been banished by her father when he was in one of his rages, although he eventually came round.

"Does Your Ladyship require more work on her shoes, or will they do as they are?"

The waspish voice of her protector was in direct contrast to what had gone on before. If what he had seen was for real – and he wasn't sure, but if it was, then this young lady needed a good thrashing.

Perhaps he might advise Kat accordingly. It gave Gad time to gather himself a little as he looked at his love, hoping she would say yes.

"Of course, Master Chamberlain," she countered her voice firm again. "I shall certainly need further fittings. After all, we must not stint on the excellent work of our Master Shoemaker."

Gad smiled with relief and she gave him an impish smile which said plainly to all present, "Silly old fool. I'm in charge here".

The Chamberlain was persistent. "May I respectfully remind your Royal Highness" – he stressed the last two words – "that we have to return to London soon, as thy father the King is unwell and may not last too long."

In fact it was a prophetic remark as he died nine months later, in 1547, as a victim at last to his malodorous ways. However, Elizabeth's thoughts did not range that far – only as far as here and now, and this sudden unexplained reason for wanting to stay.

Gad's heart took another nosedive at the news that she would have to return, and the look of panic returned to his face. But eventually Elizabeth, despite her tender age of fourteen, but looking much older, recognised the unpalatable facts which had to be faced, which included her duty too.

"Yes. I am aware of that," she said, still with an edge to her voice, but she had momentarily forgotten this, in the mental turmoil she was experiencing with this young man. However, her regained composure was complete.

She looked at Gad, holding out the shoes to him, and turned her back on the now assembled people from the anteroom. She said quietly to him, "I must go soon, but please come and see me at the Old Hatfield Palace if ye can."

Then, as if she had suddenly realised that she had the power, she turned back to her Chamberlain and said in the tone so well chronicled in later years, "Arrange with Master Rolfe De La Haye that my shoemaker may come to the Old Palace at Hatfield to continue with the fittings."

She turned away from Gad to leave, but after a few paces stopped and looking over her shoulder said coquettishly, "Until we meet again in Hatfield."

Gad left the castle with very mixed feelings. Was he in love? In fact, what was love? Should he go to Hatfield wherever that was? He had never left Hereford before, and it would be a big step, as he hated big cities.

It was in this introspective state of mind that he almost walked past an old friend of his, Brother John. The priest was the Tutor and what would now be called Housemaster to the boys of the cathedral school; but as there were only about twenty or so in attendance, he was all things spiritual and physical as well to them, mending their bodies when they were hurt and their minds when they were disturbed.

"What ho, journeyman Gadulf of De La Haye's Fine Shoe and Boot Emporium," the Priest said jocularly. "Why so glum?"

Gad smiled sheepishly, as though he had been found out in something embarrassing.

"Hello, Brother John," he said.

He liked the young lad who made excellent belts and boots, seeing in him a lad he would have liked to have been himself had he not entered an academic life and then the Church. The wise Brother, recognising the signs and symptoms of a boy in torment, said more kindly, "Let us rest awhile and talk, my young friend."

They sat next to each other on a low wall to the side of the graveyard near the cathedral, under the two spires at the eastern end.

'What about Brother John?' Gad asked, not unhappy to have his thoughts diverted from their present confused state.

Not one to beat about the bush the kindly monk said quietly, 'Why not the ladies for a start?"

Gad got up to go, but was gently restrained by his friend.

"No, stays awhile, my young sir," he said mischievously. "You aren't the first, nor will you be the last, who is just a little confused with this growing up business."

Gad grinned and then gave the Priest a sly look, saying accusingly, "And how many women have you had recently?"

This brought a huge guffaw from the unperturbed tutor and he slapped the back of his young friend playfully.

"Lord bless you, Gad – many, and why not? Am I not human? If you cut me, do I not bleed?"

"Tell me, Brother John,' said Gad, looking serious again and yet his eyes smiled. "What is it like?"

The friendly cleric's eyes twinkled and he turned an equally serious face towards Gad. Putting on his tutorial voice, he said, "Well, my son, it was given to us by a bountiful creator, and out of all his wondrous gifts it is probably his most special."

Then, in a genuinely friendly and more serious tone, he added softly, "Do I take it by that remark that the whole business of love confuses you?"

Gad nodded sorrowfully. Glad to put his bag down, the young lad sighed long and deep. Brother John's eyebrows rose alarmingly at the sound.

"Such sadness in one so young, things are bad," he added, still in a jocular frame of mind.

It was a very quiet time of the day and so not many people were passing by. As the day remained unseasonably warm and pleasant, he thought this would be as good a time as any to tackle this eternal problem of the young.

"In His infinite wisdom," he continued, "The good Lord of creation had decided that at man's beginning, it was also His need to populate this new world He had created. He also had to make this business of procreation a very pleasant business too, otherwise nobody would bother. However, the more delightful the gift of procreation was, it would mean that the more barbs or restrictions there had to be, to go with it. These He would add in direct proportion to the pleasure."

Then he turned round, plucked a small rose from the tangle of a bush behind him and held it up for Gad to see.

"Beautiful, is it not?" he enquired of his pupil. Gad nodded. "Notice the way it is made, and how the petals which are the flower's beauty increase in scent and shape as they unfold? In fact, just like a woman." Then he deliberately touched the thorn on the stem with his finger and, showing the blooded finger to Gad, added, And just like a woman if you handle them carelessly, they can hurt you too."

Gad smiled at the analogy. Gad nodded slowly, then said back to the monk, "what of my er… my… er,' and Brother John laughed.

"Your pudendum, you mean.' He laughed again. "It is called a penis, the Latin for tail. Ah, yes, that." Then he smiled at the lad once again at being embarrassed talking about such things with such an important Churchman. "Yes, it swells with blood when your body gets excited, and it becomes hard and erect and only then is it ready to insert and impregnate the woman." He lowered his voice and added with a touch of coarseness "Well, how else could it go in if it were not stiff and rigid?"

Gad smiled at the rudeness and said, "Is that love?"

Brother John shook his head. "No, not by itself – it's just part of the process of being in love. Just remember, although a wonderful gift, it is also a double edged one."

He put his arm around the tight shoulders of his young friend as they turned and strolled back to the main path. "Just remember, my soon to be journeyman Gad, not to let your penis rule your mind, as it will spoil it eventually."

They parted with a wave and a smile.

Thomas saw his friend as he arrived back from the castle with his precious bundle tight under his arm, and noticed that he was very preoccupied.

"What ho, my friend?" he called when he was a few yards away, but Gad's lack of smile of recognition did nothing to allay Thomas' fears.

"Hey, my friend, what's amiss?"

Gad replied, "Oh, just thinking," and Thomas added, unaware of his friend's mental torment, "Well, I'm off to the orchard. Master Rolfe is unwell and has asked me to tidy it up a bit. See you."

Gad wandered away too, deep in thought.

I know, he said to himself, a walk in the woods and a talk with my friends the animals will soon settle my mind, as they don't appear to have any problems with this business. Putting his bag and wrapped shoes in his special place in his part of the dormitory, he left.

Hay Wood was deep and heavy with leaves and brushwood despite the drop of autumn leaves, but the pathways were plentiful, and as the early Indian summer was pleasant, he walked swiftly into his favourite place.

He walked for about twenty minutes using the little used tracks made mainly by the animals, and was lost in thought when he heard a loud scream. Until then, he thought the woods were empty of people, as it was so quiet, and as the Royal party would be off tomorrow, most people would be gathering closer to the castle so as not to miss anything.

His mind was still very confused trying to assimilate all that he had learned when the yell happened. He slipped quietly through the trees towards the sound he had heard, and soon he could hear raised voices; women's voices.

Pulling a few sapling branches to one side gently, he looked into a clearing and his first reaction was shock and horror, followed by a strong desire to kill someone.

In the glade was a small carriage, stationary and unattended, with the reins loose and hanging down as the horse gently grazed unconcerned at the drama being unfolded. There were four people there, two women and one man standing, with fourth on the ground.

A local lout whom Gad had crossed fists with before, and who had come off worst, was towering over a girl who was sitting down, holding a hand over her torn bodice. The other man, her so-called protector, was sitting down, holding a bleeding mouth while the other girl administered to him.

But the girl holding her bodice was the love of his life, Beth!

Chapter Nine

Gad was through the bushes like a maniac and leapt at his adversary, who turned and tried to run like a startled rabbit. Gad grabbed him by the arms and turned him round. First one fist then another pounded his face in a fierce red haze of rage.

"Gad! Please don't."

He stopped with his fist poised to blacken his other eye, and he relaxed. His opponent, realising his chance, kneed Gad in the stomach and as he fell, the lad got up and raced away. Gad knew he would get him later and teach him a few lessons in manners, and it wasn't a hard blow, just winding him, but Beth came over to him and solicitously placed one arm around him and with the other, gently rubbed his damaged pride.

Once more Gad froze, just like when she had first stroked his hair and was transfixed by the excitement of her touch.

"Are you all right?" she enquired with genuine concern. "He will have a sore head tomorrow, but you..."

She giggled suggestively. Both were fully recovered by this time, and her eyes were glowing with love and pride. He was enjoying the unexpected turn of events.

Eventually he relinquished his hold on her and asked the other girl how she was; being of lesser resilience than her mistress, she was crying quietly.

The young man who had been accompanying them was still in shock and obvious pain, so Elizabeth went over to her companion, the Lady Catherine.

"My Lord Richard," she said, in that imperious voice already in her makeup, "Perhaps ye could return to the castle and advise my guardian the Lady Katherine that I am all right and in safe hands and we will follow shortly." Then she added quietly and confidentially, "Try not to tell Kat or Mistress

Parry what has happened, else all Hell's demons will be let loose on us."

He nodded glumly partly through the pain of the blow and the shame of his inadequacy, and not realising the implications of her suggestion, he helped his lady companion climb into the carriage and trotted off, with him leading the horse.

Left alone, the two young lovers held hands and looked at each other.

"My lovely Beth, is this true? Have I got ye all to myself?" he said, and Elizabeth looked roguishly at him.

"Am I safe?"

He put his arms around her and murmured, "My life is yours, and I would give it up to protect you."

Their lips met in a long, lingering kiss that set both parties on the rocky road to a situation that was far from safe and would determine the rest of Gad's life. Sinking to the ground with their arms still wrapped around each other, they kissed again, long and deep, with Gad's tongue searching out hers and she responded, moaning quietly.

Experience was on Elizabeth's side, as education and a Court of the many presumptuous men, not least his Lordship Thomas Seymour, meant that she had already had to fight off amorous Lords and Knights, whose hands wandered everywhere about her young person at times.

This time she was in love and when Gad's hands strayed into her disarrayed bodice, she did not object.

He gently enclosed her breast, which swelled in response to his touch. Her sharp intake of breath sharpened Gad's awareness of her lust, as he teased her nipple which hardened in delight and pleasure. As he caressed these wondrous orbs of pleasure, his mind was oblivious to the fact that he was being aroused to a point when he would not have any control over the result.

As he gently opened her bodice wider and buried his head in the swell of her small breasts, she stroked his thighs and groin, feeling the hard growth of his penis. Her own intimate, ready and willing erogenous cleft was eager with desire too.

Things had moved now beyond the thought of caution, as the two young people became totally immersed in lust for the very first time, and all sense of propriety, privacy or pregnancy was gone. His first experience of this wondrous gift, as Brother John had explained it, was one of complete joy and abandon for both of them in equal measure. With only the animals for company, there he straddled her willing body and wondered why he had left this pleasure alone for so long.

However, his entry was short lived, as his anxious new experience became a somewhat premature exercise rather like his first sight of her lovely breasts in the castle.

But time was on their side, and as they lay joined in lust, his body responded again to her administrations and he managed a slower, more delightful culmination of their desires.

Such moans and groans of pleasure and abandonment that they both exuded were so loud that anyone even reasonably far away must have heard them. But they were alone, except for the curious birds who watched from their perches high above them, nodding and twittering in appreciation at what they were seeing.

As they walked back towards the river and the castle with their arms entwined around each other, they said nothing. There was no need. They had both found love and lust in equal quantities. Her head was leaning against his chest and shoulder and their walk was the slow 'float' that lovers experience at these times. Just as they came to the edge of the wood, Elizabeth saw the troop of soldiers approaching at the gallop.

The two lovers very quickly moved behind a clump of trees and inspected each other's clothes for signs of their amorous encounter, giggling as lovers do. The twigs and grass on her back were difficult to remove, but together they made the best repairs they could.

Gad hoped they would not see the dark stain on his pantaloons which he covered with his hand, as the lead officer of the troop reined his horse to a stop and the troopers behind dismounted and seized Gad roughly.

Elizabeth was outraged. "What are ye doing gentlemen?"

The officer bowed and said, "Your Highness, we had been told that you and the Lady Catherine had been attacked, and we thought this lad might have been one of the louts."

Standing up to her full height, which wasn't much, and putting on her haughtiest tone, she replied, "Sir, this young gentleman is to be thanked and rewarded, for it was he who saved us from the attack which could have been of a serious nature."

Gad was almost unable to hide his amusement, but by bending his head, his eyes did not betray her.

"They are quite safe sir, and the enemy has been routed," he said and bowed to the officer.

Kat Ashley was beside herself. "I said one gentleman was not enough protection," she complained, "but am ye really safe?"

Elizabeth looked at Catherine, her erstwhile companion who was now fully recovered.

"I hope so Kat, I hope so," much to Catherine's amusement.

Gad was smiling at his wife, Meg, as he lay on his cot and she wondered what had made him smile for so long as he dreamt. He sat up and asked his wife for a drink. As he supped, he spoke to Meg.

"They have been so kind to us here, lass. I wonder what we can do to repay them for it all and what of Will? This is really a house for the actors, and we are in the way. Young Will has offered us the chance to get away from London and travel back to Stratford where his family lives.'

Meg was not happy about it and conceded that Gad being inactive would be worse than a bit of stress from making the journey, so she agreed. It was more than a couple of months, almost six, since he had been brought here, more dead than alive to this hovel in Cheapside, and now he was on his feet and able to take short walks, it was time to give them both a better place to stay.

Will had told him about his father's difficulties, not as hint to get help, but more as a self-defensive reason to explain why he wanted to leave home permanently. He desperately wanted to become an actor and writer too, and with the help of his printer friend Richard Field, he had written and had printed several plays and sonnets.

So it was decided, and late one night a string of horses set off across London in the dead of night and made for Chiswick as a first stop. From there they intended to carry on to Hounslow while they had their company of men, feeling safe, although this place was still regarded as the haunt of many desperadoes who gathered in the tree-covered marshy heath.

Will and a few of his young friends had promised to ride along with them as protection for part of the way, and what a gay group they were. There were Gad and Meg, followed by Thomas, his son, and his wife, heavily pregnant again, and their other three children from six to ten, as well as Gad Junior. He was just sixteen.

They sang and recited poetry, with each trying to outdo the other but as always it was Wil who was called upon to recite one of his many sonnets, all of which made the journey a short and pleasant one. So, despite the fact he had not yet seen his grandson on the stage, the recitations and singing by him and his many friends were more than satisfactory to Gad and Meg.

The men they had hired as protection who had been recommended by one of Will's friends and some of his fellow actors, in fact all turned out to be actors too, who were not working at the moment and needed a purse. But they seemed big and strong enough, and their flamboyant manner gave off an impression of being ex-soldiers of the Queen; after all, they were actors. Whether they could use the weapons that they carried was another thing though, as being aggressive on a stage was one thing, but in real life – well, that was another. However, they made enough noise, if nothing else.

Work back in Stratford, he knew, would be plentiful, as without doubt many of his customers whom he had left earlier when he had returned to Cheapside to see young Gad on the stage, were waiting for his work to recommence. He had assured them that once he got back to Stratford and as soon as he was rested, and began to feel better doing the work he loved, he would be welcomed back with great pleasure, as good leather workers were hard to find, and none were as good as Gad and his son.

His son Thomas was getting expert too in the art of shoe and boot making also, and so the work would be good for both of them. The big houses locally, which had a need for lots of good leatherwork, would soon occupy him full-time.

Both Gad and Meg were greatly concerned for John Shakespeare, Will's father. Will had told them that he seemed to spend so much time being a public figure with the title of Alderman that his own business went downhill quickly. He had tried to recapture some of his lost wealth, but in the end he lost his finest and most loved property, the Arden property known as Wilmcote.

It was his wife's really, and that hurt both John and Will – more in fact than his wife. But Meg's first priority was to get her husband moving, albeit slowly and with care, and not to travel too far at first. Meanwhile, Gad's grandson returned with Will one evening as they rested at an inn at Chiswick. They had great news.

Will Shakespeare had suddenly proposed marriage to a lady of his acquaintance and they wished to tell everyone about it, mainly because Anne, his bride to be, was pregnant. They came and stayed at Chiswick so that the ceremony could take place away from his father's neighbours. It went off without a hitch; however, the disgrace nearly killed Will's mother, and she had refused to come to the wedding.

It gave Gad a chance to meet John Shakespeare again, and they took to each other straight away and both felt that they could complement each other in their work. Meg could hear them making plans in the taproom as the youngsters made merry. She smiled. John would be good for Gad.

The look on Gad's face when he at last returned to Meg was a relief to her, knowing that he was getting stronger by the day.

Their grandson, young Gad, had joined up with The Queens' Men by now, who acted especially for Her Majesty, and was lost to Gad for the first time in his life. He accepted his grandfather's advice to use a pen name to hide his real identity which, he was told, was the normal practice in the acting profession, so they could acquire spectacular and easily remembered names to advance their popularity. They wished him well and Meg cried.

Thomas·was perplexed at this, as he knew the real reason for Gad's suggestion all his life he known he was someone special because of all the running and the hiding in his early years with his father, but he had never been told why.

Perhaps his father might tell him one day, so when Gad was more than a bit oiled than normal, with the wine, Thomas tackled him as they sat by the river Thames at Chiswick Reach.

He had been given the name Thomas de Witt, after his father's first true friend who had saved his father's life when they had both left for London many years ago, but that was all.

Gad was pleased to recall it, but quietly wept for his long dead friend. Gad straightened up as they reached the inn where they were staying and faced his son, looking straight into his eyes.

"Thomas, my son, all these years I have saved ye from the knowledge of who your real Ma was 'cause it'd have caused ye pain and maybe worse. But this I promise ye. When we get to Stratford and we feel safe again, I will tell ye.'

They hugged and walked on.

It was now the summer of 1581 and young Gad, the son of Thomas, was with Will Shakespeare and their company and had begun to act out some of Will's sonnets and a few five act plays.

Gad and Meg had left Chiswick and moved to Hounslow just six months after Will's marriage to Anne Hathaway. They had moved earlier than Meg had liked, because she felt they were still far too close to London. Then, after a further incident in Hounslow, she knew they had to move again that is, as soon as Gad was properly rested.

Will though, still had to earn a living as well as acting and writing, and with his newfound friends of young Gad and Thomas, they both returned to Stratford and helped in his father's wool shop. By way of compensation and the fact he could not pay young Gad, he taught him to read and write. Wil wondered whether he ought to have become a teacher, and so the exercise had a mutual benefit. His plays though were now gaining the notice of the Queen, and that worried Gad senior.

Their rest in Hounslow was short–lived, as it was not the most salubrious place to live.

The Heather there had become a haven for all sorts of miscreants, and danger always lurked when some of the inhabitants decided to try their hand outside their environs.

The incident, which created their hasty move from Hounslow, was a serious one and one which Gad recognised could involve the hand of his arch enemy, Dudley. When Gad Senior and family had moved out towards the edge of London to Hounslow, they took a house not far from an army post set up to curb the wanton outrages of the bands of troublemakers.

They gathered ever-growing numbers there, which increased after every ship, was beached and every army was disbanded. Gad felt secure with so many soldiers around the place, and had the occasional drink at the alehouse known as The Hussars.

Chapter Ten

On one such visit, he drank too much and was kindly taken home by two men in dark cloaks and wide brimmed hats. They looked sharply at Meg, and then warned her that if he was the Master Gad, the boot maker, he ought to leave there as soon as possible, as there were those people abroad who would like to see him dead.

They never left their names, but were certainly more than idle noblemen or travelling carpetbaggers. Meg was confused. Why was there all this great fuss over her husband? What had he done? He was just a humble boot and shoemaker. Why?

For the first time in her married life, she began to doubt Gad, and that hurt. Surely he was just a boot maker, not a politician or a spy or a villain. It had puzzled Meg for a long time, both the fact that Gad had been away from her for nearly eighteen months, those many years ago and then had returned with this young lad. She had never questioned her man when they had met, but trusted him with his simple ways and slow gentle caring of her during their life together.

They had met in Stratford when she was working in an Inn on the edge of town, and Gad was on his way through to find his Lady Elizabeth.

Her parents were dead a long time ago, and the hostelry where she had worked as a pot woman and where she had met Gad was not one of the more salubrious kinds, keeping a bawdy house upstairs. In her innocence, she had never queried why so many men kept disappearing upstairs so often, although she had plenty of offers to go there from her customers. But what for she had wondered?

She first saw Gad when she was being hassled by a couple of young bloods from inner London. They had got a gut full of ale before they had arrived, as their fancy shirts and doublets testified, wet from misdirected ale, and their stockings were covered in more than few rips and tears.

The older one was trying to show off and, as Meg bent over to put the jugs of ales on their table, he slipped his hand into her blouse and pulled her onto his lap. Ale and tray went crashing, and she screamed at him as they both ended up on the floor. He then grabbed her and tried to get onto her as she floundered.

Egged on by his friend, he was feverishly trying to lift her skirts up. No one else seemed to mind, and it would have got really out of hand but for Gad. He was a young strong lad of twenty and he got up and, leaning over the man, lifted him bodily off the girl, dragged him to the door and threw him out into a none too pleasant lane in the rain. He went back in and saw the man's friend smacking Meg about the face with his leather glove.

As she cowered, and with no one else interfering, just looking, Gad launched himself at the man and took hold of him by the hair. He pulled him across his lap and then he proceeded to thrash him with the fallen tray which was made of a heavy wood. The pain and the indignity were too much for him, and eventually Gad was pushed away and the humiliated young man ran from the house, holding his backside.

The accompanying noise of the laughter and drunken abuse from the now enthusiastic drinkers followed him outside. Meg came up to Gad and thanked him with a coy smile, blushing as she did. She was only sixteen and Gad had just turned twenty.

The landlord had joined them at Gad's table, she remembered, and in all seriousness explained to Gad whom he had tangled with.

"The older man was one I hadn't seen afore, but was moron like in the other's employ. His minder I suppose. I suspect they be Lunnon men." He put his hand on Gad's arm. "Take care, young sir you'm in bad trouble. The lad you soundly spanked was a relation of ye Thomas Seymour, 'im another dangerous man. So get ye far from 'ere if ye can."

Gad had not long arrived in Stratford on his way to London, which part he did not know, and he had nowhere to go. Meg was upset and frightened, and asked her landlord if she might go and "find him somewheres to hide for a while."

The landlord agreed and let the two young people slip out through the cellar.

Gad had liked what he had seen of Stratford, and the girl he was running with seemed a nice enough lass.

They stopped not far from Henley Street and Meg pulled Gad into the darkened doorway, as several horsemen came riding by with torches held high, obviously looking for someone. The closeness of the girl, despite the smell of ale on her, was a new experience for Gad, and a pleasant one at that.

Since his dalliance with Elizabeth, he had not bothered much with girls, and the death of his friend had hit him hard too.

Meg often sat in her rocking chair when Gad was recuperating and thought on those days. They were good ones. He had been a very correct man in his courting of her, although he didn't offer marriage, but inevitably they became lovers.

He had explained to her about his desire to see a woman called Elizabeth, although he didn't tell her who she was, and said that as soon as he saw her – and he was sure the spell would be broken – then perhaps he could speak more freely to her.

She was worried about this woman, whoever she was, as she sounded like a lady of quality making her much too good than her for Gad.

For about a year and a half, they had lived as man and wife in Stratford and he had begun to earn his keep as a boot maker and repairer and it was not long before he became well known as an honest man and a good and fair tradesman.

Then, without warning, he had left and returned nearly eighteen months later with this half-nourished and pathetic little boy, who was now a grown man in his own right. Together they had brought his lad up as their own and as the years went by, all memories of this troublesome time were buried. She thought.

Since the attempted hanging though, it brought all the bad things back again; if only she knew why. She was still unhappy at the mystery that surrounded Gad.

One incident happened early on, she remembered, after they had been together in Stratford for about six months. One of the men, a John Shakespeare, had got himself into trouble over standing surety for one of his friends who had then 'welshed' on him.

John Shakespeare was a good-natured man, but more in love with himself than his family. Gad nevertheless had felt sorry for him, and had helped him out with a loan of ten pounds. The meeting with this young man was to have a profound effect on Gad's life.

Meg knew that the memory of Elizabeth and their love, although now tempered by time, still gnawed away at him, and as she feared, he told Meg one day that he had to go to London alone.

The next day, he had left very early before Meg was up and about. He was just twenty two.

That were long time ago, thought Meg. The meeting in Hounslow at the Hussar alehouse with the two dark cloaked men sobered up Gad enough for him to think it was time now to explain to Meg all about his enemies, and how he had met them. She pulled up a cushion and sat in her favourite place, at his feet with her head between his thighs.

Meg had never had children of her own, despite a full and intimate life with Gad, and that sometimes worried her. Perhaps the Virgin Mary was punishing her for living in sin with Gad and every now and then she hinted strongly they ought to wed.

Gad explained that when he was a journeyman in Hereford he had met a lady in the castle there while fitting her for shoes. He said rather embarrassingly that he had fallen in love with her and her with him, but he never mentioned their dalliance in Hay Wood, nor the fact that he had not realised the full result of that encounter. He had hastily explained that at that age it was just a calf-love and of no consequence when he saw Meg pouting at the news of his 'lady'.

"I 'spec she were a pretty lady, no doubt," she had pouted.

He went on to explain how, when he became a proper journeyman and knew he could better himself elsewhere, so his friend Thomas and him had left Hereford to seek their fortune closer to London.

They had taken the direct route, which was across fields and down narrow lanes, using the sun as a guide, having been told that London was sort of west of their present position.

The River Wye was a good guide too, and soon the saw the great spire of Gloucester Cathedral.

Climbing a steep field, they suddenly heard a noise of men shouting and, knowing it was a dangerous time, they hid behind a row of bushes at the top of the hill.

They watched as a man appeared to be running for his life, followed by a group of men waving swords, sticks and an assortment of weapons.

Not wanting to see the man caught, Gad whispered to Thomas, and they stood up, shouting to an imaginary force behind them, waving them on. The chasing group stopped as Gad ran towards them, still beckoning the imaginary force. The cowardly chasers dispersed and ran off back into the woods. Gad called to the man being chased and beckoned him over.

They all ran back over the hill and to the victim's shock, there were no men.

"Where be yer friends?" he asked, turning his head around in case he had missed them.

Gad and Thomas grinned. "Just us," Thomas said with a smile.

Gad elucidated. "We've fought the apprentices in Hereford, and some were brave and some were cowards, so when we saw the rabble chasing ye, we recognised the cowards." He grinned self-consciously. "Mind, once they'm reorganised themselves, they'll be back, so we ought to move on fast."

Several miles further on, they found a high copse known as Glasshouse Hill, and settled down for the evening.

Their new friend introduced himself as Rolf Carter, a dealer in cattle. He was just on his way home when the villains saw him as easy meat and chased him. As he knew thereabouts, he was able to direct them to Tewkesbury, and they parted amicably.

After a night's sleep under the stars and a full belly from their hunting, they were in good spirits as they entered the long lane that crossed the river ahead and town of Tewkesbury.

Halfway down the lane, suddenly four men holding staffs appeared. They were led by a villainous looking man dressed as a pirate, with a headscarf tied tightly around his head and waving a much-used cutlass.

"We meet again my clever friends," he crowed in delight. "Now I wants yer hide." He swung his cutlass over his head.

As he had shown earlier, Gad had an inbuilt ability to think on his feet. He turned to Thomas, who was white with fear.

"Take off yer coat, Thomas, and do what I does."

Then they filled their pockets with stones.

As the men charged them, the two friends stood their ground, swirling their coats over their heads. As the men got close, Gad swung his coat low and threw it at the feet of two of the men.

Thomas did likewise, and it took the men completely by surprise. As their feet became entangled in the coats, they fell forward, and Gad swung his staff hard at the heads of the fallen men. Thomas also did the same, and soon they only had the pirate to deal with. He was a different kettle of fish and was obviously used to hand-to-hand fighting; quick as a flash, he slashed his cutlass at Thomas's head. Thomas dropped like a fallen tree with his head half severed and lay there, bleeding to death.

Gad's reaction was the same as that which had helped him to save his Beth from the youth in Hay Wood. First the shock at the horror, then a red mist seemed to descend over him and he roared as he ran at the pirate.

Although he was expecting Gad's reaction, the sheer ferocity of his attack was something he had not bargained for. Swinging his cutlass at the madman attacking him, it caught and stuck in Gad's staff, and the two men fell over together. The staff and cutlass were dropped, but Gad was the first to react and, still screaming, he smashed his fist into the face of his opponent. Then, grabbing the dropped cutlass, now free of the staff, and swinging it high, he slashed at the head of his enemy.

He kept on slashing until a couple of men who had arrived grabbed him and held him off.

Still shouting and crying, they held him until he stopped, and he too fell to the ground.

The men and women of Tewkesbury, a small village dominated by an Abbey, carried Thomas and led Gad back to the Abbey, where the monks treated Gad and respectfully cleaned Thomas and laid him out for burial.

The monks and residents of this small place were very grateful to Gad for killing the gang of cutthroats, who had terrorised the village for several months, taking money and goods and abusing their womenfolk. After a discussion, they awarded Gad fifty guineas.

Gad told how he had been distraught for a long time and he began spending all his money on ale and gambling, soon becoming penniless. Then he had met Meg, and for a moment they clasped each other in tenderness, as they remembered. But this urgent need to find Elizabeth again had become an obsession, and so he had left Meg and travelled onto London.

Meg remembered that she had cried for days.

He had travelled fairly light, with just a few of his tools, as he knew he would have to earn his keep; his wooden last, the sharp knives he used for cutting and shaping soles, his awl and his needle case with its selection of threads.

The small business in Stratford had been reasonably successful in the short time he had been there, and so he was able to leave Meg with a small amount of coinage to keep her through the bad times when she couldn't work.

His first journey was back to Tewkesbury. Here he had left a certain amount of his assets, although not much money, in the keeping of Jardin's the bankers after Thomas' murder not that it amounted to much. But he needed to get some good, sound clothes, a batch of soft leathers he wanted and his various daggers and a sword.

He had called back to see Meg after his visit and gave her the box of things he had kept from childhood, including the broken sabre blade that had killed Thomas and the rest of the money.

'Friends' there had found for him a sound ex-cavalry horse, one that would not startle at the first loud sound and was strong enough to make the long journey ahead.

Meg had put him up some cooked meats with dried herbs such as fennel, borage, sage and parsley, and all was particularly well stuffed into a pig's intestine, adding a variety of seeds and nuts of all kind. This she gave to him, with an instruction to keep this as his food in need. "You'm ne'er know, my lad, when ye stomach needs food where there ain't none, so don' ye go eating it on your first stop."

Gad looked at the 'sossige' and with a grin reckoned it could do as a weapon too, weighing it in his hand like a 'suader' or a cudgel. His second leaving from Meg was no less traumatic than his first, but she knew he would not settle until he had seen this woman, whoever she was.

The 'sossige' gave him the idea of making a real suader and he fashioned a leather bound one that felt just about right, with plenty of flexibility. It was to be a very useful weapon.

His journey was slow and tiring for both man and horse. The horse was not as sound as it had looked and, stopping off at a farm just outside Buckingham, he asked the farmer if he could use his barn for the night. The farmer was a kindly man, and seeing the sorry state of Gad's horse, he came out later on with some poultices and rags and bandaged the poor animal's legs, tutting the whole time.

"This lad's due for t'knacker's yard, boy. Where'd ye get 'im?"

Gad looked at the farmer's boots and, like his horse; they were in a sorry state. "A bit like yer boots, sir old and worn out."

The farmer smiled. "Aye, ye can't get a decent boot maker these days, so I 'ave to mek' do."

As he talked, the farmer chewed on some foul looking root and spat a stream of dark liquid into the ground, and then he watched with interest as Gad got out his equipment.

To his surprise, the farmer was led to a bale of hay and Gad indicated that he should sit so he could remove the man's sorry boots for him.

Later on, recounting the story to Meg, Gad smiled at her as he remembered.

"We did a good deal, Meg. A sound pair of boots and the old nag for a good strong horse."

Soon he was quickly on his way again, and he made good time to Aylesbury, where he stopped again for a while to rest up and get some money at the market. He had to work wherever he stopped so he could get lodgings and food for himself and his new horse.

The village was bustling with traders in the small square, and he found a little difficulty finding a space as he was an incomer, but eventually after doing a deal next to a farrier, so he stopped there. It was a useful arrangement for Gad, as the farrier was more interested in drink, and spent a lot of time in the local Inn at the bottom of the square than on his stand, so Gad could act for him in acquiring business the man could do later when he was sober.

When night fell and he sat and counted up his 'take', two men approached him. One was a small, ferret-faced man of about thirty, and he kept twiddling a wicked looking knife. The other seemed to have more brawn than brain and did as the little man said.

"We'm here to collect the rent," the small man said, and held out his hand.

Chapter Eleven

Gad had collected all his things together and was just off having paid the official burgher for his stay there. He straightened up and balanced himself on his feet, something he had learned as a useful way to prepare himself for a fight which he knew was about to happen.

He was also wise enough to know that when two men approach you and one talks, then it is usually the other that hits.

"I paid it, lad. Ye'm too late," he said, backing against the farrier's charcoal burner. He jumped, as it was hot.

"Not mine, you ain't," the little man said, and the big man leaned forward to grab Gad by the throat.

All he got was got was a very hot pair of nail pullers in his hand, which had been lying on the tray at the edge of the furnace, left by the farrier as he couldn't take them away. Anyway, nobody steals red-hot tools.

The big man roared with the pain, and he threw the tongs to the little man, who instinctively caught them, with very painful results. A small crowd had gathered, and as the farrier appeared, well soused but still standing, Gad told him these men were trying to steal his tools.

His roar of anger was a joy to behold, and the crowd enjoyed the spectacle of him taking hold of both men in a bear-like grip. With the strength of his profession, he gave the two men a thrashing they will long remember. They never troubled Gad again. He settled happily enough there for a few weeks to work and earn some much need cash. For several weeks he attended the market and mended shoes and made a few new ones occasionally, so that by the end of the fourth week, he had enough to send Meg a box containing a letter and several coins.

At least, that was his intention. The letter he had to get someone to write for him, because he had never learned to write nor read. He found a lawyer whom he thought was honest who said he had to go to Stratford soon on business, so he would take the box.

Meg shook her head. She had never got the box, and Gad made a mental to pay that lawyer a visit.

Soon he crossed over the boundary into Hertfordshire and the hamlet of Tring. Not that there was much there – just a crossroads and a couple of good inns – but it seemed a good place to ask for his next destination. He looked sideways at Meg. It was there that he nearly met his end.

Meg clutched him with a look of apprehension and worry. He had put up at the larger of the two inns and was lucky to get a bed in the loft above the stables so he could keep an eye on his horse. Here, the food was good and plentiful and the ale well kept.

He had just laid down for his night's rest with his things beside him in the loose straw when he felt a breeze, and he saw the big door of the barn open very slowly.

He was immediately on the alert, as this was not the opening of a regular user seeing to his horse, but a quiet, creepy, suspicious movement. It was the silent stealth of a thief; and two men came in dressed in thigh length boots, dark breeches, wide-brimmed hats and dark, heavy cloaks. Their swords hung low, which was the sign of men being used to a quick draw.

Gad remembered the funny look the innkeeper gave him when he asked the way to the Old Palace of Hatfield, so he must have sent off a servant to warn someone that he was coming.

He wondered who knew of his coming, as he hadn't planned the visit to be just then. He didn't sit up. No, these were just villains on the make. After all, who would know him? And who would want to attack him? He was now twenty two and he had last seen his Beth was five years ago. What had happened to make him such a person worth killing? What these men had in mind by the look of them and their weapons was surely not him. No, they were just thieves.

Gad dare not move, as straw is not the quietest of bedfellows and the slightest movement would alert them, so he kept very quiet.

They checked all the horses, and when they came to his, they tied something to one of its fetlocks. Then they settled themselves down in a corner facing the door and waited.

One of the men was an obvious ex-soldier, as he carefully slid out a well-used and lovingly cared for sabre and smiled as he stroked the blade, which glowed dully in the half-light. An ex-cavalry man, no doubt.

He tested the edge and found it to his satisfaction. Then he waved it under his smaller friend's nose and made him cower in fright. The frightened little man gave Gad an idea. He decided to play a trick on them to see how brave they were, and maybe they would go out and leave him be.

In the barn sometime earlier, children had been making corn dollies, and next to his head had been pinned a real beauty. It was about ten or eleven inches in height and its arms had been made to move by fixing them separately to the body with a strand of straw that went straight through the body, as did the legs.

Carefully he took it down, and even that seemed to make a noise like an elephant trudging through the brushwood, but they did not hear him. Then he pulled out several strands of grass and tied them together to make a long thread.

He remembered the Halloween tricks they played, when they were boys and people at the visiting fairs had shown them how to make puppets that danced on strings. Tears welled in his eyes as he remembered how ham-fisted Thomas was, and how it was that everyone he had made broke.

The wind was getting up outside, and all of a sudden he could hear a horse arriving. This was just the thing he needed, a distraction. The door of the barn was rattled and then the two watching men heard the rider dismount and they hid themselves in a stable at the back. Perhaps this was the man they are waiting for. The visitor came in with a blast of wind, and the hay and straw went everywhere.

The accompanying dust blew straight at where the two villains were hiding, and Gad knew they would by temporarily blinded for a few moments. As the man busied himself settling his mount, and fortunately making enough noise to drown Gad's movements, he crept around the upper part of the barn, laying his trap until he was over where the men had lain before. After what seemed an age, the stranger left and slammed the barn door closed again.

So, was it him that they wanted? The darkness had begun to lighten, as the dawn began to show that he must be the one they wanted. Gad's eyes quickly became accustomed to the dim light, as the visitor had taken his torch with him on his way back to the inn.

The two men slowly reappeared and once again settled down to wait, the big man's sword glinting in the soft light. Slowly they started to doze and Gad lowered the doll which he had positioned over the barn door. He had run the lines back over the beams to his position above the men. He practised for a while making the doll dance, and he had to admit it looked strange, with the light coloured straw against the darkened background of the door.

He looked down at the sleeping men, and with another long piece of straw, he started to tickle the nose of the smaller man. For a while he simply twitched, snuffled and pushed it away, but soon the irritation awakened him properly.

When first the men had arrived, they did not expect anyone to be there and talked quite openly to each other, even using their names – one was a Rubin and the other, the big one, was called Bart.

"Rubin, *Ru*bin," Gad's voice sounded loud, despite trying to whisper it. The doll shook and began to dance very slowly. "*Ru*bin!"

The small man was suddenly awake, and Gad watched in amusement at the sheer terror on his face as the little man crossed himself. For a while, he lay transfixed by the sight of this devil dancing by the door, no doubt ready to take him to

Hades, where he had been threatened he was going to by the local minister. He nudged his friend and as he turned to him.

Gad pulled up the doll.

"Bart!"

His friend came too quickly and reached for his sword as he stood up.

"What's the matter? Is he 'ere?"

The little man squawked, "No. But there's a ghost in here, and he spoke to me."

The big man gave a groan and smacked the little man across the face. Being awakened to hear there was a ghost was all he needed, even though his temper was full of fear.

"Oi'll give 'ee bleedin' ghosts! Gerra sleep."

"He won't get 'ere til morning, we was told."

He promptly went back to his bed. But the little man was unhappy.

"*Ru*bin!"

Slowly the doll descended and danced once again, and the little man got up, open-mouthed and staring eyes. Without any warning, he ran out through the back door. The noise of his exit was like a herd of horses in the quiet of the early pre-dawn, and the big man sat up, startled and disorientated. Then he was up and after him almost as fast.

"Come back, you damn little fool."

Gad was saddled up and away before they returned – if they ever did – and he moved on towards St Albans.

He wished that he had had time to nobble their horses, but speed was the most important thing at that point, and by the time dawn had begun its rosy red beginning to the day and the early animals and birds had begun their breakfast singsong, Gad had travelled ten or fifteen miles. He wondered if he had lost them, and nibbled some of Meg's 'sossige'.

They caught up with Gad just as he left Berkhamstead.

He heard them first as he breasted a hill on the outskirts of the small village and turning around, he saw the cloud of dust in the distance. There they were, riding like madmen with their cloaks flying in the wind, so he was able to slip into a small copse and wait.

They were hot and tired, having run their horses fast, and so he was able to prepare another little trap for them. This time he would try to question them if it was practical.

The road was narrow just about where he had hidden, and several trees bounded the edge of the road. Quickly he dismounted and, taking the strong rope he always carried across his pommel, he attached it four or five feet up one of the trees across the path, then he pulled it slackly over and into the copse on his side.

He even had time to kick dust over the rope lying on the road, but he doubted they would see it in their overanxious state.

He took out his blackthorn staff and waited. As he presumed, they were tired and irritated at having missed him in the barn. They might even have found the corn dolly he had used as a puppet so they probably had vengeance on their minds if, in fact, it was him they were after. It certainly looked like it.

The big man was beetle-browed with both concentration and anger, and neither of them was able to stop when Gad pulled the rope taut.

The two men fell to the ground with a cry, and Gad ran out and stood over them.

"What's yer game, then?" he asked as he raised his staff above their heads.

"What ye after me for? Ye got two seconds to answer. One…"

The little man was cowering and holding what appeared to be an injured arm, and the big man was still dazed by his fall.

Crack! Gad's cudgel smacked the little man across the upper arm, which was hurt already and the bigger man looked on, just waiting his chance to dodge away. The small man yelled in pain and the big one tried to get up, but Gad put the point of his staff at his throat and held him firmly.

"Ye stay there, mister."

After a few more cuffs, the little man explained that they had been paid "to do for ye". But they couldn't say who, as it was just someone in the bar.

"But 'e were a gentleman," he added, "wiv a big 'at and rode a grey.

Gad had pondered on that, as it was something he would have to remember.

Their horses had ridden away when the men fell off. Gad had no need to spend any more time with the pathetic rogues, so he mounted up and left them to find their mounts.

Someone badly wanted to stop him getting to Hatfield, but who and why?

How did they know he was travelling? This looked like it would be a more difficult journey than he thought, and he still had a way to go yet.

It was nightfall before he got to St Albans and saw it was quite a sizeable place. That was good – the bigger the place the better to hide himself in. He didn't ordinarily like large towns, but this was one where he felt he could lose himself and if possible, tries to find out why and who was chasing him.

But surely it must be a case of mistaken identity? Perhaps it was someone who looked like him.

"A man on a grey, eh?" he muttered to himself. "He wants to kill me, does he?" And he led his tired horse on, walking by its side. He looked around this new town and saw lots and lots of people. Plenty of inns and maybe a hundred or so dwellings, and of course the cathedral. He nodded to himself – this was a place where he could rest up for a while, and a place he could stay without detection, he hoped.

He made for a small inn on the south side of the town. It was a rundown place, and not the sort of place that would worry too much who its customers were, but it was on a main thoroughfare. He ordered ale and some cold meats, potage and fresh bread, and he sat facing the door, watching the comings and goings of the customers as he ate.

Like his horse he felt tired, and was glad that he had the forethought to bed his mount down before he had entered the inn, as he did not feel keen to get up and start that now. He yawned and stretched, and just as he was getting ready to go to his cot, he heard a commotion outside. With the other customers, he went to the door to look, supping his ale and belching as he went.

The two assailants of last night were being driven along the dusty lane by a man on a large grey. The little man was still holding his injured arm. The mysterious rider had a whip, and was cursing them every few paces. Gad turned to his nearest neighbour as they crowded in the doorway and asked who the men were.

His fellow drinker said, "The two men I ain't seen afore, but the fellow on the grey is the Captain of the King's Guard. A nasty piece o' work, 'im. Our Tudor 'enry 'as some real nasties working for 'im."

The men went past, and the inn settled down again to its normal behaviour.

Gad offered his informant another drink, which was gladly taken.

"Ye are new here, ain't ye?" the man asked, looking sideways at him. Then he belched and waved a hand at some friend of his across the room.

"Aye. Just up fro' Lunnun. On a visit to see my old lady, who ain't well. I promised her that when I had time I'd come by and see her. It's been many a long year sin' I bin close to the old gal, so it's about time, like."

He was not too sure about the accent, but it seemed to satisfy his companion and after a few more moment's silence Gad said quietly, "I gotta deliver a letter to a vicar too later on – he be a friend of ma's. S'posed to live on the road to the old Palace at Hatfield. D'ye know which way that is?"

"A vicar, ye say? If he's a Cathlick, 'e's probably in 'idin'. 'enry don't take kindly to they Cathlicks." He laughed quietly and got up. "Well, I'm goin' that away, so we can travel there together in the morning."

His bed was, as he expected, already occupied. It was full of lice and other nasty biting creatures, but despite this, his only thoughts were to lay down. So with a shake and several bangs on the wall with the palliasse, he put it back, slung his cloak on it, and remembered nothing more until the morning.

The sun was bright, despite being still low in the sky, so he reckoned it was time to rise and find somewhere to wash. Gad was fastidious about washing, whereas the common practice was not to, and he never felt right until he had a swill at the pump. His friend of last night was also up and about, and they both entered the main bar room for some breakfast almost on cue. Gad was caught by the casualness of their meeting, and as he could not find anything against the man in his speech or manner, they left together.

He gave another careful look around in case he saw his recent assailants or the man on the 'grey', and then he joined his new companion and they travelled on at a slow pace.

Chapter Twelve

Gad broached the next conversation with great care, so as to avoid having to answer too many questions about himself.

"How far is this Old Palace?" he queried.

The other man smiled, "Oh, about ten miles or less. I works there as a coachman, but we needed some new bolts for one of the coaches so I was sent to the iron foundry here."

Gad decided to test him and spoke with an earnestness he hoped would sound genuine. "I'm a boot and shoemaker by trade. D'ye reckon there'd be any work there?"

He turned sideways to the man and then looked at his boots, while his companion treated the question with a noncommittal shrug.

His friend's left boot was in a sorry state, with its sole hanging and the side stitching had all parted. When they stopped for a break, Gad took out his kit again and came over to the man, who was sitting on a bank as the horses gently grazed nearby.

"Give me yer boot. One favour deserves another."

He took it off him. He completed the repair and his new friend stood up and stamped his foot as he looked down, really pleased with his repaired boot.

"By the saints, ye are a fine boot mender and no mistake. 'Appen I could get ye in, and maybe ye could see the Chamberlain. He sees to all the household's needs. Nothing passes Master Knox before it gets in someone's mind."

At twenty two, Gad was in his prime, and yet he began to feel as nervous as a kitten, still holding his horse as they approached the big house. He remembered Beth's last words to him when they had parted in Hereford all those years ago: "Come and see me at Hatfield if ye can." Her words were pleading, the asking of a lover.

Though she was born a king's daughter, the young Elizabeth had been accused of being a bastard by her father all the time, and he had her mother executed before Elizabeth had reached her fourth birthday. So Hatfield was a place of mixed blessings for her.

When she had returned from her visit to Hereford and the cold faces of the courtiers, she was told that members of the royal house were not supposed to go off enjoying themselves. She felt even sadder and had they known she was pregnant, the place would have become a prison and, maybe like her poor mother, her own head might come loose.

Special staff were assigned to her by Lord Seymour who seethed with anger and frustration at her absence, and even though he wouldn't admit it, jealousy – which for a man of his advanced years and position became a source of self-mortification for him.

What all the rest of the staff knew was that the old King was in one of his many moods at Windsor, and had banned Elizabeth from his presence and meeting people. This was nothing unusual, and so they did not take it amiss. They all knew Henry's funny moods – one day smiling and gay, and the next all swishing of his cape, loud shouts and crying women.

So no one queried why this young girl should be so treated. Her brother Edward was too young to know anything, so for a while she was kept in seclusion in the old Palace without too much fuss, which pleased her, because when the baby started to show its presence, she knew a decision had to be taken and then they all had a blessed relief.

Henry died, and during all the confusion of arranging his funeral and appointing a new monarch, she was whisked away without anyone seeing her. Before she had left Hereford a week later than she should have done, Thomas and Gad had watched over her from afar, and on one occasion, Thomas soundly thrashed one of the young noblemen who made unflattering remarks about her and Gad in her presence.

Elizabeth was pleased with Thomas' action, as was Gad, and they swore that all three would love each other "until death us do part", as young people do everywhere, although they expected it to be their last meeting.

With Gad nowhere to be seen, she swore then that she would never love any other man again, a vow she took with her to the grave. Instead, she buried herself in her lessons.

Greek and Latin became as much a part of her life as her own language and helping her brother who was now due to become Edward VI. He too gave her a hard time at first, but soon they became closer and spent many happy days together. It was at this time that she espoused a dear wish to encourage the use of an 'English' language, instead of all the many tongues used around the court, particularly French.

When she was Queen, she made this 'new' language called English her main priority.

Not as bright as Elizabeth, Edward still able to master his Greek and Latin, when his coughing would let him. He never knew of her baby, which is just as well, because even at eight, he had great pleasure reading the Proverbs of Solomon.

In these he read 'to beware of wanton women', and his own sister would have been classified as one if he had known. Despite her unhappiness in her conscience, her natural sense of humour was not dimmed, and she offered to Catherine Parr a translation she had made of *The Miseries of a Sinful Soul*. It was an austere book about fornication and the straying from God's law. Kat Ashley, her governess, looked disapprovingly at her when she said what she was giving her, but not without a repressed giggle.

To her sister Mary's consternation, in Henry's will he had made it known that Elizabeth was to be fully restored to the rightful law of succession, which is just as well he died before he had heard of her illegitimate baby.

Cephar would be four years of age now. As Gad came up to the old palace, his existence was still unknown to him, and he wondered what sort of reaction his presence would have on Elizabeth. It was nearly five years since they had met.

So, with all activity going on around him, their searching for both him and the baby, here he was, as bold as brass, paying a visit to his love. Neither was he aware of the fuss and trouble that had occurred when the suspicion as to the real reason for Elizabeth's 'illness' had been raised, even to the possibility that she may be pregnant, when she was sent to Cheshunt again to Sir Anthony Denny.

Eyes were all turned to Seymour, whose liking for and close proximity to the young woman was well known. The habit of a *ménage à trois* between Seymour, the young princess and his wife was the talk of the corridors among the servants and ladies in waiting.

But these rumours persisted. If there was a baby, then they would all assume it was Lord Seymour's – who, as is usual in these matters, was the last to hear. When it reached his overwrought ears, his temper was raised to such a degree that he initiated an undercover search of all Elizabeth's apartments, including the house where she had reputedly stayed in Cheshunt during her 'illness'.

But all that drew a blank.

"Of course she wasn't pregnant – it was that awful 'sweating disease', so we have been told."

But he was still miffed at the rumour. He discussed the problem with his wife, who promptly burst into wailing and hair-tearing, until he slapped her and told her it was impossible, as he had never, (unhappily) "dallied his cockspur in her nest". But nevertheless it worried him, and he tried to persuade Elizabeth to be examined by another physician, on the pretext that he wanted to make sure she was cured of her "ailment".

However, she assured him with a withering look, followed by a sneaky grin to herself as she replied. "Have no fear, my Lord – what was troubling me has gone completely." Then her voice dropped to a harsh whisper to herself, and tearfully she said, "Never to return."

However, the suspicion remained, and at a meeting of the Privy Council in London, the suitability of Elizabeth to follow her sister after her brother, "should he die prematurely", was discussed at a higher level, even though her sister Mary was expected to follow her brother, as she was seventeen years older than Elizabeth.

But if there was an unknown, her so. The question hung in the air with a menace not to leave for many years.

The Privy Council decided on a compromise. If it became a problem, then they would handle it.

The first recorded English Compromise had been recorded.

Lord Seymour went to see her there and tried every way to trap Elizabeth by his insinuations that "virginity was kept by few women over fourteen", looking hard at her to see her reaction.

Elizabeth smiled, saying tartly, "No doubt you saw to many of those yourself, my Lord." Then added a sharp rejoinder, "But not with me, sir, eh?"

Lord Dudley, the Earl of Leicester, had acted carefully without any great enthusiasm, knowing that such proof might cause everyone great embarrassment if and when Elizabeth did become Queen.

So the court itself dropped the question as 'inappropriate', and Elizabeth breathed a great sigh of relief, as did poor Kat her governess, knowing the consequences to herself should the facts be revealed.

She came back to Hatfield.

Seymour had different ideas though, and he met the young Dudley, son of the old Lord.

"You can see what would happen if these rumours were true," he confided in the youngster. "If another royal bastard was in circulation somewhere, it would make a fine banner to fight under by those laggards at court, who have nothing better to do than to make trouble."

He put a paternal arm around the young man's shoulder who squirmed inside at such 'friendliness'.

"As for ye, young Dud, one day you will have your father's title and lands, and who knows perhaps James from Scotland might like his son to have someone like you as a friend and confidant."

This news startled Dudley. A Scottish King? Now, that might not be a bad idea. If what this man is telling me perhaps I could use this situation to my advantage and if there is no truth in the rumour of a royal bastard then maybe I can provide one, he thought.

He smiled at his host. "What, pray, can I do?"

Seymour removed his arm and, with his hands clasped behind his back, he became earnest.

"For the nonce, nothing." Then, adopting his earlier over friendly pose, he confided in the lad. "Except ye could organise a dedicated group of men who can watch her daily, to see if ye can find anything to incriminate her. Anything at all that could be construed as meaning there is a child. After all, she is a woman, and they tell me that when they do give birth, the hold the child has on the woman is unbreakable."

Dudley was ahead of him, and nodded wisely. He said, "Leave it to me, sir."

The force was set up, and this was the powerful enemy Gad walked into in blissful ignorance.

In his favour was the fact that Dudley had no time for this for Seymour, and decided that during his watching, he might uncover something that would help him to dump him, such as a connection with the Scottish rebels...

Meg took a mug of broth from the pot on the fire and began to feel peculiar, to know suddenly that her boy could be a possible King of England. Then the full realisation dawned on her. She dropped the mug in her nervousness and the liquid splashed into the fire, causing steam and smoke and ash everywhere. She shook with alarm and worry for her lad, and did not know which way to turn.

Gad too was concerned, and although more slowly, he got up and went over to her. She was shaking like she had the ague and her face was white in the semi-dark of the room.

For a moment neither spoke then she said, her voice tremulous with a mixture of fear and disbelief, "Ye mean our boy is the son of the Queen? And ye are the father?"

Gad nodded and explained his involvement with the young princess.

For a simple soul like Meg, this was almost too much to bear, and for a long time Gad could not continue with his story.

"Do anyone else know o' this?" she queried, her voice full of apprehension.

The great Queen, who had held the country together for many years and when seen close up looked like an old hag, with her wigs and painted face and her terrible teeth -she was her husband's onetime lover?

No! This could not be true. She began to weep. Why, she wasn't sure. Then she stopped and dried her eyes.

"No!' she said, her jaw jutting out in determination and resolve. "I brought 'im up. Gad gave him to me, so 'e's mine."

They both went to bed, each with their own thoughts, each a little frightened by the enormity of it, if it were true, although Gad never told lies. Her new maternal feeling gave her steely edge to her manner, which was something new for her.

His son too had a right to know the background to the origin of his birth – it is every man's right, she thought.

In the morning, it was obvious that neither had slept much, and when Thomas paid them a visit with his wife and their children, Meg looked at him more closely. He was short, but then both Elizabeth and Gad were not tall people. The red hair was the giveaway; the aquiline nose and the dark eyes too. Gad's hair had been dark but was now grey and very thin, and he too had dark eyes, although his nose was broad and flat.

Meg was more confused than ever. Thomas cocked his head sideways at the more than usual looks he was getting from his ma, and wondered what he had done wrong.

"Summit wrong, Ma? Pa not well again?"

Thomas was concerned at the look of well he wasn't sure what it was on his mother's face, but he was worried too. He put his arms around her and gave her a hug.

Meg smiled up at him. He was a good son.

"No, lad, your father's getting on fine, and we'll soon have him up and about." Then she wondered why calling Gad 'your father' suddenly had sounded so awkward now when she said it.

She remembered the time when she was rubbing her washing in the tub of soapy water, and what with that and the hot sun, it was making her sweat. Her bonnet was awry and she felt tired. There was a pounding on the door. Wiping the suds off as best she could, she had made for the door, grumbling the whole time. As she opened the door, she had nearly fainted.

"Hello Meg."

It was her Gad. Nearly nine months had gone, and he had returned to find her in such a mess.

"Oh dear, I look a mess," was all she could say then she rushed at him and flung her arms around him in a big bear hug, kissing and crying with joy. Gad had prised her off him, took her hand and turned her to look at Thomas. She remembered the feeling. It was one of complete joy.

"Ma,' Gad said. "Meet your son, Thomas."

The lad's cheeky face, smiling like a miniature Gad, completely overwhelmed her, so much so that Gad began to wonder if she remembered he was there. It was love at first sight for both of them.

Gad called for something to dry his face with, as his douche into cold water helped somehow to refresh him. It was another week before Gad was able to continue with the tale, feeling that the telling somehow purged his soul of the memory of his upset and guilt over Elizabeth and the death of his friend, the people he had killed, made love to, and most of all the trial he had been to, to his Meg. Maybe he would sleep better too.

Perhaps he might wed Meg! Aye, that was it – to show his love for her and that he no longer hankered over Beth, they would get wed. He also felt it was time to bring in Thomas and let him hear the explanation of his birth and his role in life – after all, he had promised the lad he would.

Thomas and his wife came downstairs from their rooms above and, with the children settled in bed, Gad decided that now was as good a time as any to let them know his big secret, one he had kept to himself for many years. He recounted in a shortened form of what he had just told Meg, and Thomas didn't bat an eyelid. Thomas' wife giggled.

"Well, isn't your dad funny – my husband, son to the Queen. Hehe! What a good joke."

As she was pregnant again, they took her upstairs to lie down. All her pregnancies took her in funny ways – like the time Thomas found her eating mushrooms with butter on and dipped in milk. She said she had a fancy for them.

Chapter Thirteen

When they were all settled again, Gad asked Thomas why he did not seem to be shocked, upset, or angry at what he had been told. After all, it must have been some sort of a shock to find out who your 'real' mother was.

Thomas smiled. "When I were courting my wife, I used to hang around that farmhouse at Darlingscote do ye remember? Anyways, one day I'm sitting on a fence, when this girl comes to me, all fancy like. She was about sixteen I s'pose. She asked me why I were on her fence, and I said I didn't know it were her'n as it didn't 'ave her name on it.

"Well, she laughed and then got all uppity. 'Ye're like all they Royals, making a laugh at us country girls.' Well, I was shocked, as ye can guess. I mean, me, a royal? I remembered what she'd said, and she was right."

Gad smiled at the thought that an ignorant country lass had discovered the truth and his neighbours had not, as they sat quiet to listen to the rest of Gad's story.

"The coachman was as good as his word and I was instructed to go to the kitchens."

Dudley had organised a team of men to travel a good distance from The Old Hatfield Palace in a variety of directions, and they were to visit hostelries and drinking houses that offered accommodation – anywhere that Gad might stay and leave the only description they had, which was pretty vague. A young man on a horse had visited the Old Palace, but they were too late and only got there an hour after Gad had left.

He guessed that he travelled south, but that was all. As the young Gad had entered the Old Palace at Hatfield, he had marvelled at the way the gardener had twined the lime trees into a sort of arch, his eyes and head twitching this way and that. It would make a tidy canopy, he thought, and he wished he could be a gardener.

He had never been asked by the coachman to stable his horse, as he probably expected him to be summarily dismissed, so as Gad approached the rear entrance, he tied his horse to one of the supports of the porch and tucked it around the side of the building.

The coachman just opened the door and walked down a flagged passageway to junction of doorways. Again, he didn't knock, but just opened a door and they were in the scullery next to the kitchen.

Before they entered the flagstoned kitchen, the coachman signalled Gad to wait and so he stood there, his hat in his hand, his bag on his shoulder, conscious of how scruffy he must look in such a grand place. Even down here there were pictures on the wall and shiny pots and pans stacked in piles on the floor – ready, he supposed, for the next banquet.

After a few moments, the coachman returned with a smiling, plump, friendly-looking lady. Her white mop cap was starched and clean and her apron over her long gown too was bright in its whiteness. Her friendliness did a lot to dispel Gad's trepidation. With her came the smell of cooking, and Gad's stomach began turning and squelching so much so that he moved about to try and stop it.

The cook looked him up and down and with a knowing smile on her face and said kindly, "Hungry lad?", and then added with a high-pitched laugh, "I've never known any lad of your age that wasn't."

A couple of pinched faces appeared at the door behind her, who no doubt the scullery maids were seeing who the newcomer was. They were shooed away with a sharp rejoinder, and Gad smiled at their nosiness.

"Well, now, ye come on in, my lad, while Master Beauregard goes and finds his lord and master."

Then she took Gad's arm and pulled him into the kitchen proper. If his stomach squealed and rumbled outside, the sight of so much food and the smell of the turning spit made him almost giddy with hunger. He belched.

Suddenly, Meg came alive, and forgetting the main thrust of his story, asked, "What was it like in the kitchen? Did they have lots of pans and big plates? Were they all made of gold?"

Her eyes were wide with wonder. Gad laughed; he was pleased Meg was more relaxed now.

"No, bless your heart, lass. I was so scared and I hardly saw anything."

They fed him while he waited, and slowly his heart stopped pounding and he was able to talk a little with the cook, who was busy making some cakes, her arms up to her elbows in flour and fruit.

He talked about his work as a shoemaker and looked at her own, thinking I might repair those she's wearing before she trips over the loose ends.

"Is the Princess Elizabeth still here?" he asked as casually as he could and the arms stopped. Oh dear, he thought, was it not done to mention her name? The silence became heavy and suspicious. Had he spoken out of turn?

"Why d'ye want to know, lad?"

The housekeeper had returned, and her face was far from friendly. He expected to be tossed out without as much as a chance to say he was sorry.

Gad, then realising there was a problem, just shook his head. "Oh, nothing, but I was told she was real pretty, like, and I just wondered..."

His voice trailed and he looked red and embarrassed.

The kind housekeeper seeing his predicament and, realising he was not a threat to her, said, "Sorry lad, but there are one or two little problems here at the moment. Her sister and her don't get on that much, and well, ye know. And all they rumours about her, well..."

Gad smiled. "Oh, ye don't have to tell me I have four of 'em."

Everyone laughed and the atmosphere changed again. A slight, urchin-like girl of about twelve was positively besotted with Gad; her eyes were as big and as round as some of the plates. She sniffed and wiped her nose on her wrist.

He was obviously her 'dream man', and it took a sharp slap by another woman there to get her to rouse herself and get on with her chores.

"Ye her lad?" she asked, and received another smack for her impudence.

Gad laughed. "No, but maybe I'll wait for ye to grow first, eh?"

With a boy king who was always unwell now on the throne, the threat or worry of his death made for a considerable amount of tension and jealousy between the two Royal sisters, mainly caused by those around them. In fact, there was no real antipathy – just wariness.

Elizabeth said she had no early pretensions to the throne, as she knew that Mary would be the next Queen, despite what everyone else said or thought; and it was true, but there were plenty of those who would try to use the problem for their own ends.

The door opened and a short, pompous looking man appeared, staring at Gad as though he was a dirty urchin from the streets.

"What do ye want, my lad?"

His head was held back and his nose was stuck up in the air, with the look of someone who had found a nasty smell somewhere close.

Gad smiled at his snootiness; he was used to such a look from footmen and head housekeepers in the big manor houses.

"Just a visit," he said disarmingly, "to see if there are any boots or shoes needin' repairing, like, or p'raps new ones made. I've made for they nobility afore, and I have done a proper time-served apprenticeship."

The conversation was interrupted by a silvery tinkle of laughter, which came through to them as they stood in the kitchen, and the patter of feet outside.

Gad's heart gave a lurch. Then the door burst open and a young girl ran in all hot and flustered.

"Master Beauregarde, would ye kindly stop the water boy from throwing his water over me? Oh!" She stopped her hand over her mouth and she looked at Gad. "Oh, er, sorry sir," and she blushed a bright pink.

"Mistress Garnley!" A voice sounded from down the corridor away from the kitchen, a man's voice. "What are ye doing here, and what use could ye be if your mistress called ye now?"

A tall, hook-nosed man swept down to the kitchen but did not enter. He was followed by another woman, older than him and wearing her customary black gown with a wide white cap to hide her hair, almost like a wimple. She was Mistress Parry. Gad's heart skipped a beat. The man was the one who had threatened to beat him in Hereford Castle, when Gad and Elizabeth had first met.

Master Knox was not amused, but he turned away without recognising Gad, and disappeared into his more familiar places in the old palace. The woman too – wasn't she the one who lived in Herefordshire and was 'maid of honour' to Elizabeth? She looked so severe, and Gad was too frightened to ask her about Beth.

Gad couldn't miss the opportunity though and, turning to the girl who had just been admonished, said quietly, "Er, tell yer mistress that there is a shoemaker here from Hereford and 'e 'as a pair o' shoes for 'er."

At that, everyone stopped what they were doing, and the silence hung heavy about them. They looked at him and even the cook sat down, looking paler than her flour. The housekeeper had her mouth open and her hand pressed up against it in alarm. The sheer impertinence of this lad, a common tradesman, talking like that to a lady in waiting to her Royal Highness. God's blood!

The gossiping in all the royal palaces, among every group of both women and men had said that Elizabeth's illness four years ago was more than the 'sweating disease' that was mooted then. That illness had all but died out by then, and few believed the story.

Fingers touched noses in more than one household, in that knowing way that scandalmongers had of passing around their gossip. Everyone would eventually hear of Gad, if only by putting two and two together.

After all the secrecy, the princess' visit to Hereford and her returning pregnant had been slipped out at various times – probably started by Kat Ashley who was a known chatterbox – and no doubt even their dalliance in Hay Wood will have been told many times, if not by name as what they did not know they would probably make up.

So his name, although it was nearly five years ago, was still hot in everyone's mind. It became the worst kept secret of the old palace, but to speak of it was instant death.

If the King had heard of it in London… well! Heads would roll – probably Seymour's and mayhem would be normal.

The young housemaid of about twelve who had heard the story from others of the rumoured pregnancy and birth by Elizabeth, and who was young and uncomplicated by either education or Court intrigue, certainly was not overawed by the whole potential minefield of its implications.

She guilelessly crept over to the confused Gad and with all the artless innocence of a child, and hugged him suddenly around the waist.

"I 'opes ye marry er," she said, and everyone gasped.

The housekeeper made a swipe at her, but she hid behind Gad.

He held his hand up. "Please, I haven't come to cause trouble for the princess or anyone else but..."

Before he could continue, the little housemaid continued, "I reckon you're her fella."

In all the confusion and high drama, the lady-in-waiting Mistress Parry had gone. They all sat there, with no one knowing what to say, if anything, when there was a rustle at the kitchen door.

"Your Highness!" Master Beauregard bowed low, as he said her name.

Everybody turned and all bent the knee or bowed, as was their custom.

"Hello, Beth," was all Gad could say, and the housemaid giggled. You could hear the intake of breathe from the others at his effrontery.

This scene would be told and retold by all the kitchen staff at their homes, in ale houses, in the markets – each telling would be wilder and more exaggerated and grow in importance, until probably the very sensationalism of it would cause its own downfall and it would not be believed.

Gad's eyes sparkled for the first time in years. Elizabeth was now taller and, in his eyes, more beautiful, more grown up and also more mature. Her figure had filled out too, and the lips were now rouged and powdered, but they still drew Gad towards her like a moth to a candle.

She also saw this well-built handsome young man, someone so different from the nervous gawky youth whose manner and bearing then was so awkward and clumsy. However, she also saw this someone as he really was too – a tradesman, a workman, with hard, calloused hands and rough clothing. However, she smiled with a genuine friendliness and held her hands out to Gad.

"Gad! What a wonderful surprise."

They locked eyes and the years fell away. The mature young princess became the lovely young lass of fourteen again, just for that instant.

As for Gad, his heart rose, and then sank. The sweet young innocent girl he had known not so very long ago had been replaced now by a sophisticated, confident lady of the Court, but there was something else missing too.

Ever the unflappable one, Elizabeth also realised that Gad had signed his death warrant by coming there, as he did not know of the court intrigue surrounding his dalliance with her and the ensuing child. To him, he was just visiting a person he had been in love with, someone who happened to be a princess, and with no one knowing of their coupling.

This meeting would be around London in a week, despite the hoped for secret curtain around them. Life would not be simple in those far off days either, as apart from the young cheeky housemaid, this incident was like witnessing a murder or a rape, and eventually it would come out.

His tumble with her was bad enough, but to have created a child was adding another complication in the chain of succession to the throne, and was tantamount to a death wish.

Already, she was aware of a group of selected men who had been beavering away asking questions, trying to find those involved in the plot to hide the child; if there was one.

So far there had been no progress on that front beyond rumour, but this meeting would reopen the wound and the bleeding would start again that day, as the talking would be refuelled once more.

But at that particular moment, Gad was walking about six inches off the floor as the two of them swished off into the depths of the old palace. Just like of old, her gloved hand clasped his in a frenzied dash from authority, so that they could talk and maybe he could assess what his own feelings towards her really were.

Hers was to hide him away too if she could, as this was most awkward and unfortunate just as her brother had become worse in health and the expected problems of who should succeed him should he die had begun to raise its head.

Her hand clasped his in a tight grip and they ran up the stairs. Crumbling it may be, but the old palace had hundreds of places where they could be on their own to talk. There were so many long corridors, rooms, doors, stairs and then more corridors, until eventually they reached a place Elizabeth had always kept to herself as the problems of her pregnancy had become more apparent.

It was a small room off a main bedroom, probably one that had not been used for a long time, and even then it may have been used as a dressing room only. It had a faded chaise-longue along one wall, taking up all its length, and small French table and mirror with a discoloured glass on the other, with a big cupboard next to the door alongside her escritoire. It overpowered the small room.

The latticed window looked out onto a sloping roof that led directly down into the edge of the main quadrangle. In the middle of this square of buildings was a lawn and the beginning of a formal garden, and in her quiet moments, she had often imagined Gad visiting her there, and being surprised by Kat and the guard being called, he would Gad slipping out of the window and out into the wood beyond the main buildings.

She had 'seen' him leaping on a horse, making it rear onto its back legs as he waved in farewell, then dashing off into the woods. Now he was there, the bubble had burst, and her untidy commoner was there as he was, just a 'common man'.

They held hands and looked at each other.

My dearest shoemaker," smiling at their little joke.

"My sweetest Beth," Gad breathed, his heart still beating at twice the accepted rate. His hands were shaking with a mixture of fear, surprise and affection.

Then, with an abandon not felt since their initial coupling, they fell into each other's arms, kissing deeply. This 'common man' still held a small place in her heart.

As they pulled apart, Gad too realised it was not the same, and the flame was not alive anymore. As they had kissed, her lips remained closed and cold, and whereas he had thought of this moment for years and now it was here, the magic had gone. Something was missing. Perhaps he would never know what.

Elizabeth sat him down and, holding his hands as if not wanting to let him go, bent her head and started to weep quietly. Gad was shocked, surprised and confused. She broke away from him and walked to the window, looking out onto the green sward below.

"Ye must understand, Gad that what we did, although wonderful and I re-think it many times, it was wrong and it produced a child, which I was unable to keep."

Gad's mouth opened wide in astonishment.

"Our baby was an unlawful one, and one I could not keep."

The tears began to trickle down her powdered face, leaving little lines. Gad rushed across the small room and gathered her into his arms again, and as he murmured into her hair she turned to face him.

"What we did was wrong, my sweetheart, even though at the time it seemed such a natural thing to do, and I wanted it as much as ye. Now I have another duty to fulfil, which lies immediately in front of me, and a bastard would cause a lot of trouble for our country."

"A child?" he said, still utterly confused and delighted too. "Is it a boy or a girl?"

A tearful Elizabeth said quietly, "A boy."

Gad braced himself for the bad news. "He's dead, ain't he?"

Elizabeth shook her head, her tears still wet on her cheeks, "No, my sweet, he is not."

Then, bowing her head in shame, she added quietly, "But I could not keep him, or they would have killed him and me."

Gad brightened up on hearing that his son was alive.

"Where is he then, Beth? He is safe, ain't he?"

He was shaking in surprise and joy at being a father, and shock at the enormity of it.

She had not long returned to the Old Hatfield Palace as until recently she had been incarcerated in Cheshunt at the home of Sir Anthony Denny, a doctor to the Royal Family. It was something of an ironic twist, as initially, before Elizabeth had gone to Hereford, Catherine Parr had asked for her to be sent there, as she thought Elizabeth was having unnatural affairs with her husband. It was here that she gave birth to Thomas.

Chapter Fourteen

Elizabeth made him sit down, and as they sat with their hands clasped to each other, she explained how not being an ordinary person like him, other rules govern her not the ordinary rules of life, but the rules of expediency; those that were necessary to keep her alive, and their son too.

Gad was lost now, as his understanding of the words she was using was like another language to him.

"What does all that mean, Beth?"

His eyes were full of fear and his inability to cope.

"There were so many restrictions on what I did and where I went, who I talked to and so on and so on," she said, which confused Gad all the more.

Slowly and patiently she explained that in her position, her right to rule in succession was given to her through being the daughter of Henry VIII. It was in his will, but he had as many enemies as friends, and the intrigue and fighting that would ensue if the news of her child's existence became public knowledge didn't bear thinking about.

"It would not be just a small argument, my sweetest of men," she said, her eyes sad and worried, "but just possibly it could divide the country and my enemies would use these facts against me, saying I was unfit to rule and that may cause a civil war."

Gad shook his head in wonder and simple ignorance, knowing nothing of the religious divide already causing trouble in the country, caused mainly by her father's divorce.

"So where is he? Beth, is he safe?" He took her hands again and pulled her to him. "And ye, Beth, will ye be safe?"

Elizabeth smiled and stroked Gad's soft hair as she had done those few years ago.

"Aye, my fine man, I am safe, and so far our son is too. However, there lies a problem for ye, my sweetest friend. If I give ye his address, will ye take him and bring him up for both of us? In later years, maybe I can see him, although it will have to be from a distance." She sighed. "Oh, Gad, my heart is torn with love for him, my duty and my love for ye too, Gad, but if his whereabouts were discovered, both ye and him would be killed instantly."

The look in her eyes said it all, knowing that this would probably be the last time she would ever see Gad alone, and her son too.

Gad jutted out his jaw as he took her by the shoulders and looked straight into Beth's eyes.

"Maybe my love, "he said, "but I will have ye know that I am a very determined man."

She released his hold and walked to the window with her back to him who was still standing, his mind in turmoil. God's blood! What had he done?

"We managed to keep the birth of our son quiet from prying eyes, and most people do not know of his existence. Oh, I know there is rumour, but that is all. I had it spread about that I had been taken with the 'sweating disease' during my giving birth, and the birthing time was the same time as when my father died, so it was not noticed in the turmoil. Then we were able to put him in the care of a dear friend of mine a long way from here and out of any enemy's reach and I get a report about him every so often."

Gad looked deep into her eyes but saw only fear now.

There was no love, but he held onto her and said, "What name does 'e go by and can I go and see him?"

Elizabeth also noticed that the spell was broken too and as matter-of-factly as she could, she explained about his name and the baby's whereabouts, adding with a smile, "Yes, I would like ye to go and see him, and maybe bring him up rather than Lady Frances, as she is old and will die before he grows up and what would happen then, I shudder to think."

She thought for a moment and then, making a conscious decision, she walked to her escritoire.

"I will write a letter of authority for ye to give her." Her hands were poised in mid-air as she suddenly said, "What name will ye give him, Gad?"

Without hesitation, Gad replied, "Why, Thomas of course."

He told her about Thomas' death and it obviously saddened her.

Then she smiled. "Thomas de Witt. Yes, it sounds just right." And she smiled through her tears.

They both embraced, and Elizabeth said quietly and with affection, "Dear Thomas. Yes, I would like that."

He was still holding her and, misunderstanding his touch, she pressed her hands against his chest.

With a smile, she said, "No more babies, dear Gad. Our one moment of abandonment has nearly killed me and will for ye, if ye are ever caught."

Even as they spoke, the wheels of retribution were beginning to turn. Lots of troops were being roused, and men at arms were being organised to search and arrest the intruder and the sides of an old battle were being redrawn again.

A fast horse was dispatched to William Burghley, her most ardent supporter, who now must be alerted to the trouble that would be resurrected by the unexpected appearance of the 'bastard's' father, a common tradesman.

Similarly, information was carried to Robert Dudley, Earl of Leicester, who gave his own son Dud, recently down from Balliol College in Oxford studying languages, the job of finding and killing them both.

A man capable and evil enough to do the job and yet, even with all his power, he was going to have a fight on his hands. He smiled and thought that he would relish the challenge, and went off to have another regular lesson in the art of sword fencing from his French master.

Oblivious to all the fuss that had erupted around them, the two young people sat and talked, both knowing that this was to be their last meeting. Gad began to realise that his life would not now be the same ever again. After all his years of just holding a dream which grew each time it was indulged in, it had now become a nightmare – a terrifying fight for his life and maybe the child's.

Elizabeth wept at the news of Thomas's death and then, as the conversation waned, she took his hands and holding them, she came and knelt at Gad's chair. He tried to raise her, embarrassed at a future Queen kneeling before him, a simple and common boot maker.

"Gad," she spoke softly, her voice beginning to shake. "Gad, look after our son, and one day explain to him I did love him and still do. Tell him that he was conceived in love and his future would be followed with great interest, and hope for his safety, adding, 'I shall do what I can for ye, while ye go for him, to maybe help and protect ye'."

No longer surprised, he looked with real affection into her dark eyes. "I will Beth. I only learned of it less than ten minutes ago, so the shock is still with me, but I shall care for him and I shall tell him of our love and how wonderful ye are and...' His voice trailed, "Oh Beth! Brother John was so right. 'First find love' he said, but what he said was, 'when ye have, ye will find it is a two edged sword'."

Elizabeth's eyes dropped and her shoulders began to shake as the tears came again. Then suddenly she stopped and she stood up; her back was pencil straight and her manner imperious, as she made a deliberate effort to shake off her despondency and gloom. Tears that would never be shed again, as one day she would be Queen of England and Queens do not cry. Gad put his arm around her and held her until he felt her stiffen and regain her composure.

It wasn't long; her training did not allow it. But despite all that, they had been genuine tears of sorrow. What exactly for, she was later to try to decide.

"They took him away at birth, Gad. I have never even seen him properly."

Gad was astounded, not realising the complications this birth would create.

"But why?' A simple birth of an innocent child... What harm?"

The enormity of what she had said earlier and again now did not dawn on her then, but later she cursed herself, knowing what terrible danger she had put him in. They clasped hands again.

"But dearest Gad, if ye do find him, ye must never bring him here, or in any way let anyone know who he is. He will be killed, and probably ye too."

He smiled at the memory. "So that's why I have been getting all this attention on my journey here."

He explained to Elizabeth about the various attacks on his life.

"We must make plans, dearest one," she said urgently.

She told him where the child had been sent, verbally, with no written note of his abode. It was to an elderly retainer whom Elizabeth and few others had known, a lady-in-waiting to her mother, Anne (Nan) Boleyn. When she was told at the birth she could not keep the child, she argued and said that if she had to give it up, then only she and the person looking after it would know its location. Then she used her strongest weapon.

"One day I will be Queen of England, and those who disobey me now will suffer greatly when I become Queen!"

That was enough to let her have her own way, and heads bowed in acquiescence. When the manservant arrived, the rest of the people who had surrounded Elizabeth were sent out of the bedchamber before he was seen, and the two discussed the child's future.

On bended knee, he swore unswerving loyalty to her and the child: "On my life, Your Highness, and if all fails we shall die together. I have a Lady Dorothy Fitzwilliam in the coach and she will care for him until we can give him to Lady Frances."

Elizabeth said hopefully to this man, "One day I may send the child's father to him and he will have the other half of this."

She gave him a talisman which she normally wore around her neck, in the hope she would see Gad again one day.

It was of cloth with the face of a saint on it. She had cut it in half and one half she gave Lady Frances' manservant, who took it almost reverently.

Out of the blue, Lady Frances' servant said quietly, "Many years ago, my lady too fell in love with someone in the wrong class. He was a sea captain. I know he died at sea, but his sister and I have secretly corresponded for years under the guise of her being a seamstress. My lady's family would have disowned her if they knew who he really was. She will understand your plight, so I will take him there."

Elizabeth smiled and said, "That sounds fine. Where is it?'

He gave Elizabeth the name and house, and its exact location, and Elizabeth smiled at last, mainly from relief. Looking away, one hand at her mouth and her eyes closed, she waved him away with the other hand. Never would she have a more distressing moment in her life. It was like giving birth again and having the child ripped from her body.

The servant left as he had come, quietly, but this time not alone. Now he walked in haste, imagining an hysterical call from Elizabeth's chamber, but none came. No one sought to stop a servant carrying the large sewing bag he had collected from another room and with a blind girl on his arm. She was to be the baby's surrogate mother, as her own child had recently died at birth.

When her companions returned, she had reasserted her position as Queen in waiting, and exhorted them to make a complete cleaning of the house, burning all the rubbish that was in any way involved with a baby, including its offered cradle.

They nodded and all acquiesced silently, aware of the consequences should there be any sign of a child left behind. Apparently they were more moved than the mother, but then, none really ever knew the real Elizabeth. Little did they know the heartache that Elizabeth was suffering and how it changed her attitude to men thereafter?

She smiled a sad smile, realising her choice of carrier and surrogate mother had been successful and, perhaps despite the many searches and indiscreet questions asked of her over the years, she felt happy it would remain a secret. And she was right. Until now.

"For all this time, Gad, we have corresponded secretly, using a code we made up to disguise her as a seamstress needing my charity." She looked away through the windows and added quietly, "Lady Frances will probably be in her seventies now if she is still alive, and she will be your first call, so that when ye leave here do not allow yourself to be followed. It would lead directly to both your certain deaths." Then, going to her desk, she said, "Here, my love, take this – it is the other half the talisman."

Gad clasped the torn scapular showing half a saint's face and name, but he had no time to examine it and quickly hung it about his neck.

The noise of the activity around them began to rise in quantity if not in quality, which described the hectic running about that was going on in and around the old palace.

The loud shouts from officers trying to organise the search came from different parts of the building as the chaos grew.

"Like headless chicken," Gad mused to himself as Elizabeth went for a small parchment and ink. She had lots of letters to write and friends to meet and things to organise.

She wrote a note for Lady Frances, not using her name but just calling herself 'Madam', explaining who Gad was and he tucked it in his toolbox which he still carried around with him as that was his excuse to be there if he was caught. She gave Gad details of the Lady Frances' house verbally, which was a long way away, in deepest Sussex, a place called Forde. In fact, it was near a coastal village and small fishing port called Hampton.

But Gad's first problem was getting out of the old palace, as already there were sounds of running men and the shouts of authority growing louder and getting nearer all the time. When he looked out of the window to assess his chances of escape the way Elizabeth had suggested, he saw groups of men at arms, which were running to block any exit from the established gates.

"Thank the Lord for the dark," was Elizabeth's comment.

The palace was a rambling old place, thoroughly unworthy for a princess as a place to live, but ideal for her to learn discipline, both personal and later regal of a future Queen. It was also a place with many entrances and exits and mysterious nooks and crannies.

Long after Gad had left, and when the troops found her reading quietly by the window in the main library, she simply said in her imperious way, "What is all the fuss and noise? Is the palace afire?"

It was eleven years later before she became Queen, and her years at the Old Hatfield Palace were remembered with mixed feelings.

It was a place she would learn her 'trade' to be Queen in a man's world, as no other century shows it. But as for the child and her love for Gad and the other people involved, as history records, none of these were ever entered or recorded.

Many people tried to get her to be indiscreet but the hard-faced lady was a great Queen, and she was married to her people. From the age of eight, she, and eventually her brother, Edward VI, was subjected to a most tyrannical system of learning of history, geography, mathematics, science and music.

She buried herself in her learning, and had already become fluent in both Latin and Greek as well, and as French was the court's language, she later commanded that all and every conversation had to be spoken in none of these other languages when proper English could be established. She also developed a monological style of talking, and was renowned for her diatribes when answering a simple question.

Although Gad was put on the backburner so to speak, he was never forgotten, as we shall see.

Night fell as he struggled down the sloping roof and dropped gently onto the grass at the edge of the quadrangle, catching the tool bag thrown by Beth.

The frustrated troops, who at last had decided to search more systematically, were called together and did not run around like lost souls as they had been until now. But it was already too late.

Beth could hear their progress as they searched each and every room on the far side of the quadrangle of buildings that made up the old palace. Both Mary and Edward, her brother, were away at the time in London, so there was no one else who could tell the searching men which little niche the princess liked to hide in. Kat, her governess, was not brought in to talk with Gad either and she knew no more than most other people which, being the inveterate gossip that she was irked her considerably.

Much as Elizabeth liked her, she realised early on that she was not to be trusted, and so the little hideaways that she had were kept completely secret.

From the darkened area he had dropped into, it was a simple exercise for Gad to run across the lawn, circuit the pond and disappear into the woods and away to where he had left his horse earlier.

Later, a soldier was found wandering about, holding his sore head and explaining to his Sergeant how he must have been struck from behind. When he awoke, the horse that had been discovered and he had been guarding was gone.

Gad made good progress across the open fields of East London, travelling southeast. He crossed the Thames at Blackfriars and by keeping to the coast road, he tried to make for the coastal town of Hastings, wherever that was. He would have been hopelessly lost if a man in long cloak and large hat riding a grey had not accosted him and put him on the right way.

There he hoped he could get a boat ride around the coast to Hampton, the small fishing village where his son lay, not realising the sort of journey that was.

His complete lack of knowledge of England was compounded by the fact that he had never seen the sea before either, and simply imagined the journey to be on a par with road travel, a fact he was soon to be disabused of.

It was hard ride, and he blessed the farmer who had sold him the horse, for it was a sturdy mount, no doubt having been brought up on the stony ground of Hertfordshire, leading the plough.

Several times he stopped and walked to give his beast a rest, and wondered how far he had to go.

The next town he had to get to was Tunbridge Wells so he was told by another stranger, a friend of Elizabeth, and soon the sign pointing to this famous city showed he had several miles to go yet, nearer twenty.

Chapter Fifteen

A few miles further on, he felt his horse begin to limp, and as it was late afternoon, he would soon have to bed them both down. He sat disconsolately on a bank by side of the narrow lane, lost, tired and for once not sure what to do.

He got up, lifted the horse's hoof and saw that it was bleeding slightly, no doubt cut by a sharp rock. It would need expert help and rest when he heard a voice say, "Yer horse got a problem, master?'

He turned and saw a young woman leading her horse quietly, smiling as she came over and tutted at the horse's foot.

"My da will sought that for ye – come on."

She led the way up the lane for about another mile, and then it went up sharply. As they crested the hill they looked down on a small farmhouse and stables.

As they approached the buildings, a nasty looking man appeared, holding a crook at a dangerous angle. He had an equally evil looking dog which crept towards them with its head low and its eyes menacing.

"What ye doin' 'ome this early fer?" he queried the girl.

A woman came out of the house, followed by a very large lad who looked strange and who was dribbling spittle from his crooked mouth as he walked towards them at a strange angle. His long arms and hands were huge, as were his legs. An altogether strange family, he thought. The woman spoke sharpish to her man.

"That's no way t' greet a guest, Walter." She gave what she hoped was a smile to Gad. "Get yerself down, sir, and come and have a mash of tea."

The girl grinned at Gad, and turned to the man, her father, and said, "'is 'orse be lame – it 'ave cut its foot."

The man scowled at her and at Gad.

"So what d'ye want me t' do about it?"

"See to it, yer dang old fool," said the woman, who had returned to see what was holding up the lad's progress. She took Gad's arm and led him into the farmhouse. "Sit yerself down, lad, and have some tea." She proffered Gad a none too clean mug of steaming tea.

The girl came in and threw her bag and coat onto a chair.

"That dirty bastard had another go at I," she said frowning, "so I 'it 'im with my broom handle."

They all laughed, and the weird lad who towered over Gad stood facing him close, just a few feet away, unnerving him.

"If yer man can cure my nag, I can pay 'im a shilling. 'Tis all the money I got."

He went outside to get away from the overfriendly staring of the strange lad and also to see what the farmer was doing to his horse. As he looked back the way he had come, he saw a figure standing there, looking down at him next to his horse from the top of the hill. He quickly ran into the hedge cover to hide as they looked at him.

The farmer noticed the man too. "Looks like you're being followed, lad. Run away, ave ye?"

Gad pretended he was a runaway from a factory in London where he had got a girl into trouble.

"It were probably 'er da," he said.

The old man chuckled at least Gad thought it was. Anyway, he had grinned, "Aye, well, we 'ave all done tha'," he smiled.

He called over his strange lad and said something to him and the boy shambled away, carrying a club.

It was dark now, and inside the house the women were making a stew of some dead animal, but it smelled alright. Gad started to mend a pair of badly down-at-heel boots with one side split wide open while he waited, and was soon engrossed in his work.

He next turned to a pair of tatty shoes, obviously belonging to the woman of the house.

The man came back into the house later on and said to Gad, "Well, yer 'orse be okay, but will need a rest. It don't matter about 'im," he indicated over his shoulder "as Danny 'as sorted your follower out for ye. He had a horse too, so ye now 'ave two."

He chortled and went out again.

Soon, Gad sat back and gave the shoes to a surprised and delighted woman.

"By the saints, you'm a good workman and that's no lie." Trying on the shoes, she did a little dance in them and ran outside to show her husband, carrying his mended boots.

The meal was good, and soon tiredness overcame Gad and he asked if he could sleep in the barn.

As he crossed the yard to the barn, Danny stood watching him again, making him feel very uncomfortable, so he made sure that where he slept he kept his bag next to him, with his arm through the bag's handles.

Several hours later, probably at about three o'clock in the morning, he felt a movement near him and then a body lifted his blanket and crept up to him. It was the naked body of the girl. He gently pushed her away, saying he that he had a wife waiting for him, at which she sat up looking as wild as her brother and screamed, "I wants your body", and made a grab for him.

He slid sideways and hit her hard.

As she lay there, he got up, dressed quietly and saddled his own horse, and climbed on the back of the other horse that was still saddled. He wanted to be away from this strange family, and felt his boot and shoe repairs were payment enough for the work done on his own horse.

Lifting his bag across his lap, he left as quietly as he could, as the girl was out for the count.

As he rode into the yard, there in the moonlight stood Danny. He was holding his club and was blocking his exit. He was not a pretty sight, almost ogre like with his wild looks and his twisted, drooling mouth.

Taking out his 'suader, he rode full pelt at him and caught him full in the face, making him drop his club and fall to the ground. Behind the fallen Danny, he turned and saw the eerie figure of the naked girl, waving her arms frantically at him and screaming fit to wake the dead. He rode full pelt out of the farm and up the hill to where he saw the follower, and sure enough, the mangled body was lying there.

However, he had places to go, and could not spare the time to worry about one of Dudley's men.

He now had to find his way to this Tunbridge Wells place. More by luck than judgement he rode, keeping the slowly rising sun to the left of him, and soon the lights of a small town appeared in the distance. He dismounted and walked into the dawn, watching nature come to life, which was a time he liked best, hearing the birds greeting the sun and the rustling in the undergrowth as various animals came looking for food.

As he walked, he thought over the last few days, his rides and eventual meeting with his Beth. He grinned – so he was a father was he? I wonder what sort of lad my son will be, he thought.

Perhaps he would find a princess too and become famous. He laughed at his many silly thoughts, smiling contentedly. Then he scowled; he had to find his lad yet. He gripped the reins tightly and repeated what he had said to Beth. He was a determined man and he would find him come what may. As he entered this famous old town, he was surprised at how clean it was. There was no filth, nor mess from people's bedpans. It was a nice place. He walked through the waking town until he saw an inn not too far away and stopped to see if the landlord was around.

He didn't have to wait long, as a small, broad shouldered man appeared carrying a bucket and headed into his stables.

Gad tied the horses to a post and walked over to the man who looked up, a little alarmed at seeing someone around so early.

"What can I do for ye, master?"

Gad wanted something to eat and drink for himself and his horses and the man smiled.

"Come far, 'ave ye?"

Gad answered that he was trying to get to the sea and find a boat and then he grinned.

"I 'opes the people here aren't all like the farm backaways."

The man smiled back at him and said, "Ye got mixed up with the Barters, did ye?"

As they walked back to the inn, Gad told him what had happened, adding that he had an extra horse now so if he knew anyone who would want a good mare, he would sell it cheaply.

Seeing the chance to make a few sovereigns, the man said, "Aye, well, if ye want to eat here, I will give ye ten sovereigns for it."

An hour later, fully sated and with a small pack of bread and cheese to eat later, he was on his way again with instructions on how to get to a place called Hastings, which was by the sea. It would take him several more days to get there, as his horse still limped a bit, so he decided to earn some money. He had not kept the other horse because he had seen a small mark on its rump, indicating it belonged to a Royal person, probably Dudley's crest. If he was caught with that, he could be arrested for horse stealing and hung.

Work here was not as plentiful as other places, but he still managed to get small purse of nearly forty pence.

Eventually, he decided to move on, and as he crested a hill in the distance, he saw what he took to be the sea. Something was shining through the trees along the way, and sure enough he saw a battered sign post which read 'Hastings – 10 miles'. It gave him a renewed heart in his mad dash there.

The small seaport was unexpectedly crowded, and whereas there were lots of ladies, mostly fisherman's wives, he was surprised to find that there didn't seem to be many men.

Ahead he saw a small inn, which seemed just about right.

Back at the Old Hatfield Palace, pandemonium would be a euphemistic word to describe the sheer panic that ensued after the departure of Gad. Young 'Dud' Dudley turned up, as he was on a holiday from his studies. He railed at his elderly father for being so soft on Elizabeth and was all for persuading the boy King to imprison his sister, but wiser council prevailed. He swore an oath that he would personally conduct the hunt for Gad and not return to college until the "bastard maker was hung proper this time."

So, whereas Dudley was running about like the proverbial headless chicken, not daring to talk to Elizabeth, but relieving his temper out on any other poor soul who got in his way, his archenemy was half way to Hastings, so he was told by his spies.

Why there? he thought. Was he trying to get to France? However, he contacted his man there by a fast horse. He was told of Gad's possible appearance there and to watch out for him.

Gad felt that by riding horseback the whole way, Elizabeth had said it was 'nigh on a hundred miles', it would not only be very bad for the horse, but he would be at the mercy of the many government agents and all the footpads and criminals around at the time.

He decided that he ought to go by boat. He hoped it would be like a trip down the River Wye or a gentle paddle, as he was unaware that there was a huge sea off the coast of England and it could be more trouble than it was worth.

His lack of knowledge and his simple directness had brought him thus far without incident, and he relaxed his guard.

Apart from him not knowing about seas and the like, his dress and lack of understanding why no men were to be seen in Hastings added to his furtive manner, and meant that if and when he found a ship's captain willing to take him at least as far as that part of the South Coast, which was highly unlikely, the sailor would know he was a fugitive.

One man, however, did know where he had gone and the route chosen to get there, although he had not approved of the route. He shook his head as he had watched his charge and then, making enough noise to awaken the dead, he drove his poor beast hard back across the London fields and turned back to report.

This lad would not make it, despite help from Elizabeth's own men, who had started their protection of her 'friend'. This one was in no doubt as to where Gad would end up;

nevertheless, he carried on following him after he had made his report on a fresh horse. As far as he was concerned, he could do no more.

He presumed Gad was as good as dead, but he did not know much about the determined man.

As his stomach needed sustenance as well as his horse, Gad decided to find a stable for his nag and have a drink in a quayside tavern before searching for a boat. He thought that maybe he could sell his horse to pay for the fare.

Here though, as his watcher surmised, his luck would change.

Elizabeth had no money to give him, as her position did not require her to hold any, so all he had was the little he had acquired on his journey to Hatfield and what he had earned in Tunbridge Wells.

The dark, low-beamed inn was thick with smoke from the fire and the candles and lamps lit all around, which made for runny eyes and a scratchy throat. He bumped into several people before he got his night sight, and one actually swung a punch at him in the semi-dark, but the packed throng soon swallowed him up.

It was a girl who first spotted him, as he was carrying his tools across his back with a tight-jawed look across his face. A streetwalker always had a keen eye for a good punter, and this one looked quite a promising one.

"Ye looks a strong and 'termined lad, darlin'. Buy me drink then?"

Gad was pressed up against her in the crowd and felt a hand exploring his groin.

"Big boy, ain't yer? Come over 'ere."

She kicked and pushed her way to the edge of the crowd, pulling Gad with her. Another chap watching the by-play also came over.

"Cost you a shilling matey, for 'alf an hour."

Gad looked at the open hand and spat into it.

The man lunged at Gad, who was by this time getting used to brawling, and he was not there when the pimp's fist arrived. As the body came by, Gad hit him over the head with his bag carrying his tools. The heavy equipment laid him out good and proper, and he fell flat on his face and lay there.

Several of those nearby laughed. "She's yours for free nar matey, pox an' all."

The girl was frightened and started to slide away through a door, so Gad followed. He didn't know why, but somehow he felt he had outstayed his welcome too.

The wind cut in over the harbour wall and hit the tavern square on with a howling roar, followed by a squall of rain that felt like a shower of needles.

The girl was shivering in the doorway and Gad said quite innocently, "Ye got anywhere we can go?" not realising the implication.

Nodding, she pulled her totally inadequate shawl around her thin shoulders and towed him along the drenched foreshore to an old house just off the quayside.

It had not been inhabited for many a year and was simply a very rough wooden structured house, used now as a cover for vagrants and prostitutes. Naturally, she thought he wanted her body, although her stomach growled through lack of food and she could have done with a drink. Pulling aside a pair of broken shutters below the main window of the house, the two bedraggled figures fell rather than ran into the floor of a cellar.

But they had been observed.

Gad was followed by the tall man, who was dressed in a dark cloak, with breeches and high boots turned over at the top and his large floppy brimmed hat hid his face. He grinned as he muttered to no one in particular, "I can wait."

The foetid smell as it reached his nostrils nearly made Gad throw up, and after a little difficulty, he struck his flint onto a small amount of natural tinder he found lying about. Slowly a light grew in the unwholesome darkness, and eventually he found the fireplace long unused and began a small fire. As the smoke and flames drew up the chimney, he was pleased he wasn't going to be kippered on top of everything else.

Looking around, he saw rubbish and detritus of all kinds but the most disgusting smell was coming from a small bundle near the fireplace. He kicked it and it fell apart, showing the decomposed remains of a child crawling with insects.

Once again, his stomach heaved and, turning to the girl, he saw her frightened look as she obviously recognised it.

"Yers?"

She cowered away fearfully from him as she nodded, no doubt expecting a beating and her face in the firelight showed she was used to it.

"Didn't know what to do wiv it," she said sullenly. "I birthed it two months ago."

God's teeth! Thought Gad, it's been lying here as she plied her trade, with the smell getting worse and worse.

Chapter Sixteen

He gathered up the flyblown carcass and tossed it on the fire, which was roaring up the chimney now, burning all manner of wooden bits and pieces. He felt it was all he could do, as the poor infant was no longer there, just its carcass.

The girl came over and continued to persuade Gad to lie with her, but he was so overcome with what he had had to do, apart from the sheer revulsion he felt for her, that he knocked her to the floor.

"Piss arf!"

"Yer won't snitch on me, will yer?" she asked in a plaintive voice. She added, in a sly tone, "I can 'elp yer get away."

Gad stood there drying himself off and trying to sort out what he had to do next.

Before he entered the tavern, he had put his horse in the keep of an ostler nearby; whom he seemed to think and hoped was reasonably honest. So all he had with him were the clothes he stood up in, a small purse, a knife and, on his own advice, a ten-inch flexible persuader, made of leather and filled with tiny pebbles and of course his ubiquitous tool bag.

He had made his starter after the two mercenaries tried to waylay him the other side of St Albans, as he felt he needed something quieter and less harmful than a dagger. The one he had made earlier had been lost in the mad ride from the two men.

He looked at the girl again who sensibly had stayed on the floor, but now was lifting her skirts above her waist trying still to encourage him. In the half-light he could see the heavy bruising on her inner thighs, but the very thought of indulging in anything sexual with her revolted him almost as much as seeing the dead child.

"Ye can put yer clothes down. I am not interested at anything ye've got, at any price, but I will pay ye if ye can genuinely help me to get out of this town." Then he added, in what he hoped was a menacing tone, "Any tricks, mind, and they will be yer last."

The girl gathered herself together and stood up. "Ye seem a nice enough lad. What d'ye do?"

Gad gave her a start by drawing his knife and saying in as menacing a voice as possible, 'I killed a girl for asking too many silly questions."

She cowered away. "I only arst," she said sullenly. Then she brightened up and said, "I knows a feller 'ere who has a boat, an 'e won't rob yer blind, if yer int'rested?"

Gad looked at her and decided that if he assumed he would rob him blind he might be lucky.

"Where is 'e?"

She looked out of the cellar and said, "The bleedin' rain has stopped. Come on."

With that, she jumped up and climbed out of the cellar, closely followed by Gad. As it was still pitch black, it took them both a few moments to be able to see again, so he grabbed her arm; she could be his way out of this port, he hoped.

Then, when he felt reasonably secure, he motioned her to carry on where she was going and they walked quickly between ramshackle buildings and down a narrow stinking lane between derelict houses until they came to an opening, looking directly onto the harbour. The tall, dark shadow followed silently, keeping to the darker areas. His sword stuck out behind him, a man not to argue with.

Gad's keen hearing heard the slight scrape of metal on stone behind him, and for the first time since leaving the derelict house, he realised he was being followed.

He took out his 'suader. Then, when the tall dark man realised where they were going, he moved away down a side street and ran faster on ahead of the pair. Gad looked fearfully over his shoulder deciding the man was a 'chancer' and had gone for better game.

A small broad beamed 'smack', about twenty five feet long, was moored to the quayside, bobbing up and down on the rough tide as it came in. It had an awning over the foredeck by way of somewhere to get out of the weather, and boasted a mast that looked big enough to take a fair sized square rigged sail.

"Oi! Master!" she called in a loud whisper, and banged on the side of the boat.

A thickset man appeared like a jack in the box.

"Yeah. Who's tha'?"

He stood with his legs apart, his body moving expertly with the swell. Gad had never been on a boat before, and its size and movement unnerved him, but needs must when the devil drives and he still hadn't seen the sea properly.

"This geezer 'ere wants a ride darn west."

Gad thought he was almost as broad as he was tall, but lithe and cat-like; he jumped up onto the quayside. However, on the same level he could see that he was not as tall as Gad, but he reckoned pound for pound the man was much heavier and all muscle, so he too was not a man to trifle with.

"I needs to get to the port of Hampton and I don't want to ride there," he said indicating, that he had a horse by the flick of his head. "I might sell it if ye can take me?"

The girl moved across to the other side of the man and whispered to him. The sailor spat a stream of dark spittle over the side of the dock into the wild turmoil of the sea and looked again at Gad.

No doubt she was arranging her 'cut' from the man's fare, and the whole time he was staring at Gad.

It was not a look of suspicion, but one that was sizing him up. Then, with alarming speed, his hand shot out and before Gad could respond, the man had him by the upper arm.

"Don' ye worry, lad," he smiled, his blackened and misshapen teeth giving him a piratical look. "It's just that you'll 'ave to 'elp, see? It's a long haul down there, and one man would 'ave a great deal o' hardship doin' it on 'is own like."

His grip was like steel, and one that he knew he would have a great deal difficulty breaking out from. He was dressed in a very long cloak coat, made of some shiny material for seafarers, with loose arms and a wide hem, and on his head he had a wide brimmed oily hat tied under his chin.

From head to toe he was completely covered, but had Gad looked closer, he would have seen his long hair had been tucked up under his weather-proofed hat and not 'queued' as was the custom. He was no sailor.

"Aye, ye 'ave a bit o' muscle, so maybe I can tek ye'" He paused, then knocking the stuff out of his pipe, he added as he returned onto the boat, "Now then. 'ow much?" Let us grab a bite t' eat first."

He led the way back to the inn. He looked helpless, not knowing what to offer, as he rubbed his still painful arm.

"Well, I have a good horse I shan't need, but that's about all I have of value. My tools are only any good to me, but ye could sell the horse when ye get back it's with the ostler at the tavern yonder."

The sailor grinned. "Run away, 'ave ye?"

Gad lowered his head. "Aye," he said, and using the time-honoured phrase, added, "I got the master's daughter with child."

That brought a loud laugh from the swaying man and got Gad a thump on the back. "Aye, well, we've all done tha'. Show us this nag then."

Moving off at a fast walk, they went into the stable, knocked on the Judas gate and went in. Then the two of them, the 'sailor' and the stableman, went into a quiet huddle in the stables, and the man surreptitiously giving the farrier a hastily written note.

The girl grinned at the thought of a decent stake out of this deal, showing for the first time no teeth, probably knocked out.

"'Ave a good time, mister. It's too late for Lucy Kindle, but I guess I'll be alright now. Mind yersen', alright?" Then, tugging his sleeve and nodding to the sailor, she added quietly to Gad, almost under her breath, "Word o' warnin' though. There ain't a decent man round 'ere, so don' trust 'im."

The two men in the stable seemed to have done some sort of deal, and so once again carrying all his worldly belongings over his broad back, Gad followed the sailor back to the Inn.

As the group back in Stratford all sipped their drinks, Thomas was also remembering. He said to his father, "I must have been only four or five then and I played in the sea most days when Aunt Frances took me across the foreshore at Hampton. It were a nicer beach over at Clymping."

He mused silently with his eyes closed, remembering. "One part was all stony, I minds, but if we could get a boat over the river, or walk over the rickety wooden bridge further back in the town, the other side was real good.

"The sand were all soft and warm. It had little hills, I remembers, wi' hardy, tough grass growing out of them, which hurt when I would roll down over them. That usually meant a strip bath when we got back as the sand got everywhere."

Gad smiled and listened as Thomas mused, and then he carried on with his tale.

Inside the low ceilinged bar again, thick with tobacco smoke from a badly laid fire, was a motley crew of assorted seafaring folk. Ned nodded at the small hairy innkeeper and asked for trenchers for "me an' my mate." The landlord nodded and as he called through for them. He asked Ned, "Ow long ye been in?"

"Just," answered Ned.

The big man looked about and said, "Take yer fodder into the corner over there by the small door. The press be about and if they comes 'ere you'll 'ave to scarper right fast, like." Then he held out his hand for his money before he would let go the long awaited meal of bread and meat.

"Come on lad," Ned said, "Let's pack up this food and go now before we get..."

"Hold hard, my beauties!"

They were too late. Six short and broad shouldered men with tarred pigtails, holding starters, appeared from the suggested door.

They were dressed in tight, strong shiny trousers and had a variety of shirts on, some with a shield on as though they belonged to some wealthy owner. They all wore pigtails under their tarred hats, and looked like as though they could more than take care of themselves.

These short flexible starters were used constantly aboard ship to keep the men moving, particularly the more reluctant ones as they ran to climb the rigging to alter the sails.

Gad was rigid with both fear and surprise. "Not now, dear saint," he pleaded. He looked at the man in a cocked hat with gold braid on his coat sleeve. He was holding a sword which Gad noticed had pieces knocked out of the blade, but it was still quite a formidable weapon, reminding him of the man who had killed his friend Thomas. He had a scar down his right cheek too, which gave him a permanent leer.

Ned scowled. "W'em sailors ourselves, men, trying to earn an honest living by the sea and we has 'claimers from His Majesty to leave us free from the press."

The biggest of the men leaned forward, took Ned by the jacket and simply lifted him off his feet, which was no mean feat.

"Ye're just the men we need, experienced bummers," He said, and then dropped him down.

The little door to his left was just where these men had come from.

"Damn it!" Ned said. They must have been set up by the landlord, who was watching the scene and laughing all the time.

Being a poacher made Gad a quick thinking man, so he suddenly dropped to the floor in a pretend dead faint with an "Oh, my God!" His plate and food went everywhere. The big man came over, picked him up and handed him to the men behind him, who took him outside through the little door, which meant he was no longer trapped.

Staying limp, he felt rough hands drag him away along the empty quayside, his feet dragging along the slippery roadway. Through half-closed eyes, he could see there was no one on one side of him and just as his carriers relaxed, he shot up, pushed one man against the other and broke free.

Never had Gad run so fast in all his life; in fact, it was only then that he realised he still had a fair turn of speed and, like in his earlier days as a young poacher, he zigzagged past two bystanders and was off up an alley like the proverbial jack rabbit.

It was easier than he thought, but as he kept on running, he felt the wind of a bullet pass his head and then the bang. Wow! What was that?, he thought. Ten minutes later, he was running up and out of Hastings and heading towards a place he saw was called Battle. That's a good name, he thought. But at least he was free! That was all that mattered right then, and he stopped at last under a tree panting with the exertion and his breath coming in laboured gasps as he leant against a low branch. He looked back down into the town and harbour, and there were no signs of anyone following him so he relaxed, but he had lost everything. His tools, his spare clothes, Beth's letter, his sword – in fact, all he had was just what he stood up in.

Then he had a thought. If they had taken Ned, then the boat might be free now that is if no one else had got it. Perhaps he might be able to slip back unnoticed and claim it. He waited where he was, resting for a while and wishing he still had the food he had dropped. He watched as the sun went down and evening descended on this small fishing village.

Then he made his way slowly back the way he had come, keeping a careful watch for any signs of chasing men but there were none. Poor Ned, he had become quite fond of him in a way and at his age he thought that he would be of little use to the Navy, so maybe they might let him go when they saw he was too old for that kind of service.

He reached the harbour again without any difficulty and again using his old woodcraft skills he slipped quietly along the quayside looking for Ned's boat in the dark. Then he saw it.

First though, he had to get his gear and so he ran back to the Inn and crept in. It was quiet in there now, as the press had gone. He saw the landlord clearing tables and crept up behind him. Taking out his persuader, he grabbed him by the neck.

"Now then, mister, ye 'ave two seconds to tell me where my gear is. One two..."

The man froze, and then in a panic he pointed to behind the bar.

Crack! Gad laid him out and riffled through the man's pockets, taking back his own purse and the landlord's. He took his bag, and a quick search showed him that nothing had been taken. Then, stuffing a cooked chicken and some bread off the kitchen cooker, he left.

Outside, he looked up and down what did for a quay, and there was Ned's boat, lying on its side a little way off the road in the shingle beach.

The sea was swilling around the boat making it half lift. Eventually, seeing that all was quiet, he moved off.

There were two men looking it over as though they had just bought it, and he took out his persuader again. Crouching down as he passed a low wall, he came up behind the first man as he was trying to get his lamp alight.

Crunch! One blow and he fell like an ox, and the lamp dropped with a crash. He heard rather than saw the other man coming up to the boat's gunwale from the inside of the boat, and with just the front of his head showing, he too received a smart tap there and he slid peacefully back down into the boat.

Gad looked around him and it appeared that his little fracas had gone unnoticed. He pushed the first man away from the edge of the low wall. Not that Gad knew it, but the tide was on the turn fortunately, and as he slipped over the side of his boat as the water had begun to lift the boat upright, he cast off and began to steer it out to sea.

More by luck than judgement, and not without a few bangs against other moored and anchored craft, he pointed the boat for the open sea. But which way to go?

While his companion was asleep, Gad went through his pockets and threw overboard his knife and the gun thing.

The sun had gone down on his right, so he turned the craft to keep the hidden sun in the same place. He wasn't sure if he was right, but it was the best he could do.

The man who had fallen in the boat was coming round and he groaned, feeling the front of his head, where he had a lovely bruise spreading over his forehead. Gad had deliberately left him on board because he knew he would need someone who knew about boats to help him get to Hampton. If he was a buyer then he should know something about boats. He tied the steering arm to the side of the boat and clambered across to the man, before the boat got too far out, as needed all his new friend's attention. He quickly searched the man, removing a knife and what looked like a bag of stones.

Then he found the pistol, but threw it over the side. He tied the man's ankles together just as a precaution against a sudden attack. He had heard of these gun things, but thought them more dangerous to the user than the victim and never had any plans to get one, so he had disposed of it. He took a handful of seawater and threw it over the man.

"Wake up, master – we have sailing to do."

The man shook his head and looked across at Gad who was holding the tiller. "Oo might ye be?" he said angrily.

"Me?" said Gad. "Oh, I'm the person whose boat ye were going to steal. Now, ye have two choices. One, ye can jump over the side and swim for it, or ye can help me get to Hampton which be along the coast somewhere. Then ye can keep the boat and no hard feelings." He waited. "Which is it to be?"

Gad gripped the tiller, hoping this new man would help, as he knew he could never get to his destination alone, after all he didn't even know for sure which way it was.

The other man looked over the side and judged the distance to the dark strip of land and shrugged his shoulders. "I don't 'ave a choice do I? I'll help ye".

"Right!" said Gad moving over to the sail. "Ye take the rudder and I'll hoist the sail. I'll cut yer legs free later but should ye move away from that steerer or try any tricks, and they'll be yer last."

He figured that a fight out here would only destroy them both and as expected, the man nodded. Gad did as he had seen Ned do in reverse before they went to the tavern, and soon they were creaming along.

Chapter Seventeen

"As we shall be together for a while,' the man said, 'we'd better introduce ourselves. My name's Og Vetch and I own the chandlers on the quayside. My friend ye 'it, was a fisherman I sometimes worked with, name o' Tommy Dickson."

Gad gave him a false name and told him he had a wife waiting for him in Hampton who had last seen him being pressed for the Navy, so this time was his second escape.

Og was impressed. "Ye're a difficult man to hold then?"

Gad smiled. "Aye, and a worse man to cross, so point me in the right direction and let's be going."

The night was a dark one, with just a few stars to sail by, but with a dark mass of cloud ahead, which did not auger well. As he had no idea where he was heading, things could get tricky.

His companion was quite a talkative man who seemed to take the trials and pleasures of life with equal measure. Soon the water became rougher and the seas started to loom larger than Gad had ever imagined them; in fact, so high that he feared for his life. His reluctant tiller man shifted his seat, bracing himself against the rising sea.

"Ye'd better lower that sail, young fella, or else we'll all be in the drink and ye'd better cut I loose. Have ye never sailed a boat before, lad?"

His look was one of considerable consternation. Gad smiled at his companion's worries about drowning, and after he had stowed the sail neatly tied, he answered his newfound friend.

"Oh aye, I watched the man who brought me here and learned from 'im." He ducked as a large wave washed over them amidships.

"Ye'd better get bailing then, or we'll have more sea in here than outside and that's not good," the man said.

The anxiety in his voice was real, and he soon realised that Gad did not know what bailing was either, so he kicked a bucket that was lying in the scuppers over towards him with his feet.

Gad bailed for three solid hours and still the water poured in, and so Og tied the tiller down and came over to help.

"We are about four hours from our destination yet, so don't let up on the bailing. I have set the tiller pointed towards the shore because as soon as we pass the Beachy Point, the land will protect us from the main fury of the sea, but we must keep well into the shore. The next half hour is the testing time."

As fast as they threw water out, a lot more of it seemed to come inboard. Then suddenly, the waves died down and the sea became less violent; they had passed the high promontory, which made Gad look at it with sheer horror at its height and closeness, and then their next task appeared.

This was to keep themselves from being dashed against rocks which were looming too close for comfort on the lee-side, and they had to find a route close enough to shore but far enough out to sea to clear the rocks.

Og went back to the tiller, asking Gad to come and help him and together they wrestled with its wooden arm, praying it wouldn't snap as they fought the battle for survival. But it held, and after one scary moment when a large incoming wave lifted the small craft high in the air and prepared to dash it against the waiting foam covered rocks, when they slid sideways down and shot under the curl of the wave to a sort of comparative safety.

"I thought we'd had it then," Og said, as the two completely soaked and exhausted men desperately bailed and bailed again until their arms ached with a pain neither had experienced before.

As they moved under the guidance of the sea towards the coast, both men laid back exhausted and the boat rocked and rolled alarmingly with the water in the scuppers rushing from one side to the other.

"Fancy a life at sea, me lad?" the older man said with a tired grin.

But Gad, sitting up and checking how much gear they had lost, turned and said, "It's bad enough on a horse. No thanks."

Once again, Gad had that feeling. This man seemed well enough educated and spoke properly without much of an accent and the clothes he was wearing were of good quality. God's bones! He will be frightened of his own shadow next, he thought.

Og stood up and said, "Aye, we've passed the Beachy Point so we should be all right now."

For the first time, Gad saw his friend properly. He had been right this man was no sailor, he had rings on his fingers, good quality ones. No, he was a landlubber and a wealthy one at that. I wonder! Gad's mind turned to the earlier events and wondered if he was the man in the cloak who had been following him. He was about the same size.

The swell had been almost as bad as the waves. One minute the boat was high on a crest and the next it was rushing down into a black hole. Gad had never been more terrified, and if he had time to think he probably would have been sick too. He had clutched the mast so hard that he felt he would break it, but slowly and not so surely, the little craft guided by the inexperienced hands of Og and himself crept towards the shore.

Lights could be seen from the fishermen's houses high up on the beach, and the lighthouse on the pier shone out brightly.

"Where do ye want to go?" he asked Gad. He was standing now and saw a runway for a fishing boat ahead.

"Look! Just there."

Gad pointed to a flattened area where the wide beamed fishing boats slid down, hoping they wouldn't damage them against the solid timbers of the ramp.

He was soaking wet and freezing cold but ahead was solid land, and he felt quite relieved.

The gravel beach slowed the boat down to a stop as they made their approach. Gad turned to his assistant and thanked him saying, "The boat is yours now, as poor old Ned has a bigger one to sail."

Then, with his kit clutched over his shoulder, Gad jumped over the side. As he turned, he saw the man who had helped him raise his hand as though in farewell, but it was the flash of steel above the man's head that alerted him.

He pulled his gear in front of him sharply as the large knife that Gad had left behind by the tiller thumped into it, cutting his arm. Gad dropped his gear into the scuppers as he leapt back into the boat.

"You tried to kill me why?" he yelled as he clutched the man around the throat.

As they wrestled, Gad using his weight as an extra force, the man's jerkin burst open and a fine doublet was underneath. He held the man down and close to a pool of water in the rocking boat.

"Speak, man, or I drown ye here and now."

The man croaked, and said with difficulty, "Ye cannot get away, Gad ye are doomed. Now we know where ye are, others will follow."

Already mad with the thought that this man had tried to kill him, he began to realise that Og, if that was his name, could not return either.

So far only he knew where they actually where. But he was forgetting Ned. For him, he thought it would be a useful piece of information to trade against him being 'pressed'.

Slowly and deliberately, Gad squeezed the man's throat until he went limp. Then he shook with terror when it dawned on him what he had done, as the boat rocked with the movement of the tide. He had never killed a man in cold blood before, and only then it was in a fight when Thomas was killed. This was so awful, so awful. However, he shook himself, after all, it was either him or me, and if he had failed in his quest to find his son it would be his life too. Now what should he do? He couldn't leave the boat and the man here – it would bring the whole Army on to him. Looking about in the semi-dark, he saw an anchor off one of the fishing boats lying on the beach. It was not big, but enough, he thought.

He waded back through the surf and onto the stony beach, put the anchor in the boat and pushed it off again. Waist deep in the bitterly cold water, he continued to walk the boat out until it was in deeper water; then he clambered aboard, his teeth chattering with the cold, and he swore he could not feel his legs. The tide thankfully had begun to move out to sea again and the craft continued to drift out as well, so Gad tied the anchor to the man's legs, making sure he would go down and stay down long enough for him to disappear.

He knew he had to do this, or else all would be up for him and his son would never know him.

Gad watched Meg's face, which was a picture of horror as she looked at his crooked hands in front of him too. Thomas shook his head.

"But ye had no choice, father. If ye had left him to return to Hastings, we might never have got out of Auntie Frances' house alive. But how did this man know about ye?"

"To be honest, lad, I didn'' find out. Dudley, a friend of the Seymours, had many spies all over the country looking for me it seems and particularly at the ports I expect too and my Lords Seymour and Dudley had men sent out to track me down, so it could have been any one of them. They could have used fast 'orses and passed messages to the port officials; they may even have used some kind of signal towers put onto the highest hills, like the bonfires we lit during the war with the Spanish. 'member? 'appen they made signals every time I were seen."

Meg was still horrified by Gad's admission that he had killed a man in cold blood.

"But to kill with yer bare hands, my dearest." Meg's face was still fixed in shocked horror at the realisation of what Gad had done.

Gad stroked her hair. "I knows my love, and every day I ask yer God to forgive me. But those were violent times and when yer own life is put against another's well..."

Thomas was wrapped in a mixture of wide-eyed excitement at the telling of the tale, and a hero worship of his father. He felt Meg soften against him as his father expressed his genuine sorrow at his killing of another human being. Then she began to realise that out there, away from her house and immediate locality, where the only violence was a drunken husband, there must be lots of people ready just to kill.

Her own sheltered life was one in which she only met violence in local situations, at the tavern where she used to work, or a drunk on his way home, and occasionally a husband beating a wife, but that was different.

Bedtime had arrived, heads began to nod. For a while Gad called a halt to his tales of his 'daring-do', and they all took to their various cots. Eventually he decided to go to his on the first floor of this comfortable house, and he rose stiffly and awkwardly to his feet, declining Meg's help a little roughly.

Then he stopped and took hold of her into his arms and they just stood there, feeling each other's body close and warm.

He felt that, despite his fascination with Elizabeth in the early days, he doubted whether he would have been as comfortable or so well looked after as now, or indeed as cared for as he was by Meg in the future. He let out a long sigh, which caused her to smile up at him, and letting go his hold he followed her upstairs.

No sooner had they undressed and actually climbed into the high four-poster bed and drawn the curtains, there was a hammering on the door downstairs loud enough to wake the whole household.

Thomas was the first down, being the more agile, and before Gad could gather himself again, his son was standing in the room holding a candle.

"'Tis Will's servant, ma. 'e says Annie needs ye, real quick like."

Thomas was standing there in his shift in the candlelight and made Gad see himself at his age when he had found out for the first time he was a father at The Old Hatfield Palace. He smiled. Was he as scrawny and as wiry as that? His lad's hair was still tied back, and he detected the serious growth of facial hair. He smiled contentedly.

He patted the bed when Meg left in a matronly flurry, as this was something she could help with alone and men would only be in the way. Thomas snuffed the candle and sat next to his father.

"Yer life has always been in danger, Thomas, through my lust, and it worries me that ye might not like me as much because of it," Gad said.

The concern in his voice as his hand searched the bed for his son's hand was evident, and Thomas chuckled quietly.

"Lust always seems to play a part in all our lives, father, so ye are no different than anyone else including me." He paused then said in a more serious voice, "No father, that's not true no man could have done as much for his son as ye have. Your tale so far has been one of such richness in the way of fatherhood that I hope I don't have to do anything like as much for mine. But if I have to, then let's see if I can do as well as ye."

He smiled, hearing the soft breathing of his father in the dark, and saw that Gad was becoming a tired old man. He offered a silent prayer to his saint that "he is spared to us for many a year yet".

Dawn forced its way through the slatted shutters of the big bedroom window and the sun sliced across the bed in a slow arc. It then followed and passed the drawn back bed curtains which were not set back. All of which was after Meg had rushed out during the night, until it had reached the sleeping man. As it hit his eyes, it disturbed him and he moved over and away from the intrusive light.

Once again the noise downstairs started up with women's voices all talking at once. Gad sat up with a groan.

"Women!" he exclaimed in his early morning irritation.

Then, with a yawn and a scratch, he looked about him just as the bedroom door burst open with a loud bang and Meg arrived, all disarrayed and in a state of high excitement.

Her bonnet was slewed across her head, with bits of loose hair poking out all over it, and there were spots of blood on her cheek. She carried an apron with something all wrapped up inside, which looked decidedly unpleasant. She was sweating and her face was a rotund angelic picture of excitement, relief and tiredness.

"A beautiful girl!" she explained. "A lovely, squawking brat, as bright and healthy as ye ever did see."

Then she poked an apparent disinterested Gad as he lay there just smiling at her.

"What ye grinnin' about?" Gad stroked her hand. "Poor Will. Another mouth to feed and I expect all he can do is write another poem for 'er."

All the excitement over the birth of Will's first child Susanna had died down after a week. Once again the three members of Gad's family were gathered around the fire as the cold wind began its ululating sound, whistling through the timbers of the house, while Gad junior was in London, still with Will, his new teacher.

Once he had started his tale of Thomas' life and rescue, there would be no letting him forget it. Mind, things were still not safe nor secure for their family; with men needed for the new Navy, every able-bodied man hid during the day and only worked at night, still keeping a sharp lookout.

Thomas had been busy with the making of new harnesses for a local carter, and Gad had started to get back into the fine trimming and sewing needed for a pair of soft bootees for Will's little Susanna.

Life was beginning to get back into some sort of order, although Gad knew it couldn't last.

New men were being seen in the town of Stratford, men who swayed as they walked. Gad knew of old that these were an advance party of the feared Press Gang.

He had heard about the distant trouble with Spain, wherever that country was, which they discussed in the inn whenever a new man came in from London, and news was wanted about a new Navy which was being formed, so Thomas was advised that all the times that this danger was coming. He was only to go out after a careful looking at where these men where and to be constantly on the alert.

"What's the news, Thomas?" Gad asked, meaning about the pressmen.

Thomas looked at Gad under downcast eyes. "I was nearly caught today."

There was an intake of breath all around as they turned and looked at him.

"How, boy?" Gad's eyes blazed with concern.

Thomas told them he had been mending a workhorse's collar that had split badly and had never heard the approach of the two men from the Nore. As they came close, he turned and saw them getting ready to tackle him and to tie him if necessary. Both men keeping well apart from each other to avoid getting in each other's way if it came to a brawl.

He reacted just like his father would have done years ago. He paused to weigh them up then ducked under a beam and stopped dead. Both men dashed forward and as the first man bent to go under the beam, Thomas hit him hard across the nape of the neck and he fell, poleaxed.

Chapter Eighteen

The second man grabbed him and they wrestled, and again, just like his father had shown him. First you fight hard, then suddenly relax. It was an old trick, and the man fell for it.

As the man felt Thomas go slack, he automatically relaxed too, and that was when Thomas lifted him with a grip he had learned at the wrestling; one arm between the other man's legs gripping his belt behind him and the other across his opponent's chest, holding his coat lapels. With a heave from his haunches, he lifted the man over the bran box and threw him hard against the wall. The man did not get up either.

Now Gad was worried. Had his boy killed one or both of them? He was a strong lad. There was nothing for it, he had to go out, casual-like, and see if there is an uproar.

When Gad reached the stable with his slow walk and leaning on his stick, he heard voices.

"Oi tells 'ee it were 'im. 'E 'ad red 'air. We'd better tell 'is Lordship."

Gad opened the door to the stable and went in.

"What you men doin' in 'ere?" he asked as sternly as he could. "This be private, see, and unless you 'ave permission..."

He saw the two men. One was holding a badly broken arm, and the other was rubbing his back ruefully.

"Who was the lad we tussled with?" one of them asked Gad, who replied, "Oh 'im, 'e were a casual lad from somewhere up north. Why?"

"We thought perhaps he were a Lunnon lad."

Gad shook his head saying nay, he spoke with a funny accent. Behind Gad came a couple of his friends.

They soon took in the situation as they saw it and asked Gad what the problem was. He bent down and lifted up an unlit torch that had been knocked down in the fight, and was lying on the floor of the stable.

"They was trying to set light to the place."

The men protested but to no avail and they were carted off to jail by the summoned constable. Gad hurried home to an anxious family.

"Sorry lad, but they recognised ye they know who ye are."

Thomas' wife cried and Meg complained, but Gad was adamant. Thomas would have to leave, at least for a while.

First though, Gad had to find out what was happening to these men, and while Thomas was preparing to go away for a while, he went to the town hall where he met the mayor, who was a friend of Will's father.

"Ye say they were trying to burn the stable down, Gad – did they have a flint with them?"

Gad shuffled his feet. "How long can ye keep 'em there, Cecil?"

The Mayor was surprised at Gad's request. "Can I ask why?", suspecting all was not right with this affair.

Gad took the Mayor's arm and they walked back along the dusty street. He had to think of something quick that would not give the Mayor the opportunity to discover something he shouldn't.

"When my boy was fixing the horse collar for Master Roddens from Pinkers Farm in the stable here, these men tried to take him for the press gang." He paused and stopped for breath, milking his frailty for all he was worth.

The Mayor looked at his companion with concern.

"They fought, Cecil. No one likes to get pressed as ye knows, and he hurt them bad. I thought he might have done for one on 'em. I was frit of their revenge and when I saw they was alright, I dreamed up the charge just to keep them, while Thomas slips away awhiles 'til they cools off, like."

His friend smiled at Gad's cunning. "They always said ye had a sly streak, Master Gad. Now I knows." They both laughed. "Don't 'e worry, Master Gad, I'll see they'm sent packing with a warning in a day or two, and not to return else

192

they shall feel the full rigours o' the law. But keep yer lad hid a while." Gad thanked him and relaxed.

That night, as they sat about the fire again and before Thomas went a visiting the next day for a few days, Gad continued with his tale.

"Aye, that was some sailing." Gad smiled at the memory. "Him not knowing what he was doing either."

Eventually they spotted a beach, and a small line of boats were on a sort of ramp where fishermen had left them. The two men somehow managed to correct the boat's antics, and the boat joined the boats on the edge of the ramp.

He was here, and being excited at the prospect of finding his son, and not bothering to keep his eyes on his companion, he just leapt over the side of the boat holding his bag.

As he turned to thank the man, he saw with horror his raised arm was not a wave, but that he was holding a large knife. As it slashed down, he managed to pull his bag in front of him, which parried the bow, but cut his arm. He jumped back in the boat and shouted at him.

"What are you doin'? Why are you trying to kill me?"

He grabbed the man by the throat and they struggled.

He managed to force the man down into the water, which was slopping around in the sump of the boat.

"Ye will not get away, Gad," he said, gasping for breath, "now we know where ye are heading."

Gad was shocked; he didn't know his real name, but he must be one of the men Dudley had sent to try to kill him.

"Who are ye?"

The man just grinned, so with nothing to lose, he held him under the water until he stopped thrashing about.

He got back in the boat and having turned around with great difficulty, pointed it out to sea. The weather had begun to worsen but fortunately the tide had turned again which helped him manoeuvre the boat. So pulling the sail up again as far as he could with all his effort (even though his arms were aching painfully), it helped to get it moving seawards. He found the ship's anchor in the bottom of the boat and he tied it to the man around his neck. Then, when he felt he was far enough out, and with his last remaining strength, he managed to heave the body over the side.

The land was not in sight anymore, and the beacons on the hills to warn shipping seemed far away now, but at least he could see where the shore was by the darker colouring of the distant sea's edge.

He staggered back to the stern and fell rather than sat next to the tiller. He hoped and prayed he was going in the right direction, as the boat began to move sluggishly towards the darkened distance.

He must have dozed off slightly, because the next thing he knew was the sudden stopping of the boat as it hit the fishermen's ramp. His injured arm ached painfully, and his back was almost breaking, but managed it. Many weeks later, he marvelled at what he had achieved with a slashed arm and aching limbs. It was amazing. His next worry was finding the land.

More by luck than judgement, he had actually run aground on the Selsey Bay, near the village of Pagham, which was inside the peninsular jutting out from the main landmass. It was not far from Chichester, and he wondered how far he was from Hampton.

Worn out, hungry and sore from his many knocks, he managed to tie the boat to a stake that others had used before him and then he fell onto the grassy mound above the sand and fell asleep.

He was wakened by the cold. It was a bitter wind that was ripping his jacket back and forth across his face and he staggered to his feet once again, banging his numb limbs to restore some life to their deadened flesh. Slowly he made his way, aching in every muscle and bone and clutching his bag of tools, falling many times until he reached a hut used by fishermen, which was easy enough to get into as the users never locked it. There was nothing there to steal.

When daylight came, he looked out to the sea. It was a mighty long way away, and his boat was lying in the sand on its side, seemingly miles from the water. He shook his head in disbelief, but he was refreshed enough to try to gather himself together and make tracks for somewhere inland, wherever that was. It could be France for all he knew.

As he rose, he found he ached like he had broken something. Every muscle he had ached, even the aches pained. But after a twisting and a turning, stretching every which way, he moved off, slowly gritting his teeth in agony.

Soon houses appeared; poor affairs, low lying and only one room high, with thatched roofs, using any and everything for the thatch, and spirals of smoke were coming from the holes there.

A dog started barking, and soon a man appeared, then another and another. They watched him struggle painfully towards them in a silent, mocking inactivity. The dog was growling and slinking towards Gad.

"I got a boat to sell," he said, jerking his thumb behind him, "'an' I needs an 'orse and some supplies and a meal." He had stopped and was facing these silent men.

The front man spat into the grass and smiled a crooked smile at Gad.

"What's to stop us taking it? Yer fagged out."

Gad stopped, stared and straightened up and squared his shoulders.

"None, 'cept I'll come back and burn yer house and ye all in it if ye do."

Unafraid, the men spread out.

A woman's voice cut into the scene like a sharp knife. "Abel! Francis! What's that ye said, ye thievin' bastards? Ye'd steal from a tired fisherman his boat?"

Her voice rose on the last two words and in disbelief and anger she gathered her shawl and skirts about her, pushed her way into the gathered men and looked at Gad. "Who are ye?"

Gad looked back at her with just as sharp a look. "I ain't a thief like these'n o' yers."

She turned swiftly back to her menfolk, her voice rasping harsh and critical, but with an authority they all obeyed.

"Get to work and find this man a good horse from the farm. Say as 'ow ye'll pay for it later and put its bridle and saddle on it too."

She could see the boat and knew it was worth a great deal more than a horse and supplies.

The men moved away, slouching and looking back at Gad in anger, humiliated by their mother. "Where's ye from, lad?" she asked as they walked back to her cottage.

Several little children scuttled about like ants around Gad's feet, and one or two touched him and ran off.

"Git back indoors, ye little sods," she cursed them and swung her hand.

Gad smiled. "Don' ye mind them lady, they's jus' 'avin' fun."

Indoors, she pointed to a chair by the big fire, and Gad thankfully dropped his bag and, after standing for a while, sat down with steam beginning to rise from his damp clothing. She dished something into a bowl and brought it over to him. It was a fish stew including seaweed and some rough bread.

He never finished it, as his head lolled forward with all the tiredness that had built up in him since leaving the last stopping place overcame him, and he slept.

Then, as the bowl slid down his lap and the bread dropped, a kindly hand caught the unfinished meal and slowly lifted his feet onto a box.

He awoke, stiff and still aching all over. It was dark, but he was dry and rested. As he tried to get up, his legs would hardly move with the stiffness. After a few moments of fruitless struggle in the dark, he gave up and dozed off again.

The next time he awoke, the sun was streaming in through the open door and a child was standing, staring at him. She was dressed poorly in old boots too big for her, a torn dress, another hand-me-down and a face that carried too many fears and pain for one so young. Gad smiled at the young girl and once again tried to move.

This time, he was able to sit up but the pain in his back and legs was almost unbearable. The child vanished as he cursed and sweated in his labours. He started to get up, using his legs and bent them against the pain and his feet and his arms followed. Then, as he stood and tried to bend, he had to grip the mantle shelf for support.

"'Avin' trouble lad?" Her voice, though full of authority, had a kind edge to it and carried with it a wealth of knowledge of stiff and tired men back from the sea.

Gad smiled ruefully. "Aye. 'Tis like as though I've been run down by an 'orse, then he's turned around and stomped over me again for good measure."

She smiled through her grimy face and, flicking a rebellious lock of hair away said, "I knows. Most fishermen have the same trouble after a long voyage. But ye'll live, I 'spect."

She went over to her 'kitchen' which was a box near the fire on which she prepared meals, and started assembling some cold cooked fish and bread from last night.

Gad had begun to move about, swinging his arms and lifting his knees in an effort to free the constricted muscles.

"We found yer boat and she's a good 'un and worth a lot more than an 'orse and supplies. We ain't got any money times is 'ard but the men agreed to get what ye wanted and anything else they can beg, borrow or steal for ye."

Gad gratefully ate the food and drank the poor beer and nodded his agreement.

"D'ye know these parts?" he asked casually. The woman stopped what she had been doing and turned to face him.

"Yer on the run, ain't ye?"

Gad nodded, Aye. I killed a man who tried to steal from me in Hastings. They wanted my boat, but he had friends and they came after me." He showed the woman a long cut on his forearm recently acquired from Og.

She nodded. "I knows hereabouts."

"I 'ave to get to a place called Hampton. It's along the coast here somewhere, but I missed it last night."

She turned as the sound of her men folk came from outside. She hushed him. "Don't ye tell my men what ye done, as they'll as like as not call the watch for the reward. I shall point ye on the right way to Chichester. When ye gets there

there's several ways to go, but keep yer face to the wind and ye'll get there."

The men had found a reasonable looking horse and it was saddled and a few bags of supplies were tied to its rump. One of the men came over to him, twisting his cap in his hand, and with a hangdog expression on his face.

"We'm sorry we crossed ye las' night, Master. 'Tis the ale, it's mighty strong sometimes. Sorry."

The other men came over and held out their hands, but their handshakes were not firm, and if there was one thing Gad always knew, was that a limp, soft handshake meant trouble.

"That's fine, I hold no grudges. 'Cept I'm an 'onest tradesman an' don' take kindly to pushy sort o' people." He looked down from the horse at the assembled fisherman and the woman and children. "Thank ye kindly, ma'am, for yer 'ospitality. I just 'ope I don't 'ave to spoil it if ye are making plans to cause I other trouble."

The men looked at their feet and the woman pointed up the beach.

"Up yonder is a wide track, deep rutted and it leads to a proper road. Turn to yer right 'till the next track on yer left an' follow tha' all the way up over the hill. Ye can see the spire from there."

Gad nodded and kicked the horse into moving.

When Gad got to the proper road the sign pointed to the left to Itchynor and West Wytering, and he stopped. He knew those men were going to try and get the horse back and so get the boat for nothing, so he turned left. The wind was behind him now and he knew the woman's message of "keep the wind to yer face" meant that he was going the wrong way.

He turned again at the next lane on his right and pushed the horse through the brambles and on, until he crested the rise of the hill when he saw the spire of St Richard's Minster in the distance.

As the light was beginning to fade and the evening was drawing in, it would be dark before he reached the city. It was surely somewhere to ply his trade and perhaps replenish his empty coffers, as his kind, good Samaritans had stolen the money he had taken from the Inn in Hastings, so he had only a few coppers in his pockets.

He saw the old barn at the far edge of the field he was passing, and decided that that was the place to stop for the night. It was passably free from the wind and there was a lot of loose straw and hay for the horse to nibble on until it got dark, when he would turn him out for an hour or so into the field on his rope. He opened his supplies and discovered some dried fish, some raw, limp vegetables and a stale loaf, there was also a scrawny chicken cooked over her fire, as it was burnt in several places. Well, he mused, at least it's something.

Chapter Nineteen

Several hours later, with the horse safely tethered inside the barn beside him, both watered and fed, he lay down and was soon asleep.

Next morning as he rose very stiffly to his feet again and once more he exercised painfully, to rid himself of the aches and pains he had picked up at sea. Then he saddled up and made his painful way towards the city. He crossed a large wooden bridge over a wide river called the Lavant, which was some forty odd yards across, and noticed he was joining a column of traders going into the city for their day's selling. That was good – now he hoped could slip past the watch as they looked closely at everyone who entered, and he would have more chance in a boisterous crowd.

Just as he came fairly close to the gate, a little ferret-faced man three in front of him panicked at his own guilt about something, and turned and ran. The guard at the gate shouted to a couple of mounted soldiers inside the walled gateway and, during the ensuing pandemonium, Gad followed several others who were also anxious to enter the city unquestioned for one reason or another, and he moved swiftly through, unchallenged.

Once inside, one of his new companions spoke softly to Gad.

"That'll cost 'ee two coppers, master. We always pay little Jack after he does 'is running trick, so's we can get in w'out paying any dues."

He chortled again as Gad handed over two of his fast dwindling collection of coins. Although he had no leather he had his tools, and soon settled down on a pitch near the baker's stall in the market. His stomach was beginning to rumble with the smell of the fresh bread after what he had eaten earlier. Still, as he knew from earlier days, no work, no food.

He took his boots off and made a great show of repairing them until a shadow fell over him as he worked. His stomach turned over and his heart pumped as he looked up, mentally alert to twist out of trouble if that was what was needed.

The man standing there was holding a large pair of thigh boots.

"Can ye mend these?' he asked brusquely.

Gad took the boots and saw they were coming apart where the leggings part joins the calf of the boot. "Aye, mister, it'll cost ye five pence."

All that, morning he worked and soon his pocket of money had grown to thirty five pence, with some more to come when they collected their goods. About one o'clock he stretched, still painfully, and got up to get his lunch.

"Ye're a good worker my friend," the baker's wife said and, smiling at him, she gave him half a small fresh loaf, a scrape of butter and a cut of ham. "Where you'm from?"

As he paid her the two pence, he was intrigued by the accent and by the drawl of her voice, which he assumed she must be very local. Stuffing some bread and ham into his mouth to hide his lack of a local accent, he raised his hand and indicated by his thumb that he was from somewhere up there, behind him.

"Ah, the Goodwood – I knows there. I have an aunt 'oo lives there," she said, but before she could ask any more embarrassing questions, she had to serve a line of people waiting for the loaves which had just arrived at the stall by cart, which they just had.

As he sat back enjoying the first decent food he had had for many a day, he realised that he hadn't even made a plan of how to actually get to Hampton. Each time he had sat down to make some sort of journey route, if only in his head, he knew then how little he really was aware of where he was, and something cropped up.

"Where's a good place to wet my whistle?" he said with his best smile, and she turned and pointed him to the other side of the market. He stopped. "D'ye 'appen to know how to get to Hampton?"

That stumped her. Several people in the queue said it was that way and others said, "No 't ain't it be that way?", pointing in the opposite direction. She knew where it was, but how to give him a direction that was something else. Eventually after many attempts, she called a man over who was some sort of market watchman.

He pointed out of the East Gate and said, "Aye, master, follow the road to Arundel and go by the river. 'T'will lead ye there."

The inn was packed as tight as a virgin's corset he thought, as he pushed his way through. He eventually got a tankard of ale then went out into the small garden to sit awhile and try to sort himself out.

For the first time in a long time, he felt full and pleasantly tired. The next thing was to get his horse fed and watered so that he could ride through the night, a time he liked best. As he made his way back carefully to the place he had been working, although he had brought his tools with him, not trusting to leave them behind, he saw one of the fishermen.

He was holding his horse and was talking to the man who had given him directions to Hampton.

"It's mine, I say, a young seaman stole it fro' me last night."

Gad stopped as the crowd gathered. He had to think quickly. Then it dawned on him spread a tale. He moved back a couple of paces and shouted into his cupped hands so as not to be seen by his adversary, and spoke in a loud voice. "I 'ear the Queen's come to St Richard's." He had heard the large cathedral's name in the pub.

The effect was electric. There was a stampede, as everyone started to run towards the cathedral as the word was passed. He quickly circled back behind the group by his horse and smiled as he watched even the watchman move smartly in response to his ruse. Soon the man holding his horse was by himself, and Gad took hold of him by the scruff of the neck and twisted him round.

"I told ye what I'd do if ye crossed me. So ye'll burn tonight."

The frightened man broke free and ran off as fast as his legs could carry him. He hoped his threat would give them a few sleepless days and nights. Gad mounted his horse and, helping himself to another loaf and leaving a copper on the board from the abandoned stall, he moved off quickly, adding "Thank Edward for me, Beth."

Like many towns and cities in England, Chichester was surrounded by a high wall with four gates, one at each end of the cross of streets. He had entered the city over a bridge which crossed the River Lavant, and had entered by the south gate without any great difficulty, although this side of the city was the most heavily fortified indicating possibly that the greatest threat came from the sea, and it would be the first side that would be attacked by invaders.

Things were fairly quiet in that direction at the moment; even Spain was friendly, only because their Philip II had married Mary. France was always causing irritating little problems, but they were always under control. So far so good, but everyone knew it would not be long before trouble would flare up with the frog eaters.

Lady Frances had originally moved to a place near Hampton a few miles from Arundel and then she was left the family house there in her father's will. It was a grand mansion not far from the sea at Forde, which was a tiny hamlet hardly worthy of a note on a map.

Gad was cursing himself as he rode quickly across the lower part of the city of Chichester until he reached the Minster. He stopped just beyond the cross, which was where the four roads joined, and he scratched his head. Which way I wonder? he asked himself, still not sure which was east.

A man in a long black cloak over his clothes and wearing a large brimmed hat had followed Gad at a distance, but unseen by him, his well-repaired boots fitting comfortably on his feet.

He had followed him ever since he had arrived at Selsey, and had a good look at him in the market, marvelling at his quickness of thought that had got him out of a difficult situation there. He was determined that his duty to Elizabeth's men to protect him would be redoubled.

Gad stopped under a chestnut tree and looked about him. He was just about to move off when the fluttering of dark clothing caught his eye behind him and he turned, ready for action, his persuader in his hand.

"Whoa, sir, art thou Master Gad?" a voice said.

Looking down at this strange figure in clerical garb, he replied, "Aye, whose askin'?"

"Ah, good sir, I am the Reverend Tooken, and a friend of Lady Frances."

Gad started. 'Lady Frances, from Forde?" he said, mouth open in surprise and his heart fluttering.

"The very same, sir, and she awaits you follow me."

At last, after all his trials and hardships, he was going to see his son. Then his in built caution kicked in. As they walked towards the cathedral's little side door, both men holding their horse's bridles, across the piece of grass at the side of the great cathedral, they were soon hidden from the main city roads.

Was this priest real? Was it another trap? His mind was turning all these thoughts over as they reached the door. Nevertheless, he was holding his 'suader in readiness as he tied his horse to a stanchion like the clergyman. The little cleric disappeared through the small door in a flurry of black, swirling cape and cassock. Gad though was still not sure, and held back and waited.

The cleric, finding Gad was no longer following him, returned to the door and looked out at Gad.

"Do not be afraid," he said, realising Gad was unsure of him, "I am not one of the villains chasing ye, but a good friend and follower of the Ladyship, the Princess Elizabeth."

Somewhat reluctantly, Gad followed, still prepared for the worst. He entered the cathedral through this small door into the Minster with his 'suader at the ready and twisting his head every which way.

The size and the smell of the place made Gad think of his own cathedral back home and Brother John, and he felt quite homesick. As he quietly crept along the side flagged passageway, tense and ready for any sudden attack, he approached the main altar and then turned right along another walkway, leading to a small side altar, still looking around him nervously.

However, the few people that were there were kneeling in prayer and with their heads were bowed, seemingly oblivious to the mind numbing events which were about to unfold.

The priest turned to see if Gad was following him, and they both moved quickly and swiftly towards another small door set in the wall, which was the sacristy.

The Reverend Tooken stopped and said quietly to Gad, "Before we go in, let me explain."

He paused nervously, twitching his cassock in fear. "The two people here are the two who were charged with the task of looking after your son. Last week, the house was raided by men in disguised tabards and after slaying the man who was trying to protect your son, they beat her Ladyship to the floor, grabbed your lad and have taken him away."

Gad stopped, open-mouthed and in rising anger. Not now after all he had gone through, this!

"I am telling you this as you will meet two very upset and tearful people, and I wanted you to know what had taken place before you meet them. Come."

Gad was dumbstruck. All his dashing about, his near death at sea, plus the closeness of being taken by the Press Gang and all the other problems he had faced and endured, was all for naught.

Inside the room were two women. One was her Ladyship, and the other was her maid. Dropping his bag, he took out the letter, much dirtied, that Beth had given him and gave it to her Ladyship.

Then he showed them the torn half medallion from around his neck and sat down, his head in his hands.

"Dear Gad," a tearful lady's voice sounded loud if a little shaky in the small room. "What can I say?"

At this point, the Minister coughed and said, "Her Ladyship was very brave, and they had to beat her before your son, on hearing the noise, quite innocently entered the room.

Whereupon he was roughly grabbed by these soldiers and they rode off with him."

He paused and said quite cheerfully, "However, sir, all is not lost."

Gad's head snapped up in surprise and hopefulness.

"By the way, my name is Robert, and I have been a devoted follower of Her Royal Highness, the Princess Elizabeth, even though if I were caught out, I would no doubt be hanged. But as I said, all is not lost. I have discovered that the villains were probably from the castle at Arundel, which is not far from here and is a Catholic stronghold. I have a plan".

Gad put his arms around the shoulders of her Ladyship and said quietly, "Do not fret, madam you were kind to my son for many years, and for that I am grateful. I have not given up hope yet, and I swear on my sacred oath that I will find him and bring him home and revenge the death of this man, his guardian, who also helped him get away from Hatfield."

The Priest got up and went over to a large wardrobe, which filled one wall completely and was used for the dressing of the priests before they went on to the Altar. After rummaging around inside for a while, muttering and making very un-priestly comments about the cleanliness of his fellow Ministers, he withdrew a cassock and a flat hat worn by these priests outside.

"Now then, sir, try these for size."

Gad was astounded. "Er, what for?" he said suspiciously.

"I have a friend, a Minister, who lives near the castle and who, like me, is an ardent follower of Elizabeth, and a Protestant as well." He paused and sat down, facing Gad. "Now," he spoke quietly in conspiratorial tones, "Next to the castle is a small chapel, which is attached a little vaguely to it. I have spent many hours there in the old days when I could practice my faith. During my time there, we discovered a small door behind the High Altar, not much used in these Roman Catholic days, but on a further examination one evening we found that it led into a small corridor, which in turn led to a room in the castle where young orphans are normally kept by the ladies under the Duke's patronage."

Gad was all interest now and he was ahead of the Priest in his thinking. "So if can get into the castle and then I can maybe get my son?"

The Priest was fiddling with the cassocks and asked Gad to stand up and see if one of them fitted him.

The housemaid came over, as this was her province. "Let me see, Reverend," she said a little peremptorily, and picked one out that fitted him very well.

Gad shook his head. "No," he said, "If I am to find my son and carry him away, he will have to get under the robe and, by clutching me around the waist we can both be covered. It will have to be bigger one".

Robert laughed. "I see you are a master magician, sir," and they all laughed, which relieved some of the tension.

Lady Frances had been hurt badly by these men and everyone was concerned that she might not recover, as she was old and very fragile. She just sat there with her eyes closed and tears slipped out from under her lids as she quietly wept over the loss of her charge.

Robert looked at Gad and shook his head after casting a look at her Ladyship. Quietly, another door opened and two nuns came in carrying a tray with hot food and a porter of ale for Gad and something to drink for her Ladyship. Then, after she had drunk a little, they took her under her arms and led her away, gently calming her.

A little while later, two priests, one more portly than the other, left the cathedral clutching books of the Bible and riding their sturdy horses.

Had they seen his rugged boots under his cassock, wondered what one of them had in the pack behind him on the horse's rump, or took notice of his purposeful, forthright demeanour, they might have been a bit more suspicious of this odd couple.

But as it was dark now, no one noticed them particularly, nor became curious, so they rode gently together across the green sward in front of the cathedral and passed the preaching cross situated in the centre of the city at its crossroads.

They increased their pace as they trotted down East Street, and soon were able to gallop a bit faster after they left the city by the eastern gate, waved through in a friendly manner by the guards there. They passed through the woods and fields until they saw it in the distance.

Chapter Twenty

The impressive castle, surrounded by woods and a small village on one side and a river down the other side, stood out like a beacon of hope for Gad. Robert had to restrain him, as it was very late and the children would be asleep in their little cots by now.

He said, "So, let us wait 'til daylight."

Before they came too close to the castle, they had to obtain food and water both for himself and his horse, and hopefully his son. Robert had contacts here too and so they knocked on a lonely farmhouse to find shelter.

The farmer and his wife seemed to know Robert, and after a splendid if simple meal, they retired to their beds.

Bright and early the two 'priests' continued on their journey to the village of Arundel and rode down the hill with the gardens and chapel on their left until they left the road and entered a small lane on their right, which in turn led to a very impressive mansion.

People were about now and they touched their forelocks to the two men, which brought a smile to Gad's face for the first time in a long time.

Meg was giggling now; the thought of her Gad as a Pastor amused her, as he had no religious leanings at all. Thomas too smiled at the thought, although if he was to be honest he remembered nothing of the 'priestly men', except the excitement of his escape.

The atmosphere in the room had lightened now, after the trauma of the revelation that the Duke's men had seized the boy and that his guardian had been mollified.

"I never saw Lady Frances again," Thomas said sadly, and he was cross that she had been hurt badly by the Duke's men. She never recovered from these injuries. What happened to the companion he never knew, but he hoped she had found peace at the convent next to the Minster.

Tying their mounts at posts near the rear of the house, they walked around to the front and pulled the bell cord. A maid carefully opened the door, but when she saw two priests, she smiled and let them in.

"My dear Robert, it has been all too long."

The tall, grey-headed man came bounding down the hallway to greet them, with arms outstretched and enveloped Robert. He turned and saw Gad.

Robert introduced Gad as, "The Reverend Albert Blake from London. He has heard of your unusual Chapel and wishes to see it before he goes back."

"Come on in, come in," he said. "We are about to break our midday fast, and perhaps ye could do with a rest too. London be a long way away." He laughed.

Reluctantly they followed the man into his dining room, a large ornate room, with lots of hanging portraits of various long dead Ministers on the walls. A large fire was burning brightly in the centre of the far wall, and everything looked homely and friendly.

Maids rushed about laying places and they served warm bread wrapped in napkins, which Gad, following Robert, broke into two pieces. They offered up a prayer, whilst holding up the pieces above their heads, mumbling.

This brought a hilarious scream of laughter from Meg.

What seemed hours later, full of meat and a heady wine, the three men went off to the proffered beds and they slept like logs.

In the morning, after another hearty meal, the three men rode off up to the big gate.

Leaving their horses tethered there, they all walked down past the neatly trimmed lawns and flowerbeds towards the main door of this lovely church, which Gad thought was remarkably large, not small as described by Robert.

He had already primed Gad on what he had to do, marking out pages in his missal of the common service, adding, "Keep your 'suader out of sight, as it is not something a clergyman would carry."

Gad watched his friend carefully and copied him in whatever he did. Removing their hats, they knelt in silent prayer.

Meg was almost in a paroxysm of mirth at the thought of her Gad acting out priestly motions.

"What did ye pray for, my love?" Meg said with a smile, and he answered, "To get out of that uncomfortable garb and see Thomas".

They walked down the aisle and entered a small room called a sacristy, where Ministers usually changed and dressed into garments for their services.

"All I wants is to see the little door up there," Gad said, pointing up the high altar.

Robert's friend's face changed, and he tried to explain about Gad's kidnapped son, who was held there by the Duke. It didn't make it any easier when Robert's friend now realised Gad was not a Pastor, and he felt that Robert had betrayed his friendship.

"Ye know how we all hate this 'Cathlick' Popery, so help us please."

The Minister turned to Gad. "I don't know what ye are about," he said, "but I must warn ye that I do not stand for people causing us trouble here. Long after ye are gone, we shall have to face the wrath of the Duke's Men."

Robert smiled at him and said, "Ye don't need to worry, my friend. When we leave, ye will be tied up and your cassock torn a bit to show that ye put up a struggle."

"Hmm," was the reply. Then he smiled. "It would be nice to put a trick over that evil man, the Duke he said."

Satisfied, but still not understanding his guest's sudden change of character, with Gad only seemingly only interested in the little door behind the high altar, so he showed them how it opened and gave Robert the key.

"Give it me back to me when your friend and his son have gone".

He went back to the main door of the chapel they had come in through and closed it, giving the gardener a blessing that was standing looking at them from the outside.

He returned a moment later and said, "Afore ye go in, then perhaps ye'd better tie me up and tear my cassock."

This they duly did, wiping his friend's face with dust and dirt from the floor.

Having done this, and before Robert could stop him, Gad smacked him over the head with is 'suader. Likewise he hit Robert, saying, "sorry, but ye too need an excuse for this 'appening."

Both men were lying unconscious halfway down the steps behind the altar. He took the keys off Robert's friend, so he could close this little door after him and open the entry door they used to come in and get out.

As the steps behind the high altar ran down both sides of it, he left Robert on the steps on one side, knowing he could return and go down the other steps.

The silence was eerie as he went through the door and soon he found himself in a long passageway. He stood quietly and listened. Voices!

He could hear children's voices and he walked forward, opening his prayer book, and put his hat back on. After about fifteen paces he came to a door, which suddenly opened and young girl came out.

Oh, sorry Reverend" she said, curtsying and went to go back in.

"No, please," Gad said, 'Tell me is there a small redhaired boy recently brought here?" Her look was quizzical.

"'Oo are ye?" she said, then clapped her hand over her mouth, seeing Gad's rough clothes under his opened cassock. "You ain't no Reverend, are ye?"

"No, I ain't," Gad said, "But I need 'elp."

She smiled. "Are ye this Master Gad I keeps 'earing about?"

"Aye, I am," he admitted. "But don't ye scream or shout out, please. All I wants is my son. 'e's 'ere, ain't 'e?"

She began to giggle and then threw her arms about him and kissed him on the cheek.

"All us girls 'ad 'oped ye'd come for 'im. These 'orrid men hit 'em and makes the little ones cry." Then she said, "I'll get 'im for ye, but ye'll have to hit me so they don' blame me for his escape." Then she slipped back into the room. "Come on Cephar, time for yer poos."

Gad smiled, thinking, I suppose that's baby talk for a shit.

Then he was there.

Gad put his finger to his lips as he looked at his son for the first time. The girl kissed Cephar and turned her head for the hit. Gad turned her around and kissed her firmly on the lips "thank ye, lass," he said, and then hit her hard.

Cephar didn't seem upset by this action and just smiled and waited with his hand out.

Thomas said, "I remember that, as I had seen and heard a lot of violence and another bit of it didn't seem to be of any consequence." He clutched is father's arm and said, "Ye know, father, that was the happiest day of my life".

Gad returned the contact and said, "Me too."

Getting out was easy, after all the trials and tribulations of his earlier troubles. So with no sign of the gardener, they raced up the lawns to the horse which Robert had strategically placed at the entrance to the gardens.

Soon an overweight reverend, sitting none too comfortably on a horse, was seen to gently walk out through the village of Arundel. On his early advice from Robert, he followed the signpost to Hampton. At last he was able to talk the little lad.

"Hello Thomas," he said.

He tore off his cassock and threw it and the hat into the fast running River Arun. The boy looked quizzically at his father.

Gad smiled. "Aye, lad, that's your new name and ahead is a new life for ye with a proper mother and father, and no hitting."

The smile was positively beatific. Gad could hear the lad saying to himself, Thomsers", as he struggled to pronounce it.

Robert and Gad had discussed his route in great detail, and surprisingly Robert had suggested that they made for Forde and stayed at the house where he had been living. He said that as he would not be able to out run the Duke's men, the last place they would expect him to go would be back there. They arrived at Wick just as the sun was going down and a light wind was blowing. Soon Hampton came into view, and he could smell the sea. Eventually they crossed a rickety wooden bridge and followed the sign to Forde.

He was corrected by Thomas as he took a wrong turn, saying, "No Da, it's down there," pointing down a very overgrown narrow lane. The sound of him calling him 'Da' was like music to his ears.

The unconscious girl was found after about an hour later, and the place erupted.

Robert and his companion were discovered as well, and finding the little door to the church locked by Gad, the soldiers turned back, went into the village and started to search it like madmen.

The Duke then divided his men into several groups and sent them off in different directions, not knowing which way the fugitives had gone.

Gad had disposed of the cumbersome cassock into the river they crossed and hoped it would float down to the sea.

Although Robert and him jad discussed the route he should take, Gad wasn't too sure it was the right one.

If he was the Duke, he would think that as the two runaways had to go to London, that therefore they would take the straight forward route. This was to follow the river Arun that flowed through Arundel, Pulborough to Horsham, to Dorking and then they would cross over the Thames and home. That would be his plan, and not surprisingly it was also the Duke's. But, like all the best laid plans of mice and men, things often have a mind of their own. Crossing the Downs was the obvious route.

As Robert expected, the men charged off, shouting and even laughing, on this obvious route, when all the time they both were securely ensconced in the Lady France's house, not a million miles away.

Gad could see the irony of it and grinned at Robert's understanding of the soldiers' minds. He was also advised not to make any alterations outside either, as it must remain just as they had left it.

Another thing, he added, "Stay indoors, as there are a few people still about and a reward may have been offered, which will tempt local people to start prying."

When he arrived at the house, Thomas leapt down and ran towards the house when an elderly lady appeared, who had been a companion-cum retainer called Margaret, who acted as a housemaid, cook and, no doubt, bottle washer.

Gad dismounted and putting his arms around her, he said sadly, "I be dreadfully sorry, but her Ladyship will not be returning. I'spect the Nuns at the Minster will be looking after her."

The companion looked sadly as Gad, and said, "I know, they treated her very badly, those nasty men."

Another person arrived, who was some sort of gardener and handyman, called Marvin.

He looked at Gad and, touching his forelock, said, "Aye, they bastards sorry Margaret, but they killed Cephar's guardian an' beat her Ladyship to the ground. They'd 'av 'ad I if I hadn't seen 'em arrive."

Gad explained what he wanted to do, and so they all settled in with the knowledge that the Duke's men may return at any time.

The Duke was in fact incandescent with rage, and several people were summarily executed, but not the young nursemaid whom Gad had smacked, as he had to admit that she couldn't have stopped him taking the boy, so she had several days to savour the kiss and smiled and hugged herself for ages.

Back in the Old Hatfield Palace, Lord Salisbury's house, Katherine was talking to Dudley, who was looking decidedly crestfallen.

"My Lord, do I take it ye have been bested by a simple tradesman?"

"What does your father think, eh? Pleased is he?"

"No, your Majesty, he ain't. But maybe His Lordship, the Duke of Arundel, might do something right for a change. He let Gad slip into the castle and out again with the boy without a challenge, and they simply rode off."

Katherine was flabbergasted, and it did not help her pregnancy one bit. "Me thinks a word with his Lordship might not come amiss. Meanwhile, ye are to stop what ye are doing and go down to Sussex yourself and sort this mess out once and for all. Tell his Lordship that if the boy is not caught and disposed of soon, I may have to see about removing him from his position." Her voice rose at the end of the sentence.

Chapter Twenty-One

Her sister had a lot to answer for, if the child was hers; so far she had just smiled cheekily, but said nothing.

"Now go," and, turning to a lady-in-waiting, she added, "someone ask my sister to visit with me, please. At her convenience, of course," she added sarcastically.

Dudley left, bowing respectfully, but inside he was seething with rage.

Elizabeth dutifully visited her sister, and knowing Gad was still at large with their son her own spies had reported most of what had gone on, including the murder at Forde, of the boy's guardian and the injury to Lady Dorothy she felt confident in her meeting with her sister. Her sort of tolerance and even respect for her sister had slowly drained away, and she knew the time was close to her reasserting her claim to the throne.

"Tell me, sister, did ye actually birth a brat from some common tradesman?"

Elizabeth's eyes narrowed. "Ye ought not to listen to such rumours, sister dear. The next thing ye know is that they will be saying the child ye are carrying is not your husband's."

She immediately apologised, as the look of anguish on her sister's face made her ashamed at what she had said.

A week went by, and by then Gad had met the gardener again and they had buried the boy's guardian, whom they had summarily executed, deep in the far end of their grounds so that it could not be despoiled by any of Dudley's men should they get into to the grounds.

That man had a lot to answer for, thought Gad and together they hatched a small plot.

The man, Marvin by name, went out every day and surreptitiously enquired as to the state of the searching, but soon Gad realised the inevitable would happen and that the man would be followed as he was known locally, and so the two fugitives decided to lay a false trail. They got Thomas to draw ships in his baby way, indicating that they would have gone the other way, by sea to France.

It was dark and raining when the two left; this time, Thomas was dressed in a girl's frock and his red hair was uncut and had a ribbon on it, which Margaret said would confuse any one if they were looking for a man and a boy.

They left the safety of the house, but only after Margaret had done what she called her "John her Baptist bit" first.

To the uneducated Gad it meant nothing, until Margaret explained that Saint John the Baptist went ahead of Jesus to prepare the away for him when he began his Ministry.

So, when she reported back and said everything seemed alright to travel, they said their farewells and travelled through Hampton on the road to Rustington, and along the coast road and on towards Brighton at least, according to Robert.

He had also mentioned a landmark he should look out for when he left Brighton called the Cissbury Ring. This was a ring of trees easily seen for many miles in every direction and was a marker for him to follow across the Downs. By evening time, the horse needed a rest and they could both have done with some food too.

They reached Angmering, a little hamlet, but as the Duke's men no doubt had already been there, he decided not to speak, nor be seen by anyone so they picnicked out in the woods and slept rough.

The Duke, meanwhile, had no reports of any sightings whatsoever, and on a whim, decided to revisit the old house in Forde to see if any of the people there knew anything more. If they did, he would make them talk.

He felt the that two priests had some Elizabethan connection with this event, as he knew that she would dearly love to have her son returned to her unharmed, so her agents must be here too.

After his persuaders worked on the Warden of the chapel in Arundel, he admitted that two priests had arrived yesterday and said they wanted to see the chapel before they returned to London.

No, he didn't know them, but they seemed genuine enough.

"Two priests, ye say," now, that was interesting. "Our Gad has a devious mind," he said, rubbing his chin in contemplation. "Well, so have I.'

Hence his visit to Forde again. They rode noisily into the house's grounds and were met by Margaret, who disarmingly said, "What a pleasant surprise, Your Grace. If you would like to come in inside, I will get…

"none of that nonsense, madam. Where's the brat?"

At that moment, a soldier appeared at the Duke's side with the sheaf of drawings made by Thomas of ships.

The Duke looked at them and then he smiled.Turning to Margaret, he said, "Why ships?"

Guilelessly, she replied, "because that is where they have gone."

"Where?" asked the Duke, beginning to lose his temper at the self-assured woman.

A Sergeant trooper stepped forward. "Shall I beat her, my Lord?'

Margaret stood tall and said in a cross voice, "Why, I do believe ye are Mistress Lander's boy, aren't ye? I shall have to tell her what a very uncouth son she has birthed."

The rest of the troopers were enjoying this repartee and the putting down of their Sergeant.

The Duke snapped, "Don't interfere; madam now, where is it they have gone?"

Margaret said, "Can see where the troopers get their manners from too, my Lord." Then, pushing it a bit, she added, "A 'please' would not come amiss, my Lord."

He was treading on dangerous ground and his Lordship was fast losing his patience. The Duke raised his riding crop to strike her when she said, "Ye strike me, my Lord, and ye will not find the answer to your question."

They stood toe to toe, and it was the Duke who had to back down.

"Well, Madam, *please*, where have they gone?"

"Thank ye, my Lord," she said, stressing the 'Lord' again. "I know they discussed going to France, so I 'spect they have gone to Portsmouth or somewhere similar but all I know is that the boy was drawing ships, 'cos I showed him them from books in the library."

The Duke was not happy and immediately sent two of his fastest men to find them.

With that, he turned and rode out, just as quickly, furious and muttering, "Thinks he can outfox me, does he? Well, we'll see."

Meanwhile, Gad had dismantled the boy's ribbon and tied all his hair back in a queue and rode on. Soon they saw a crowd of people and a lot of horse drawn caravans ahead, all circled in a field.

"A gypsy campsite," he said. "Now, that would be helpful."

Once again his trade would come in handy, and so he rode in the site brazenly and dismounted.

A large man dressed in travellers' garb and smoking a long stemmed clay pipe strolled over and said, "Ye want something, mister?"

Gad said, as disarmingly as he could, "Aye, master, a meal and a bed for me and my lad for the night, and maybe someone to travel with."

The man grinned at Gad's impertinence. "Alright, 'oo are ye, then?"

Gad lifted his boy down and said, "My name is Gad and this is my boy Thomas, and we be running from the Duke's men from Arundel.'

A small crowd had gathered by now, and one said, "There must be a reward for ye then?"

Gad smiled. "I expect there is, but I could earn my keep 'ere wi' ye. I'm a boot and saddle mender". He looked around and saw a lot of badly worn boots.

The big man grinned again and said, "My name is Griffin, Ben Griffin, and I rule here. Okay, Mister Gad, ye have a deal. We don't like the Duke's men and we do need a boot mender."

He turned to his group and said harshly, "And any of ye 'oo go slinking off to the Duke, they 'ave to answer to me and our code." That meant death by burning. "Mergit!" he shouted, "Get 'ere, sharpish like".

A small woman about Gad's age came over and tried to take the boy's hand.

"No!" said Gad. "I've fought men and the sea to rescue my son, and I don't wan' 'im out o' my sight."

The big man grinned again. "We're going to get on fine, you an' me, Gad. Like you, we look after our own, but Mergit has no child and no man, so she will be your wife and the boy's mother as long as ye want."

"Okay," he acquiesced. He didn't have a choice really.

This part of the tale he didn't tell Meg, as it might have upset her. So far the tale had just been one of daring do, and other women were not part of it for her sake.

Settling into their routine by living in a wooden horse-drawn caravan was something new to Gad, and they were both able to relax and rebuild their strength and get to know each other for a few days.

Soon he had a lot of badly worn and damaged boots to see to, and he began his work. She wasn't a demanding woman and, as Gad explained, "Although I needs a woman occasionally, it don't mean it's permanent, like". She nodded and said no more.

The campfires, the freedom of movement around the countryside, the music and the camaraderie appealed to Gad, but they were not getting him any closer to home.

After a week of shoe and boot repairing, he wanted to get on and as he discussed with Ben Griffin a route to take, there was a sudden alarm raised by one of the young men. Gad was quickly rushed out of the group and hidden in a collection of pipe smoking men who were chopping wood. Thomas dressed as an urchin of the road with his red hair, a giveaway, was tied and hidden under a cap. He was in dirty knickerbockers and a torn and filthy shirt, once worn by a woman and poorly cut down to size. His dirty face, legs and arms completed his disguise.

The group of soldiers trotted wearily into their campsite and Ben Griffin went to meet them.

The officer was a Germanic mercenary who growled and snarled as he spoke. "We looks for a man and a boy. Zey vill be strangers to you, and are wanted for killing a woman and a manservant. Have you seen any strangers like zat?"

Ben smiled a crooked smile and said quite subserviently, "Nay, sir, we'm just gypsy folk not bothering with others. Sorry."

The troopers were mixing with the men and women, and several women made suggestive advances to the soldiers who were suitably distracted until the Officer called them back and they rode out to the taunts of the women.

Ben called Gad over to him and Gad stood among the biggest group of them as he questioned him.

He angrily denied killing anyone, and then, pointing to Thomas, he said, "Ask him, he 'asn't learned to lie yet. Tell these people, Thomas lad, who hurt your Aunt Florence and Edward."

He clutched his father's hand tight and, with a frightened look he pointed to where the soldiers had gone, with tears beginning to run down his cheeks.

"They had hit her and killed my friend with a big sword."

He sniffled and Gad looked at the men and they smiled, and almost as one they said, "Aye, the boy tells the truth," nodding their heads. One or two women wanted to cuddle Thomas, but he wouldn't let go of his Da.

He could see they were satisfied. Ben came over and put his arm around Gad and said, "Aye, they be evil men and we have no truck wi' 'em."

Thomas cried and clung to Gad again. "Are they coming back, Pa? They knocked Auntie down and killed my friend," and he cried again.

Ben looked at Gad and said, "We would have guessed that, but the boy don't tell lies, do 'e? So it be alright."

The men all agreed, and soon he was drinking at their fire and tried some of the weed they were all smoking. He told Meg they were the worst few moments of his life there, as he coughed and coughed and tears rolled down his cheeks. The men thought it was hilarious, and he swore he would never ever smoke again.

But for Gad, the visit of the troops was too close for comfort, and maybe one of these people might tell the soldiers and get a reward despite the terrible punishment. No. It was time to move on.

That evening, he gathered all his bits together quietly, and going over to Ben who was yawning and stretching with the need for his bed, he said, "Thanks for your hospitality, Ben, but that visit were a warning, so we'm movin' on."

Ben, who understood his companions too, said, "Aye, p'raps you're right. Some of my folk might find the reward too tempting, so I won't ask ye which way ye are heading, but get Mergit to gather some travelling food for ye and I will talk to her about not saying anything about ye to anyone."

"The weather looks good for a few days, but keep looking behind ye, they be nasty bastards cunning too." He shook Gad's hand and pressed a small purse into it. "That's for your work."

Gad smiled and thanked him warmly.

Later that night, as everyone slept, Gad told Thomas to be very quiet and, giving Mergit a cuddle and a kiss they left in a way sadly, for they were good people.

They walked the horse out of the camp and headed in what he hoped was in the right direction. Then, out of sight of the gypsies, he altered his direction, taking a different one from that which the soldiers took. He had noticed that the soldiers had gone towards the ring of trees direction and the Downs, which learned later, was called the Chanctonbury Ring. He decided to travel sideways, almost going back the way he had come, only in more northerly direction too.

He headed through the woods to where he hoped was in the direction of Harrow Hill, just north of Arundel.

It was late afternoon now, and although still bright, he knew he would have to get on back on track soon, otherwise he could end back where he had started, and that would disaster.

Later that day, they stopped for some food that Mergit had prepared for him. There was a nicely cooked chicken and some good fresh bread. There was also a skin of wine, although where she got it from…He smiled and guessed someone would be asking, "Who 'as took moy wine then?"

"Thanks, Mergit."

Woods covered this area for many hundreds of miles, giving cover for many kinds of inhabitants, not least of which were human ones and not all of whom would be welcoming.

This made Gad extremely careful, and he understood why Beth had said him before he left Hatfield to "travel by sea if ye can and avoid the countryside as there be many vagabonds and villains there old soldiers and sailors, mostly with limbs missing, or half blinded." He was lost.

The noise, when he heard it, came surprisingly quickly close to him, before he had time to hide.

It was riders, and men with noisy gear too. The Duke's men, Damn!

He looked about and saw that Thomas dismounted and when he turned around, Thomas had gone, simply disappeared.

Chapter Twenty-Two

He looked about in panic, but before he could move, he was surrounded by a small troop of soldiers who had burst through the trees ahead of him. But where was Thomas?

The inevitable gentleman appeared, dressed as a man of substance, wearing a dark brown jerkin over loose pantaloons and riding boots. His floppy hat was like those worn by tax collectors, covering a head of curls and a sharp pointed beard. He was wearing a large gold chain and medallion around his neck.

He smiled a crooked smile and rode gently over to him. "Good day, sirrah, and who might ye be?"

Gad sat tall in his saddle and then he tried to relax these were not the Duke's men.

"My name is Gad O'Hereford, and I am just trying to get back to my family in London. I thought it would be a nice change to ride among the trees."

"Mm," he said. "Well, sir, ye are in my woods. Did ye not see the sign?"

Gad smiled. "Maybe, sir, but as I can't read, it would not mean anything to me."

A trooper started to try and take off his toolbag, and Gad's hand snapped down on his. He backed off, scowling.

"Are ye thieves, sir?" he asked, and the man bristled.

His voice changed to a harsher tone. "Ye are on my land, and so what is on it belongs to me and your bag is now mine."

Gad also bristled and backed his horse towards a thicket to avoid anyone coming behind him.

"So ye are just common thieves, then sir? But there's naught in there of use to ye, just my tool kit and leathers. I be a shoemaker and repairer. If you want it, sir, why don't ye come and take it?"

The stand off was silent then for a few moments, except for when another trooper came forward. Gad turned to him.

"Not you, sir, your master if he's man enough?"

The troopers were enjoying this now, and were all smiling. The silence was broken by the snorting of the many horses, the occasional clink of the men's harnesses and their armour and swords.

Gad's insult had confused this man, and he was in a quandary, not knowing what to do. Unknown to everyone, there was another watcher.

A woman's voice broke the deadlock, entering the circle of men riding side-saddle on a beautiful grey horse of about sixteen hands, Gad thought. Aye, and she was a beauty too. She sat tall, with authority, tapping her thigh with a short leather covered persuader crop about twenty inches in length. But it was her porcelain clean face that Gad was enchanted with. It was partially covered with the most beautiful, lustrous fair hair he had ever seen and with no hat, just a silken scarf entwined in it.

"Well, Marcus?" Her voice carried an authoritarian sound. He blushed and turned towards her. She turned and looked at the man facing the troopers, and with a smile in her voice she said, "The gentleman is right, Marcus ye sound like a group of thieves and vagabonds yourselves." She looked at Gad. "My apologies, sir, but my brother does not have the best of manners. We are the family De Montfortes, and my name is Jessica." She held out her hand, and Gad moved forward and kissed it gently. "We own the manor house at Fittleworth, and ye are welcome to come and be refreshed and perhaps we can repair some of the damage to our name by giving you food and shelter."

Gad relaxed. The troopers were all smiling at his Lordship's putdown, but Gad had lost his son.

"Pardon me, your Ladyship," he said, "But my son ran away when your men appeared. I must call him." In a loud voice, he called, "Thomas! It's alright, come here boy." Silence.

Gad became worried, when he heard a little voice some distance away calling "Pa!"

Gad was sick with worry and anger made him scream, "I'm coming, Thomas," and he charged past the startled troopers and galloped towards where he thought the sound came from.

Jessica shouted, "Hold on, Master Gad, we know these woods wait, listen."

Gad was restrained by a trooper. "Hold hard, sir, he's not that way. Harken."

Gad reluctantly stopped, and they all sat and listened to the woods.

Jessica came over to him and said, "These woods talk to you if you stop and wait for them to answer."

The cry came again. "Pa!" This time it came from a different place. The men and her ladyship nodded to each other, and they all raced off in a different direction followed by Gad.

There were sandstone outcrops in the woods and they tended to bounce back sounds quite alarmingly.

A trooper raised his hand and pointed. They all raced off, and eventually they saw a group of men in armour milling about, seemingly confused.

As the two groups met, Gad realised that these men were the Duke's soldiers, mercenaries from Arundel and supporters of the Duke. They were diametrically opposed to those supporting Elizabeth, which these other men and Jessica were. They stopped and looked at each other. The leader of the Duke's men was holding Thomas, with a dagger against his throat.

Jessica arrived and held Gad back with a hand on his arm.

"Wait, Gad, let us not harm the boy."

There was a moment's pause as she turned her head and nodded and Gad said to the man holding Thomas, "If you spill a drop of his blood, ye scum, I will castrate ye and hang you up to be eaten by the animals in the woods."

There was suddenly a twang and a rushing sound. The trooper fell off his horse with a bolt through his neck, missing

Thomas by no more than an inch or two. It was followed by Gad. He raced over to the fallen man and Thomas and, lifting his lad up, he stood, ready to defend him with his life.

The fighting became rather one sided, as the two groups met with a whirling of swords and yells of pain and occasionally exhortation from Jessica's men.

It didn't take long, and when they stopped, the troopers belonging to the Duke all lay either dying or dead. A few of the other troops were holding cut arms, but no one was killed or seriously hurt.

Gad went over to Jessica and thanked her with a very courtly bow. He said, "Your archer must be something of a champion, your ladyship that was a fine shot."

Jessica smiled and said, "Aye, meet his Lordship, Richard, Marquis of Nutbourne."

Gad looked at this very young man, no older than fifteen and who, by his fair looks, was the brother of the Lady. He was smiling and even blushing. Gad rode over to him and proffered his hand which the lad took embarrassed and lowered his head.

"Twas nothing, sir."

Surprisingly, the young Thomas was apparently unfazed and even smiling, not realising how close to death he had been.

Jessica sent back for the woodsman's cart and the dead men were loaded onto them, ready to be delivered to the Duke. They all rode back to the mansion with Gad both relieved and shocked, holding Thomas with an almost desperate, fierce grip, which made the boy wince.

Meg was sitting with her mouth open in constant surprise and Thomas said with a half laugh, "Aye, Pa, they were nasty people those Duke's men – but me, not knowing the danger, it were like a big game."

Gad turned to Meg and said, "Aye, these people didn't seem to have any understanding of human life."

Meg decided it was time to get a meal, as they had eaten nothing once Gad had restarted his tale of daring do, and soon they were all eating one of her special stews with fresh, crusty bread that she had baked earlier.

Gad was also concerned about the men they had met and beaten from the Navy Press gangs, and he took Thomas aside and said, "I know it's hard, lad, but ye must hide away. While these men are about, go back to see Will and young Gad for a while."

So reluctantly, Thomas packed himself a good parcel of food and drink and rode off into the less likely places these men went, with his wife crying and wailing.

Meg was itching to know what the mansion was like and pestered Gad to tell her.

The Duke of Norfolk was furious and almost insane with rage as he met the cart full of dead men, which was left outside the castle's drawbridge, as the driver and his mate raced away on their horses, knowing they would be summarily executed if they were caught.

The mansion was huge, although not as big as the one at Petworth, but it too had sweeping lawns, fountains, fruit gardens and even a vinery, from which Jessica proudly opened a bottle of their own wine as they all sat down to their long awaited meal.

Meg was constantly asking about the crockery and the tableware, the cutlery and the glasses. She wasn't interested in the wine or the food, except when Gad told her that the servants entered the dining room, holding a stuffed and cooked swan on a dish, surrounded with all sorts of vegetables. It too was stuffed with another fowl, and that one was also stuffed with a different one.

Meg positively refused to believe him. "No, you'm making that up, my love."

Everyone clapped, and soon they were all tucking into various slices of meat and piles of vegetables, most of which Gad had never seen before, including balls of herbs mixed with breadcrumbs and roasted. More food arrived fish, rolled in something Gad had never seen before either, but tasted of vinegar. He didn't like that. Next came dishes of a cream, frozen and covered in nuts and biscuits, which Thomas was scoffing with great relish. Everyone was laughing at him, as a lot of the cream was spread all over his face and hands. More wine, fruit and cheeses, and soon Gad was quite drunk and he lolled sideways in his seat.

Eventually he fell over and remembered no more until he awoke in the dark with Thomas beside him, fast asleep.

His head was thumping with a terrible noise, as though there were demons inside hammering to get out, and he moaned and went back to sleep.

The noise of women laughing awoke him and reluctantly he got up to see if he could go somewhere to pass his piss, when he saw a half open door across the room.

He went over and to his surprise, he saw Jessica was standing stark naked in a large tub as two women doused her with cold water.

Before he could slip away unnoticed, Jessica called out, "Come in, Master Gad come and join me in my ablutions. The cold will cure your sore head while my ladies clean your clothes."

The women soon stripped off his clothes and he stood naked in front of her as she held out her hand to draw him into the tub. He entered it, almost falling, and grabbed hold of her arms, which led him to clutch at her breasts.

They stood nipple to nipple, the cold water lapping around their knees. Gad's body reacted as it should and he had an erection the size of which he had never had before. As they came together she rubbed her hands over his back and drew him to her tightly.

With her firm breasts pressed hard against him, he soon inserted his erection into her willing erogenous cleft.

All this he left out of his tale to Meg he was not wishing to cause her any pain or suffering. After much pushing and pulling, they both soon sighed and moaned until they just stood silent and sated, joined in an unholy alliance.

Jessica smiled and said, "Not what ye expected, eh, Master Gad?"

Gad grinned mischievously. "Ye neither, I 'spect."

Later, as he sat at the table eating a buttered cake of sweet dough, his newly cleaned clothes smooth on his back, he heard a patter of little feet. Thomas stood there in a pair of new pantaloons and shirt with fancy stitching all around the edges.

One of Jessica's maids had taken a fancy to Thomas and spent the afternoon playing with him. When he got tired, she removed his clothes and put him to bed to sleep on a small chaise. Once she had his measurements, she set to and made him a new outfit.

Gad now felt that he had to repay these kind people for their hospitality. He took out his last and began mending and re-stitching worn and damaged footwear.

However, Jessica was becoming obsessive, and insisted he bedded with her each night, much to the dismay of Marcus, her brother. She began making things unpleasant for him. Her lovemaking was constant and frankly more than he could bear it was becoming too much of a good thing. After a week of this attention, he quietly started to collect his things together and, making sure his horse was well fed, shod and fit. He waited his chance.

A near neighbour wanted to meet him, so Jessica rode out to arrange a meal and took her cook with her.

He slipped out and walked his horse with Thomas on top for about a mile, and then rode fast and furiously towards Petworth. The next day, he headed for Midhurst.

While he was looking around at the mansion, he found their library completely fascinating, and although he couldn't read, he found a book with maps in it. With the help of the ostler, who was a very bright and intelligent man, he memorised his next journey, bearing in mind it would have to be a somewhat convoluted one to avoid being traced by Jessica and secret enough to stop the ostler telling her which way he had gone.

He had left a small love token on her pillow, as he couldn't write to soften the blow of running away, as she obviously was a very lonely girl.

Several days later, he entered the quiet market town and looked for an inn to stay at. He had also run out of soft leathers and hard soles for boots.

Although suspicious, Meg didn't want to sound as though she was checking up on him all the time. I 'spect he must have met lots of pretty women on his way back, she thought, but as he came home to I, he must love me and they were only passing fancies. Although not wholly convinced, she began to accept this fact and got on with her work.

Back in Pulborough, the Duke exacted a terrible revenge by attacking the mansion and burned it almost down, killing staff and beheading Marcus. He took Jessica as a hostage and returned to Arundel.

When the news got around to the various houses and mansions, a large force of troops was organised and they laid seige to his castle.

Even Mary was shocked, and she sent a force to intervene. The Duke surrendered to her, thinking she would understand and spare him, but she didn't and she had him put in the Tower while she made up her mind what to do with him.

Dudley pleaded for him but to no avail, and he was banished to France, which, using his words, "were worse than the axe."

Gad did not hear of this for weeks and so he lost precious time trying to cover his tracks. He felt now that he could travel openly, still stopping wherever he went to earn his keep and it was a slow journey.

Chapter Twenty-Three

It was this complacency that nearly cost him and Thomas their lives again. He found a small hostelry called the Bear's Arms, which he learned was rudely mispronounced by the locals.

However, he needed time to settle and make some money. He found a local tannery and bought a small selection of their leathers, which took some sorting. His knowledge of these items came in very useful, and at last he found some reasonable ones.

The tanner was not best pleased, as he wanted Gad to buy his rubbish, but, as he said, "Your rubbish makes my work rubbish."

The marketplace was surprisingly large for the size of the town, but he was told it was on the main road from London to the coast and Hayling Island, wherever that was.

Before he sought out a site, he walked through it, looking for other boot makers and repairers, as competition sometimes bred trouble. At the far end of the market there was a good site, close to the small barracks there, and he set up his stall, which was an upturned wooden box, long since discarded by someone. He explained to Thomas that he was not to go off anywhere, but stay close and help him with the people who stopped to look.

A girl came over and sat in front of him to watch him. After a while, with nobody coming to him, she said with a smile, "Ye needs a sign, master, to let folk know what ye are doin'."

Gad said, "Aye, but I can't read nor write. I were never schooled.'

She went off and a little while later she returned with a piece of flat wood, no doubt off a building. On it she had scrawled 'Shoos and Bootes Mended'.

She proudly offered it to Gad, and then withdrew it, saying, "make I a pair of walkers, and it's yours."

So a new friendship was started, until her father came over and remonstrated with Gad for stealing his daughter.

Gad laughed and said, "Aye, I could do with an assistant, but she would have to be able to mend boots."

The sign did the trick though, and soon he was mending and repairing a variety of footwear. His purse grew to over a sovereign, with more to come.

Later on, as he was bending over his last he heard Thomas say, "Pa!" in a frightened voice. As he looked up, he a saw a man holding Thomas' arm with one hand and in the other was a short stubby 'suader.

He bristled and stood up, with his leather knife in one hand and his last in the other. He felt rather than heard a sound behind him, and turned and ducked at the same time, as a stick was wafted over his head, missing him by a hairsbreadth.

Quick as a flash, he swung his last at the new assailant, catching him across his jaw. He went flying into the side of the dusty road and stayed there.

The man holding Thomas was not too confident now, and as a small crowd had gathered, Gad could see he was wavering, and his eyes were flickering side to side.

He walked over to the man who was still holding his son and said in a quiet, low murderous tone, "If ye do not return my son to me unharmed, you will wish you had never been born."

The crowd waited expectantly, adding their own remarks, like, "'e needs a good smacking, master." The man paused, then, realising his hopeless position, gave a sob. With his eyes full of fear, he dropped the lad.

Gad said to his boy, "Go and sit by my box, Thomas, and don't ye move."

Then moving forward, he hit the man hard in the stomach. As he doubled over with the pain and shock, Gad grabbed his belt and lifted him up. He started walking over to the water trough and doused him well and truly, plunging him in and under the water.

The crowd by now were suddenly brave and rushed forward. They kept pushing him down as he tried to get out.

Two of the men watching then picked up his semi-conscious friend and did the same to him.

Eventually, the two chastened men managed to climb out of the trough, soaking wet and almost drowned.

The people's mood was now raised to fever pitch, and they began throwing all sorts of rubbish at them as the two villains limped away.

The folk came back to Gad, cheered and patted him on the back. Thomas was beaming with pride at the sight of his pa being feted, and clutched his hand as they walked back to the inn.

Apart from that, he had had a good day, as he sat outside and counted his takings fifty pence and five half sovereigns.

By now, of course, the event had become a popular talking point in the small village and the landlord of the inn came over to Gad.

Seeing him counting his money, he said in a loud voice so everyone could hear, "Put that away, master, as here ye pay for nothing today. They bastards have been robbin' us for days' and our Constable, Joe Rowlands, is laid up wi' the gout."

After his meal and drinks, they went to their room and were glad to be on their own again.

Gad looked kindly at his son, and explained to him that when he said "stay close", he meant just that, as there are "those who would take ye back to Arundel Castle". That frightened the boy. They slept well that night in a nice, clean, warm bed, the first time since Pulborough.

The next morning, as he and his lad sat eating a hearty breakfast, a man wearing a cloak and wide-brimmed hat came up to the window and beckoned Gad outside.

"I be one of her Ladyship's men, and although your action was very good yesterday, other people might not find it to their liking. This will have been sent to Dudley who wants ye and the boy dead, so I reckons ye ought to move on quick, like."

Then, like his predecessors, he disappeared as silently as he had arrived.

Gad went back into the bar, saying to himself, "I s'pose a nod's as good as a wink to a blind horse". He then grinned at the stupid saying. He explained to the landlord that he was expected in Arundel on the morrow, and so he ought to leave now as he "didn't want to be late, like." Then he asked him if he could make him up a parcel of travelling food and drink, which he was pleased to do.

After all, he had done something which "our Constable Joe would be pleased ye done". Gad and his boy rode towards Arundel to avoid suspicion, but as soon as he could, he rode cross-country and then back to the road, to where he was told Guildford was.

When he was at Jessica's house, the clever ostler there showed him the maps in the books in the library and even drew a sort of plan for him to get to Guildford.

As they sat by the roadside just outside the small village of Liphook, they met another travelling man. He was extremely upset and explained why to Gad. Apparently he had come from Petworth, where he had heard what had happened at Pulborough. When the Duke had seen the bodies Jessica had sent to him, he immediately despatched a large troop of soldiers, who not only killed or maimed the people there, but set fire to the house and nigh on destroyed it.

The lady of the house had been taken as a hostage. Gad was really upset poor Jessica but he could do nothing for her. Little did he know but when Queen Mary heard of the atrocities committed there, she sent a huge force to the castle and, having taken it, had the Duke arrested. He was incarcerated in the Tower.

Later, he was despatched abroad and Dudley was executed for treason for his association with the Scottish Mare.

After the man had left on his way, another problem arose, one Gad had never thought about.

At that point, Meg interrupted the story and asked Thomas what the problem was.

"Well, Ma, I weren't used to riding 'orses like, and I had been on one for a long time and me little arse was red raw."

Meg looked at Gad and tut tutted. "He were only a little lad, my love no wonder he were sore."

They walked into the village, Thomas being carried by Gad. As they passed a small, neat, thatched cottage, a woman was looking at them as she sat outside smoking her long clay pipe.

"'as your lad a problem, master, eh?"

Gad stopped and said rather shamefacedly, "Aye, Mistress, 'is little arse be sore from riding."

She shook her head accusingly at Gad. "Come 'ere, master and let I look at it."

He hesitated, not sure about this woman, who looked for all the world like a witch. But as he didn't know what else to do, he walked over to her, and the woman took the boy's hand, saying in a cross voice, "Some Pa's ain't got the sense they had been given by the Good Lord."

She put Thomas onto a small table, took off his pantaloons and swore softly under her breath. His little arse was red raw, and was beginning to bleed in one or two places. Going to a cupboard, she brought out a pot of cream she had made from a mixture of herbs and other mysterious countryside things, and spread it all over his little blunt end.

Thomas smiled as he remembered and said, "Aye that was some mixture – in no time at my entire backside was cool and no longer tender to the touch. What a relief.

"'Tis good', he had said, visibly feeling better. Gad was full of attention, watching carefully in case she would hurt his lad, keeping his truncheon. Soon she made a pair of padded underdrawers for him too, and fastened them with a scarf like band. Washing her hands in a bowl by the side of the table, she put his pantaloons back on and lifted him down.

"Have ye got far to go, master?" she queried, and Gad told her where he was headed for.

"That be a long ways," she said, and then added, "If ye can get to Haslemere, which ain't far, ye can sell your 'orse and get the coach to Richmond by the river from there it'll save any more riding."

237

Gad thanked her and said, "Can I pay ye for your work, Mistress?"

She smiled. "Nay, lad, I have no need for money. Just ye look after the lad – 'e's had a hard time somewhere, ain't 'e?"

Gad nodded. "He were taken by some vile men and I 'ad to rescue 'im. 'Is Ma is waiting for 'im. Thank 'e kindly for your help."

Thomas was pleased with his new under drawers and said he felt fine and ready to ride again.

It was only a short distance to Haslemere, and after a short search, he found a stable which was able to give him a fair price for his horse and its accoutrements.

The two forlorn figures, much worn by their travelling and exertions, stood side by side holding hands. The big man was grasping a tool bag, and had that look of almost desperate determination on his face.

As they waited they began to relax, and soon they were rubber necking, as everything seemed new to them, as each new event appeared: the flower sellers, even the odd juggler, who was struggling to keep his torches in the air much to everyone's amusement. Thomas giggled the loudest.

Eventually the coach arrived in a cloud of dust, and a trumpeting noise and the two figures, with Gad acting as lead man, pushed their way onto the coach and sat side by side.

Gad had reluctantly had his bag thrown on top of the coach, but at least they were unfettered by luggage and were able to sit close together. They watched with growing excitement as the large coach set off, with its horns trumpeting and men shouting.

As the initial flurry of the excitement settled, the two of them nodded and eventually slept, as the rolling coach coaxed them into a much-wanted sleep.

They both awoke with a start as the coach arrived at Guildford with the accompanying sounding of the long horns, and they watched as the horses were removed and replaced with fresh ones. Soon they were on their way again, and the countryside flashed past as they rolled along at a fair pace.

They began to feel safe for the first time in their longhaul from the small village of Hampton.

Richmond and the river appeared in a haze of warm sunshine and the inevitable clouds of dust and noise.

Thomas had never seen so many people who crowded the foreshore, and the rancid smell of the river made their nostrils twitch with its unpleasantness.

They disembarked from the coach, and Gad caught his thrown bag. The two bedraggled creatures made for the covered entrance to the river and a large barge type boat.

Meg wanted to know what the place looked like in greater detail, but Gad said that they were so overwhelmed that little of what they saw stayed in their memory.

"The river trip was the best bit," Thomas said. He liked the smell of the whole place, despite the river being a flowing cesspit. Buildings floated by and they saw large warehouses and even a castle, until the large and impressive Tower Bridge and the houses on it came into view.

Disembarking was less of a hassle as they had time on their side, and they waited until the man crush had gone before they walked down the gangplank and onto London's noisy, smelly city.

A man who was travelling next to Gad said with a wry smile, "It don't change much, do it? Still smells of every kind of rotting fish, and even the people don't seem to change either." He added, "I don't know which smell the worst. Your first visit to our fair city, be it?"

Gad explained no, that he lived in Cheapside, if he could remember how to get there from here.

The man was quite helpful and said, "Aye, I knows it, but how about a drink first? And the lad can have a whelk or two."

Thomas smiled at the memory and said to Meg, who had never tried those weird looking things that smelled of salt and dirt, despite living so close to the fish market.

They knocked on the door.

While all this was going on, Elizabeth was having her own problems with her own sister, Mary. She even had Elizabeth incarcerated in the Tower, until better sense intervened and she was released.

Now, many years later, with her battles almost over, with wars and financial problems in the country behind her, she had hoped for a quieter time.

It was time to reflect on her past life. That included Gad and her son.

Her spies had told her that both of them were living quiet lives in Stratford, by the Avon River, and she was tempted many times to sneak out and visit them, but common sense overrode those ideas, and all she could do was just to hear to about them.

Meanwhile Gad, now rested, had decided the time had come to go home to Hereford. Meg was not best pleased, as she had found a lot of good friends and neighbours.

But her man had said they were to go, so she meekly acquiesced.

Later that month, as the evening drew in, two coaches were laden with all their personal things and they set off, hopefully without any fuss.

They had not counted on their good friends, and as they left their house and turned onto the main road, all hell seemed to break loose.

Torches were lit, and a large crowd had gathered. Meg was in tears and as they dismounted from their coaches, another sound was heard.

The people were dumbstruck as soldiers appeared and lined the road just where they were. Soon, a small group of horsemen arrived soldiers in full armour and military dress, followed by a large coach.

The coach stopped in a circle light from the torches almost as though it was prearranged, which it was. The Mayor smiled secretly to himself.

"I 'ave got one over ye at last, Master Gad," he said to no one in particular.

The door of the coach opened and a very elderly gentleman who was having difficulty extracting himself from the coach got out eventually and walked over to a very surprised group.

He said, a little testily, "Master Gad, yer presence is required with a lady." He added a little unnecessarily, "She be in the coach."

The crowd was absolutely silent. There was not a whisper, nor a whimpering child as Gad walked over to the coach.

"Get in then," a waspish voice said, and he got in and sat opposite the great Queen who was lying on a pile of cushions.

He smiled. "Beth!" Then he corrected himself and said, "Your Majesty."

The great Queen smiled and said, "Here and now, my lovely man, Beth will do." She shifted her weight and aid a little plaintively. "Is our son here, my favourite shoemaker?" They both laughed.

"Aye, Beth, he is shall I bring him over?"

But she said, "Alas no, Gad. His life is always going to be in danger from my enemies so this meeting is just between ye and me." She took a fat parcel from her robes and said, "I cannot do this officially for his sake, but what is in here has been approved by my judges in the greatest secrecy, and I want ye to give it to him. Give it to Thomas with my love, and say that I have always followed his life as best as I could through my trusted aides and spies." She held Gad's hand and smiled. "We did as we promised, didn't we? Ye found him as ye said ye would, my determined man, and I have kept this for him now that ye may be leaving." She smiled. "Ask him to stand with ye as I leave so I can see him. I would like to see him one more time."

The coach turned and moved off. Gad and Thomas stood side by side and as she left, a white kerchief fluttered in the window. They both bowed.

Needless to say, the crowd were agog with shock and surprise at this obviously Royal visit.

Gad stood and said, "She wanted to come and apologise to me personally for what her courtiers had tried to do to me."

Gad was now in a fix, but taking the easy option, they returned home.

As they all sat around the big table, Gad opened the parcel. In it was a small miniature of herself in a gilt frame. The rest was in writing, and so young Gad was called on to read it.

The gilt and red print document had the Royal Seal on the bottom and it read,

'Be it known to all her subjects that Her Majesty has great pleasure in raising one Thomas de Witt to the title of Lord, and bestows on him the land and property and incomes from the Manor at Forde in the county of Sussex.

Signed Elizabeth R.'

They all turned and looked at Thomas.

Smiling, Gad said, "Well, my Lord, it looks as though my return to Hereford is cancelled, as we have a home to go to."